"You must r... **he said, "rui**... **clothes on in this weather when your body is still fighting hypothermia."**

"I need to get answers about what happened to Faith. Tonight. Once they kick me out in the morning, I'll never make it back inside Benediction. I'll never learn the truth."

"In this town, the truth won't set you free and it won't bring your sister back, but it might get you killed." He shifted in his seat toward her. "So, do you?"

Hope tensed. "Do I what?"

"Have a death wish?"

She blew out a heavy breath and lowered her head. "I can't live with not knowing who killed my sister and why. I won't let a murderer get away. Someone has to be held responsible."

He looked around at the darkness. "What's your plan?"

"From here, I'm winging it."

ROGUE CHRISTMAS OPERATION

Juno Rushdan

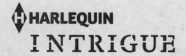

HARLEQUIN
INTRIGUE

To my husband, thanks for being my hero every single day.

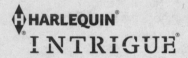

ISBN-13: 978-1-335-48921-0

Rogue Christmas Operation

Recycling programs
for this product may
not exist in your area.

For questions and comments about the quality of this book, please contact us at CustomerService@Harlequin.com.

Harlequin Enterprises ULC
22 Adelaide St. West, 40th Floor
Toronto, Ontario M5H 4E3, Canada
www.Harlequin.com

Printed in U.S.A.

Juno Rushdan is the award-winning author of steamy, action-packed romantic thrillers that keep you on the edge of your seat. She writes about kick-ass heroes and strong heroines fighting for their lives as well as their happily-ever-afters. As a veteran air force intelligence officer, she uses her background supporting Special Forces to craft realistic stories that make you sweat and swoon. Juno currently lives in the DC area with her patient husband, two rambunctious kids and a spoiled rescue dog. To receive a FREE book from Juno, sign up for her newsletter at junorushdan.com/mailing-list. Also be sure to follow Juno on BookBub for the latest on sales at bit.ly/BookBubJuno.

Books by Juno Rushdan

Harlequin Intrigue

Fugitive Heroes: Topaz Unit

Rogue Christmas Operation

A Hard Core Justice Thriller

Hostile Pursuit
Witness Security Breach
High-Priority Asset
Innocent Hostage
Unsuspecting Target

Tracing a Kidnapper

Visit the Author Profile page at Harlequin.com.

CAST OF CHARACTERS

Gage Graham—A former CIA operative with a specialized skill set. He's on the run and hiding out. His team was set up, and he's found a safe place to stay under the radar in Benediction, Virginia. But causing waves in the small town would draw unwanted attention, putting him in the CIA's crosshairs.

Hope Fischer—This photojournalist is in pursuit of the truth surrounding her sister's death. When Gage saves her life, she realizes he may be the one person capable of helping her. She knows Faith would never kill herself and she's determined to prove it, even if it costs her her own life.

Faith Fischer—A scientist who worked on a secretive project for a big pharma corporation in a closed town with strict travel and residency restrictions.

Ryan Keller—He's the sheriff in Goode, the neighboring town to Benediction.

Claire Coughlin—Gage's stepsister. She has reasons of her own to keep her stepbrother's secret.

Jason Coughlin—He is Claire's son and has a grudge against Gage that could cause trouble.

Hunter Wright—The former leader of Team Topaz.

Chapter One

Her rental car slid across the ice and swerved. Hope gripped the steering wheel tighter, regaining control.

The night was pitch-black. Storm clouds that threatened to unleash more freezing rain blocked out the moon. To her right, beyond the darkness, was a steep slope that led straight to Goode Mountain Lake. No streetlamps or guardrails were along the side of this godforsaken road—*the only road*—that led in and out of the insulated town of Benediction, Virginia. There were only the bright lights from the SUV behind her.

High beams blared into her sedan. She glanced up at the rearview mirror. The light reflected was blinding.

Raising a palm to shield her eyes, she squinted against the harsh glare, but her car swerved once again. Hope put both hands back on the wheel as her heart drummed faster.

The dark two-lane road was slicker than she'd anticipated tonight from the rain earlier and the dropping temperature. She needed to slow down, but the driver behind her picked up speed, riding her bumper.

Misgivings stirred in her gut, crawling through her like worms beneath her skin, but she ignored them. She had to do this. For her sister, Faith. For her own peace of mind. She had to keep going until she made it inside Benediction, got answers about Faith's death.

No matter the cost.

Steeling her nerves, Hope tapped the accelerator. Just enough to get some distance between her and the SUV.

Nothing was going to stop her.

Raindrops hit the windshield and pounded the roof in a frenetic beat, ratcheting up her tension. She winced as she turned on the wipers. The downpour only obscured her visibility and made the road even more treacherous.

Wiper blades whisked aside the rain from the windshield, giving her a spotty view.

Headlights from an oncoming vehicle ahead pierced the darkness. A car had left Benediction. In the distance, she barely made out the lights from the lampposts marking the electric security fence surrounding the restricted town.

She checked the rearview mirror.

The SUV roared up behind her, too close on her tail. She touched the brakes to back him off, but the vehicle tapped her bumper.

She jolted forward in the seat, holding tight on to the steering wheel. Heart racing, she accelerated. A little farther and she'd make it.

The rain picked up, the torrent battering the car. Anything past sixty feet was erased by the deluge. Headlights from the vehicle that had left Benediction were no longer visible.

The SUV rammed her again. The steering wheel jerked in her hand as the back end of her car fishtailed. She forced herself not to struggle against it. Steering in the opposite direction would only make things worse.

Hope flicked a glance at the hazard button on her

dash. She could hit it, slow down, stop the car and turn back to Goode, the neighboring town. Turn away from Benediction. Give up her search for the truth.

She'd been warned. That's what everyone wanted. For her to leave it all alone. To go back to California and bury her head in the sand.

But then a murderer would go free.

She had failed her sister once. Not again. She swallowed past the ball of anxiety in her throat. *You can do this.*

The SUV zoomed up alongside her, sending a new wave of fear crashing through her. What was he doing?

No sooner had the thought crossed her mind than the SUV swerved sharply. The front end slammed into her side of the car, propelling it into a wild slide toward the edge.

Hope panicked, hitting the brakes. The wheels locked. Her vehicle lost traction and went into a skid. Everything was happening so fast. Too fast.

Spinning out of control, her car missed a large tree and slid over the edge of the slope. A high-pitched cry escaped her lips. Dirt and rocks spit up. She tried to straighten the steering wheel and pumped the brakes. Her car fishtailed, clipped a tree and went airborne.

The sedan flipped. Rolled end over end down the gradient. Metal crunched and groaned around her.

Hope's seat belt jerked hard across her body, cutting off her oxygen for a second.

The airbag deployed like a hot fist, knocking her head back against the seat. Dust and chemicals saturated the air.

Her lungs seized as a scream lodged in her throat.

The car slammed to a stop with the impact of crashing into a brick wall. Her skull smashed into something hard.

A riot of pain flared…everywhere. In her head, chest, bones—even her teeth hurt.

Her vision blurred. Not that it mattered. She couldn't see past the airbag, which was the size of a large beach ball in her face.

Hope pushed on the light fabric, and the airbag deflated. Coughing, she wiped at the wetness coming from her nose with the back of her hand. Blood. Her nose was bleeding.

She switched on the interior light and pushed the deflated airbag out of her way.

The headlights were still on.

Water.

The car was in the lake. Beneath the water, or at least half of it. The weight of the engine pitched the front end forward, so that the car was almost pointing straight down. She looked back at the rear window. Rain and darkness.

Water was starting to seep inside the vehicle. The foot well was filling up as water rushed in. Faster and faster.

Hope pressed the button to release the seat belt. But nothing happened. It was stuck, jammed tight. She yanked on the belt, trying again, tugging and pushing. Praying.

Oh, God. She was trapped.

Icy water rose past her hips to her waist. Shockingly cold. Her toes were already growing numb, and she was shivering. She had to get out. Now!

Her purse floated up on the passenger's side. If she reached it, got to the Swiss Army knife inside, she could cut herself free.

She extended her hand in the water. Her bag was inches from her fingertips. She stretched out as much as she could, straining her arm muscles. A pang wrenched through her chest, her eyes tearing at the intense pain, but she didn't stop. She kept reaching for her purse. Almost had it. The bag was so close—she needed to stretch a hair farther, but the seat belt had her pinned.

The car shifted, still moving. Down and down it sank. The car tipped to the side, and water carried her purse away, out of reach.

No, no, no. It's not supposed to happen like this.

Pressure built in her ears, making her head pound. The headlights flickered and died. Then the interior light blinked off. Everything went black.

I'm going to die. In this cold, dark lake without ever learning the truth.

This was a mistake.

She screamed, venting her grief and rage, until her lungs were empty.

Faith. You deserve justice.

Even if the seat belt was useless, Hope had to try. She got back to work on getting the hell out of there. With her last breath she'd fight to get free.

Tugging harder, she pushed on the seat-belt release again as a surge of water wrapped its icy arms around her chest.

"WHAT IN THE HELL?" Gage Graham said aloud to himself, slowing down his truck.

An SUV had just run a car off the road right in front of him, wheeled a U-turn, and the driver was hightailing it from the scene.

In his thirty years, he'd seen a lot of insane stuff, most of it horrible, but nothing quite so bizarre.

Gage tried to make out the license plate number of the SUV, but it was impossible in the dark with the raging storm.

It burned him to the bone to let such a vicious piece of work get away, but he didn't have much choice. The driver of the sedan might be hurt or worse.

He pulled to the opposite side of the road and stopped at an angle with his headlights pointed in the area where the car had gone over the side. Switching on his high beams, the lights illuminated the area well enough for him to get a decent look at the situation.

The car had gone into Goode Mountain Lake. A fifteen-thousand-acre reservoir. The whole front end was submerged, and the rest was quickly sinking. It'd only take minutes, maybe five, tops, for the entire car to fill up with water. By his count, more than sixty seconds had already lapsed since the car went off the road.

Calling 911 was pointless. Goode was twenty-five miles away, and first responders wouldn't make it in time.

As for the residents of Benediction, they didn't respond to anything outside its gates. One of the many iron-clad rules. Most of the road was considered no-man's land. Luckily for the driver of the car in the lake, he wasn't a typical inhabitant and believed if a rule couldn't be broken, there was usually a way to bend it.

Gage pulled his Sig Sauer P220 from the ankle holster and stowed it in the glove box. After switching on his hazard lights, he jumped out of the car.

Icy-cold rain pelted down on him like tiny daggers, soaking most of his clothes. He only had on a down puffer vest over his turtleneck, since he hadn't planned on being exposed to the elements. The weather had turned from bad to nasty with the inbound winter storm that was going to drop an estimated foot of snow tomorrow. The temperature had already dipped into the thirties, but it wasn't below freezing yet.

He hustled around to the back and popped open the door to the under-bed storage compartment. Fished out a flare from his emergency roadside kit.

The last thing he needed was a passerby sideswiping his truck, exacerbating the situation, because they didn't see his hazard lights until it was too late.

Gusts of wet wind lashed his face and stung his eyes, but he'd been through much worse. This paled in comparison to what he'd endured in the CIA. Besides, he'd take cold rain over sand in his eyes any day.

With the flare lit, he tossed it a few feet away in the direction of oncoming traffic. He grabbed the flashlight— a floating, waterproof one that was impact resistant and could be used as a weapon in a pinch. He slammed the trunk closed and took off for the embankment.

A patch of ice had him slipping on the road but didn't take him down thanks to the traction on the soles of his thermo tactical boots. He made his way along the slope. Moved quickly but carefully over the slick grass.

There wasn't a second to lose. The smashed-in trunk of the sedan slipped underwater.

He dived into the lake.

Although he'd braced himself for the cold, the brutal chill of the water was startling. A jolt of pain ripped through his whole body, but he didn't stop swimming.

Diving deeper, he swam to the driver's door and shone his flashlight inside.

A woman was trapped behind the steering wheel. She gasped for her last breath of air as the water inside the car overtook her completely, and then she was under.

She moved her head, her dark hair flowing in the water, and looked at him. Terrified, pretty and about to drown if he didn't get her out. She pointed to her seat belt and yanked at it.

The belt was stuck.

Gage tried the door handle. Locked. He tapped the window, gesturing for her to unlock it.

She glanced down and hit the button. The lock disengaged, and he pulled on the handle as she pushed. But it didn't budge.

Doors didn't jam when submerged, but they became very heavy due to the pressure exerted by the water pushing it toward the car. It'd be nearly impossible to open until the car completely filled with water. Then the pressure would be in equilibrium, but she didn't have that kind of time to wait.

Gage slammed the hard case of the flashlight against the window. He swung again, and the glass held. Blunt force wouldn't work.

Too bad she hadn't rolled down the window before the car had lost power. The windshield was a spiderweb of cracks. From the inside of the car, it could be kicked out. Trying to do the reverse, from the outside in, wouldn't work.

He was almost out of air. His lungs strained for oxygen.

Gage pointed to his chest and then up.

She pressed her palms to the glass. Her eyes were wide with panic as she shook her head. For him not to go? That she couldn't hold her breath for a minute longer?

Either way, it'd serve no one if they both drowned. Still, something in his chest squeezed at what he had to do next.

He had to leave her.

Chapter Two

Hope shook her head, desperate for the man not to leave. Help had come. The stranger from Benediction had stopped his car. Had dared to jump into the lake against the odds. Tried and failed to open the door. Only to abandon her.

She banged on the window, frantic. *Please! Don't go!*

He held up one finger. Then he turned and kicked off the car with his feet. He swam away through the darkness, leaving her behind and taking the light with him.

No! Hope screamed the word in her mind.

She yanked at the seat belt. Kicked the dash. Pounded at the glass. It was no use.

The car sank deeper, leveling out. The pressure popped her ears, and she was now dizzy.

Her lungs began burning, starved for oxygen. Fear inundated her. No matter how hard she fought to get loose, she was helpless. Probably ten, twenty feet from the surface, but it might as well have been twenty miles.

Was this all a lost cause?

He'd warned her, told her not to do this. *Mark my words, you'll end up dead, just like Faith, if you don't let this go*, he had said to her.

Desperate for the sweet taste of oxygen, she clutched

at her throat. Her lungs ached like they were on the verge of exploding. The weight of the water, the strain of holding her breath hurt so much.

She couldn't fight the urge any longer. The impulse was as instinctual as it was overpowering, even though she knew it would it mean the end, but there was no stopping the inevitable. She gasped and sucked in water.

Excruciating pain mixed with blinding panic as her lungs filled. She flailed like a madwoman. Frantic to get out.

Something brushed her head. She reached up and grabbed it. Smooth leather in her hand.

Her purse.

Hope struggled to unzip it. Her hands were shaking so badly. She gagged and choked.

God, oh, God. She was drowning.

A bolt of agony and sheer terror went straight through her. But a sense of calm quickly followed as everything slowed and faded.

Suddenly, she wasn't afraid to die anymore.

Soon, she'd see Faith again.

GAGE POPPED TO the surface. The torrential rain pounded against his face. He sucked in a few deep breaths, easing his lungs while he thought of a way to quickly get the woman out. Teeth chattering, he shed his soaked-through down-filled vest and heavy wool turtleneck, leaving his long-sleeved thermal undershirt while keeping a grip on the flashlight.

His knife. He could use it to get her out.

He took another breath, the deepest, longest one he could hold, and dived back under.

Before he'd left the woman, he had held up one finger

to the car window, letting her know he wouldn't abandon her. All he needed was a minute and then he'd be back.

Hang on.

The car had settled into the muck at the bottom close to shore. He swam to the driver's side and cast the light inside.

Her arms were floating up by her purse, and her eyes were closed. She was no longer conscious.

Damn it. He'd taken too long.

Gage dug into his left boot, his fingers numb from the frosty water, and pulled out his Venom double-action knife. It had a lightning-fast release button, but he didn't need the four-inch blade yet. He angled the handle at the window. On the end of the knife was a pommel designed to break glass, though he'd never used the feature prior to today and for a moment had forgotten it was even there.

One hard tap pierced the window, fracturing the glass. A second tap and the pane shattered.

Gage hit the button on the side of the knife, releasing the blade. First, he cut the shoulder strap, followed by the one across her lap. He shoved the knife back in his boot, grabbed her purse and let go of the flashlight.

Taking care not to hit her head on the door frame, he pulled the woman from the car. The flashlight was floating to the surface, the beam of light providing a guide.

The cold pressed in on him from all sides, icy teeth sinking into his skin, deeper to his bones. He pushed off the car with both feet for a boost, but it wasn't nearly enough. Keeping one arm wrapped around the woman's chest, he swam with one arm, pulling at the water, scissoring his legs with all his might.

Blood pounded in his head along with his thundering heartbeat. His lungs screamed for oxygen, the cold knotting his muscles. Every cell in his body burned from the cold.

He clawed his way through the water, following the light.

They were close. *So close.*

Slowing down wasn't an option even as his lungs ached and heaviness set into his limbs.

Darkness danced on the edge of his vision. He was growing tired, but he ignored the fatigue. It was only a product of the cold. He ran six miles a day, lifted weights, stayed in peak condition since he'd been disgraced and disavowed from the Agency. There was no doubt in his mind that he had the strength to make it to the surface.

He was not going to let this woman die. *Keep going. Don't stop.*

The flashlight was right there, and then he broke the surface.

"Uh!" He raked in rejuvenating air as he also sucked droplets of water into his heaving lungs.

Relief whooshed through him, but he was nowhere near done. He pushed onward, doing a sidestroke while ensuring her head stayed above water until he reached dirt. His body ached from the exertion, and the chill spearing through him only made it worse. He wanted to rest for a moment, but the rush of adrenaline kept him moving. If he was going to save her, he had to act quickly.

Panting, Gage hauled the woman up onto the muddy bank and into the brightness from the headlights. Her face was pale, nose bloody and her lips had turned blue. Getting her breathing was paramount, and getting her warm would be equally important.

The freezing rain hadn't let up. It was coming down hard at a vicious angle, making his next task even more difficult.

He rose on his knees beside the woman and began chest compressions. The heel of one hand on the center of her chest, the other hand on top of the first, and he used his entire upper body, not just his arms, to push. Counted to thirty.

No response from her.

Come on.

He tilted her head back and pried her lips apart. Pinching her nostrils closed gently in case her nose was broken, he sealed his mouth over hers, wasting no time. He blew life-giving breaths into her. Two, long and steady.

Still nothing. He resumed chest compressions, pushing even harder this time. "Breathe for me. Come on!"

The woman jerked and pushed him away with a forceful cough.

Gage rolled her onto her side, swept her hair back from her face and helped her expel the brackish water. Those first few breaths must've felt like fire. He rubbed her back and her arm, encouraging her while she wheezed and sputtered.

Once she finished hacking up the liquid, she dug her palms into the mud and rolled her upper body off the ground. She looked him over. Brilliant eyes took in his face as her lips quivered, body shaking, chest rising and falling in the desperate rhythm of the utterly spent.

Gage exhaled hard himself, white puffs of breath leaving his mouth.

"Thank you," she said, still gulping air. Her soft voice was barely audible over the pounding rain. "You...okay?"

Gage was fairly sure he was the one who should've

been asking that question. She'd nearly died but was concerned about his welfare. That told him plenty about this woman despite the fact that he didn't know her name.

"I'm fine." He pressed two fingers to her carotid artery. Her pulse was slow and thready. He had to warm her up. Frigid water lowered a person's body temperature faster than air. Hypothermia was already setting in. At least she was conscious and talking. "I've got to get you out of this rain. Can you make it up the embankment to my truck?" he asked, sliding his hand up to cup her cheek. Her soft skin was like ice.

It registered to him on some level the gesture was too forward, too intimate between strangers, and at the same time, the impulse to comfort her after saving her life was as natural as breathing.

She nodded weakly, though she didn't look as if she even had the strength to stand, much less walk uphill.

The wool jacket she wore would be burdensome on the climb, and it was only transferring heat away from her body at this point. "Better to toss the jacket than lug it," he said, teeth chattering. "Don't worry, the truck will be warm."

She reached for the zipper, but from the way her body shook, he doubted she could mange it. He pulled down the zipper for her and peeled the sodden wool jacket off.

Refusing to give in to his own fatigue, he grabbed her purse, cupped her arm and helped her up to her feet.

She swayed and staggered forward two steps before her legs gave out from underneath her. Gage caught her, expecting her lack of coordination and the fragility of her limbs.

Nearly dying took a lot out of a person. He'd know better than most exactly how much.

He lifted her, putting her slender body across his shoulders in a fireman's carry. She went limp on him. Soaking wet, she was heavier than she looked. Not to mention the added drag from his own wet jeans weighing him down, but in this position, he was capable of carrying a grown man almost double her size.

Lurching into motion, he began scrambling up the slick ground. The embankment was slippery and rocky, but he made decent progress, even if it wasn't as fast as he would've liked.

Grunting with effort, using the last reserves of his strength, he climbed to the top.

He caught his breath and then hurried around the front of the parked truck and opened the passenger door. The cabin was toasty from the heat he'd left running, and he welcomed the rush of warmth that escaped. Carefully, he set her down on the seat.

Once he closed the door, he ran to the driver's side. He hopped in and turned the heat up full blast, angling all the vents toward her. On the console between the seats he spotted a zip-up hoodie he'd taken off the other day and forgotten in the car. Just what she needed.

"This will help." He handed her his lightweight jacket and set her purse down. "Better if you take off your wet shirt first." When she hesitated, he added, "You'll get warmer faster that way."

"Y-you're n-n-not try-trying to get me...naked?" Her words slurred, which was a bad sign, but he gave her points for the humor, considering.

"I'm positive." Though staring at her pretty face, the idea of seeing this woman unclothed—*under different circumstances*—was unquestionably appealing. "Promise not to look." He turned toward his window.

She had on a simple pullover sweater. No buttons. No zippers. As long as she was able to lift her arms, she shouldn't have a problem.

Glimpsing her reflection in the glass, he watched her for a split second to be sure she was all right before lowering his eyes. He was nothing if not a man of his word.

"I'm Gage, by the way." He deliberately neglected to mention his last name. Force of habit. Secrets were his constant companion, but she'd learn his surname soon enough where they were going. "And you are?"

"Hope." Hard to miss that she'd done likewise with a similar omission, but her purse was on the console and he was willing to bet two forms of ID were inside.

"Any idea who ran you off the road or why?" The sound of the zipper trying to close was his cue. He shifted, facing her. "Need an assist?"

She nodded. "C-can't feel f-fingers, t-toes."

Keeping his gaze on her face, he got the zipper closed for her.

She pulled the hood up over her head and settled back in the seat like she was ready to close her eyes and fall into a deep sleep.

Another bad sign.

Questions would have to wait for now, but eventually he'd get answers. No chance he was going to let the bastard who'd run her off the road get away with it.

He backed the truck up, spun the wheel, turning them ninety degrees, and shifted to Drive. Benediction was ten minutes down the road. A quick and easy ride.

Getting her through the gate was a different story.

Benediction was a closed town, with strict travel and residency restrictions. No unauthorized personnel were allowed. Only assigned government or military personnel and grandfathered-in residents who kept the town running with the essentials—diner, grocery, pub, auto shop, tailor, one-school K-12, nondenominational church, funeral home/crematorium and the clinic. Special dispensation was granted on a case-by-case basis only to relatives of residents.

They rode in silence with the blasting fan from the heater on high, static noise in the background. The patches of black ice on the road were the worst at night and early morning. He'd only ventured out to go to Goode and stock up on essential supplies that weren't available in Benediction before the storm hit. None of which he'd gotten and all of which he needed.

The rain eased from a downpour, turning into a relentless drizzle. The bright lights of the front gate cut through the darkness as they approached. By daring to go a little faster on the road, it had taken them less than eight minutes. He slowly pulled up to the guardhouse, mentally kicking his brain into gear for some quick thinking and smooth talk.

Gage glanced at Hope. Eyes half-open, she was still shivering, and her breathing was a bit shallow. The tremors racking her body hadn't improved. Didn't help that she was stuck in drenched clothes from the waist down and soaked shoes.

A predicament he understood all too well. The steady shudder running through him had his hands shaking on the wheel.

"Pull the hood back. The guard will need to see how bad you are to let you in," he said, bringing the car to a stop under the overhead canopy.

Hope slid her hand up and pushed the hood down to her neck.

"For the next two minutes, say as little as possible until I get you through the gate." That shouldn't be too hard, with her suffering from the effects of hypothermia and fatigue.

Two US Army soldiers came out of the heated guardhouse. Sidearms were holstered on their hips. Pepper spray was clipped to the other side of their belts. Gage knew from witnessing an incident with his mouthy teenage nephew who'd gotten drunk and belligerent one night that they also carried handcuffs in a side utility pocket.

Gage rolled down his window. The specialist checked the underside of the truck with an inspection mirror while the corporal came up to his window.

Benediction was small, population 250, including the rotation of military personnel and government contractors. The guards working the gate got to know faces, names, and make and model of vehicles fast.

In turn, Gage made it his business to learn as much as he could about everyone.

"Corporal Livingston," Gage said.

"Evening, Mr. Graham. Surprised you're back…" Livingston stopped short, studying him with a wide-eyed gaze. The kid was a baby. Couldn't have been more than twenty-two years old. "What happened, sir?"

"Car accident. A few miles down. This woman was run off the road." Gage indicated his passenger, and the corporal peered inside the truck. "Her car went into the lake. If I hadn't gotten her out, she would've drowned. I need to take her to the clinic inside."

Corporal Livingston shook his head. "You know the rules. I can't let her in."

"She needs immediate medical attention."

Specialist Porter finished checking the undercarriage and was now inspecting the truck bed.

"You'll have to take her to the hospital in Goode, sir," Corporal Livingston said.

"Perhaps you missed the word *immediate*. She won't make it to the next town. Look at her."

Livingston's hard gaze shifted from Gage to Hope but didn't soften. He took a flashlight off his hip and shone it inside, getting a better look.

"You've got no choice," Gage said. "You have to let her get medical treatment unless you want her death on your conscience. Either hypothermia or pulmonary edema will kill her before we make it to Goode." Gage believed that deep in his gut. "Never mind the fact that I might not make it there myself. There has to be some kind of exception for a medical emergency."

Conflict twisted the young man's features. "I can call my sergeant. See what he thinks."

The specialist finished in the back and came up along the passenger door.

Gage sighed. "In the twenty minutes you'll take regurgitating what I just explained to your superior, who can't see firsthand the dire state this woman is in, and going back and forth, debating, I'll need medical attention, too. You want to be responsible for two deaths in one night?"

The specialist climbed up on the running board, casting his flashlight on Hope. "Oh, man, Corporal Livingston. She looks really bad. Maybe you should let her in."

Porter was new, had been in Benediction less than two months and hadn't had a full dose of the isolationist Kool-Aid yet. All positives in Gage's book.

"It'll be my butt on the line," Livingston snapped. "Not yours."

"I didn't save her only to watch her die in my truck because you're worried about getting a slap on the wrist," Gage said. "Let us go straight to the clinic and get her checked out. You'll be hailed a hero after the doctor and I speak to your superior."

Livingston lowered his eyes and rubbed his forehead. "If anything goes wrong, you understand it might be grounds to have you kicked out of Benediction permanently?"

Gage was aware he had to watch his every step. This town was the best haven, where he was hiding in plain sight. If he were ever forced to leave, it would mean he'd have to go back on the run. Then his days would be numbered, but saving Hope's life was worth the risk.

"I understand," Gage said.

"All right, but Specialist Porter will follow you and provide an escort. I need to see her ID for the report."

Thank goodness, sanity prevailed.

Gage turned toward the console and reached for her purse, but it was gone.

"L-l-ost...lake," Hope said.

Easy enough for Gage to chalk it up to him being mistaken. Perhaps he had forgotten her purse on the bank or had dropped it in the water during the swim. A lot had happened quickly. His had brain misfired more than once from the cold.

But he knew better. After eight years with the CIA, he didn't make rookie mistakes.

Hope's purse wasn't lost. She was lying.

Her gaze bounced up, and those sparkling green eyes

met his. She looked frightfully fragile and impossibly tough all at once—a beautiful contradiction.

A person's life could pivot in a second—with a single word, the smallest choice that might not feel like any choice at all. Destiny often whispered a promise or a warning. All you had to do was listen. Gage was listening right now.

This woman is trouble.

He attracted trouble —was attracted to it, same difference. Basic magnetism, like a lodestone to iron. There was no changing his nature, what compelled him, any more than one could alter the laws of physics.

At that moment, his gut was telling him that if he brought Hope into Benediction, she was going to toss his house of cards upside down.

Chapter Three

The past week of prying and pushing and, most recently, nearly dying had led to this moment. Nothing was going to stop Hope from getting inside Benediction now. If the soldier saw her ID, it'd take him thirty seconds to learn that she was on their blacklist and then he'd sooner let her freeze to death than allow her through the gate. Of that she was certain.

Gage might be her savior, but that didn't make him her ally. *Yet.*

Hope placed her shaking hand on top of his. "P-please." She only had the strength to utter the single word.

By plunging into the freezing lake twice, Gage had risked his own life to save her, a stranger. That meant he had guts *and* he was a good man. She prayed it would be enough.

For a split second his dark eyes narrowed, then they brightened in a way that warmed something inside her. Gage looked back at the soldier standing at the driver's side. "Her wallet was lost in the lake," he said, and relief loosened some of the tightness in her chest. "Let's get her to the clinic. Once she's warmed up and they examine her, she'll have to fill out forms with all the pertinent information. Specialist Porter can call you and pass along the details for a full report before your shift ends. Okay?"

The soldier nodded. "All right, sir, but I've got to let my sergeant know." He waved the other young man over, spoke to him a moment and sent him running toward a parked vehicle on the other side of the controlled entry point.

After the soldier ahead of them had started his car, the guard pushed a button and the long-arm barrier lifted.

Anticipation whispered through her in a dizzying rush from the top of her head down to her belly, perhaps even lower, but her legs had grown numb. The ringing inside her head was loud, shutting out everything else in that instant. No pain. No cold. No doubts.

Gage hit the gas, passing the gate, and they entered Benediction.

I'm in! I made it.

Hope's stomach flip-flopped, part exhilaration and part nerves. This was the farthest she'd ever been, but her battle was just getting started.

A parcel of land covered with evergreens was a buffer zone between the gate and the town. From the outside, it was impossible to get a clear look at Benediction, even with a telephoto lens, due to the trees. She had hired a local tour guide who specialized in the Goode Mountain area to take her out on the lake, so she could see the town from the water.

No luck on that front, either. There was a similar swath of dense trees on the other side of the electrified fence around the rear perimeter of the town. The only thing visible was the top floor of a building—steel and tinted privacy glass—and half of a sign for Nexcellogen Industries. Forget about renting a helicopter to do a fly-by to give her a chance to snap some photos from over-head. The town was protected by a strict no-fly zone. No pilot dared violate the statute for fear of having their license permanently suspended.

This town was hiding something. Hope knew in her bones it was the reason Faith was dead, even though she couldn't prove it.

Beyond the evergreen woodland, Gage drove through the tiny town, which was little more than a well-planned community. This was the one main road, she realized when they came to a large roundabout. At the center of it stood a fifty-foot tree decorated with luminous multi-colored lights and a crystal star on the top. The Christmas tree made the creepy town almost look normal.

A street lined with shops was off to one side of the main road. Twinkling white lights had been strung up in rows. On the other side of the road were homes decorated for the holidays. Town houses and a variety of one and two-story homes within walking distance to the shops.

After they took the second turn out of the roundabout, staying on the main road, they passed a large park with a playground, a school and a church.

The one building that stood out like a sore thumb, set apart from everything else, was the sprawling three-story Nexcellogen research facility, where Faith had worked as a scientist.

In a few short minutes, she spotted a small volunteer fire station and the clinic.

The soldier parked his car in a row of spots across from the building. Gage stopped the car beneath the emergency entrance's awning, near a lone ambulance awash in eerie sallow light, before running around to the passenger side.

He opened the door. "I'll help you inside."

She scooted off the edge of the seat and slid, more so than climbed, down. Gage drew her from the step rail. He scooped her into his arms without letting her feet touch the ground and *helped* her into the clinic by carrying her through the automatic doors.

If she hadn't been drained to exhaustion and needed his assistance, she would've protested, but she didn't even have the energy to enjoy it, either. Where the man got the herculean strength to lift her after everything else that he'd already done was a wonder.

He wasn't a large guy. Six feet tall with the hard, honed body of an athlete. Or a man of action. Impossible to miss, since his sodden thermal top hugged the curve of his muscles. And he was handsome, as in make-your-jaw-drop-and-forget-your-name kind of gorgeous.

The automatic double doors whooshed closed behind them. She squinted against the bright fluorescent lights as Gage carried her into the clinic. The soldier was right by their side.

A woman in her late twenties, maybe early thirties, wearing scrubs, caught sight of them. "What happened, Gage?" She jumped to her feet behind the front desk and came around to meet them.

"Her car went into the lake. She took in a lot of water. Lost consciousness. She almost didn't make it."

Hope's heart clenched at how close she'd come to drowning in the lake, but she'd do it all again to get inside Benediction.

"She's an uncleared outsider," the soldier said, staying close on their heels.

The woman's gaze bounced from the armed guard back to Gage. "Follow me." She led them to an exam room, where she hurriedly grabbed a few foil blankets and spread one out on the exam table. "Set her here."

Gage laid her down.

"Hi, my name is Danielle. I'm the physician assistant on duty tonight." She draped another foil blanket on top of Hope and tossed one to Gage.

"I need her name for the report, and Corporal Livingston said that as soon as she's warm I'm to escort her back to the front gate."

Hope's stomach twisted in dread. She turned her head away from the young man and pulled the foil up to her chin.

"Do you expect her to walk twenty-five miles in the freezing rain all the way back to Goode?" Gage asked. "It'd be best, safest for her to leave in the morning."

"Not my problem, sir," the soldier said. "I've got my orders."

"I need both of you out of my examination room," Danielle said.

The two men turned toward the door.

"No." Hope reached out to Gage. "Stay." He'd proven himself an ally, for the time being, anyway, and the prospect of him walking out the door and her not seeing him again was too much to bear. It dawned on her that she couldn't accomplish the monumental task ahead without help from someone on the inside.

Gage came back to her bedside and took her hand in both of his. "I'll stay if you want," he said. The concern in his eyes calmed Hope with the sincerity she saw there.

The soldier hovered on the threshold. "If he stays, so do I, ma'am."

"I need to get you out of these wet clothes and examine you," Danielle said to Hope. Then her gaze dropped to their clasped hands, and she straightened with a look of distaste on her face. "That means both of you gentlemen will leave. Now."

Gage nodded to Danielle, and then he looked at Hope. "I won't go far. Promise." Unwavering sympathy resonated in his voice despite his chattering teeth.

"Doc has a clean set of sweats in the locker room," Danielle said. "Warm up and I'll check you out when I'm done with her."

"Okay," he said to Danielle, giving another nod but without taking his eyes from Hope's. He squeezed her hand once, and the dread that had been bubbling inside dissipated.

Gage ushered the guard from the room and closed the examination room door on his way out.

Danielle put a stethoscope to Hope's chest inside the zip-up sweater. "Take a deep breath as best you can," she said, and Hope drew in as much air as possible. "A few more for me." She moved the stethoscope around, listening. "Sounds good. What's your name?"

Hope considered lying. Something she should've done with Gage and would've if she'd been thinking clearly. Since he already knew her first name, it made little sense to lie to the PA. "Hope."

Danielle took out a small electronic device and clipped the gadget onto Hope's index finger. "This'll measure the oxygen level of your blood." She opened the drawer of a cart beside the bed and took out a pair of medical scissors. Danielle slipped off Hope's shoes and began cutting her jeans. "How do you know Gage?"

Hope tensed at the question. "I don't." The stutter from the cold had left her, but she was still chilled down to the bone.

"Hmm. Well, he seems sweet on you," Danielle said, a hint of something in her tone Hope couldn't quite pinpoint—it made her squirm.

Was it jealousy? Irritation?

Danielle was attractive, with deep-olive skin, keen eyes alight with curiosity and an athletic build. It wasn't hard to picture her with Gage.

"Why do you say that?" Hope asked, intrigued to hear the answer.

The woman shrugged. "The way he interacted with you. The blatant show of concern. He's got a big heart, but he doesn't wear it on his sleeve."

"It must be a rescuer-rescuee thing, I suppose." With the mounting hurdles she had to overcome, the last thing she needed standing in her way was a jealous girlfriend. "Are you two together?"

Danielle snickered, but the sound was forced. "If we were, my wife might have something to say about that. It's just odd seeing Gage take to a stranger. Or to anyone, for that matter." Danielle tossed the wet pieces of denim in the trash and threw a wool blanket on top of the foil one over Hope. "He's the oil in our water. Doesn't quite mix, but we don't mind him, either." She removed the device from Hope's finger and took her blood pressure.

"Like all the other government contractors here?" It was clear from the conversation at the gate that Gage wasn't military, but Hope needed to know his connection to Benediction and, more important, if he had any professional ties to Nexcellogen.

Taking off the blood pressure cuff, Danielle held her gaze. "No. The military and the contractors are a necessary evil. Benediction never would've been born without them. Gage is different. He's a resident. A townie, sort of. But what do you know about the government contractors here?"

"Nothing. I heard rumors in Goode, though." Rumors that came with stern warnings.

"Did those rumors bring you to Benediction?"

"No." Hope forced herself to maintain eye contact and reminded herself not to fidget. "I was run off the road."

Danielle looked at her closely, her gaze taking in every detail of Hope's face. "The one road in and out of Benediction. Tell me about your car accident."

"There isn't much to tell," Hope said, her blood suddenly running cold again. She struggled to avoid the woman's scrutiny. "Someone sideswiped me and sent my car over the embankment into the lake."

"No one finds that road unless they're looking for it." Danielle put her hand on Hope's shoulder. "One of the pledges I made as a medical professional is to hold in confidence the information shared in the course of practicing medicine. Anything you tell me in this examine room is between us."

In theory, that sounded lovely, but Hope had earned a degree in the harsh realities of life the hard way. Danielle could be on Nexcellogen's payroll, for all Hope knew. This town safeguarded the company's and the military's secrets and clearly was indebted, since Benediction wouldn't exist without them.

"I told you," Hope said. "There's nothing more to it."

Danielle pulled back and folded her arms. "Let me put it to you another way. I believe in and practice first, do no harm. I can tell that soldier out there that your vitals are sufficiently stable for you to be transported to Goode within the hour. Or I can recommend that you stay the night, which I honestly think would be best in your condition, as does Gage. His opinion means something to me, but I need to be sure that your presence isn't going to do harm to anyone in my town. So, what's your story?"

Hope took a deep breath.

Trust was a precious commodity, and she wasn't about to invest one drop in this woman.

Chapter Four

Sighing with relief to be in dry clothes, Gage stuffed his wet things into a plastic bag and headed for the locker room door. He gritted his teeth at the icy sting from every step thanks to the soaked boots on his feet, but he'd have to tough it out until he got home.

He pulled the door open and rounded the corner, going back toward the front of the clinic. Hope had looked terrified at the prospect of him leaving her. Then again, Benediction could be a terrifying place for someone who didn't know how to navigate the endless land mines— some seen and others well hidden.

But one question kept repeating in his head. *What was she doing on that road to begin with?*

A military police patrol car pulled up out front behind Gage's truck. The blue and red flashing lights were on, but the siren was off. A minute later, the double doors of the clinic opened and in walked Staff Sergeant Burton.

Holding a clipboard in one hand, he removed his patrol cap with the other. He marched down the hall like a man on a mission, his thick-soled boots pounding against the linoleum floor until he reached the front desk.

Livingston had called his supervisor, which Gage had expected. He hadn't expected Burton to throw on a uniform and leave the comforts of his house, where he had a sleep-deprived wife and a four-month-old baby, to race over to the clinic.

"Where is she?" Burton asked the specialist.

Porter hiked a thumb at exam room two. "Inside with PA Varma."

Staff Sergeant Burton stormed over to the door and banged a fist against it.

Gage charged across the hall, bypassing the specialist, and came up alongside Burton as Danielle opened the door.

Burton didn't acknowledge Gage's presence with so much as a glance. "I need to speak to the woman in there."

"We were having a chat, but I'm starting to get dizzy from going in circles." Danielle stepped aside, letting him in.

"I'm Staff Sergeant Burton with the military police." He held up the clipboard in his hand, facing it out toward Hope. "Ma'am, is this you?"

Hope pursed her lips as all expression drained from her face.

Gage strode up to the bed and glanced at the front of the clipboard. There was a black-and-white picture of a woman standing at the gate next to her car, speaking to one of the guards. It was clear as day the image was of Hope and little point in her trying to deny it.

Specialist Porter joined them, taking a position next to the staff sergeant.

"Ma'am, is this you?" Burton asked again, his tone harsh, his expression hard as granite. "Are you Hope Fischer?"

"Fischer?" Danielle shot a worried glance in Hope's direction. "Are you related to Faith Fischer?" Her question reflected typical Benediction suspicion.

Everyone in town knew the name Faith Fischer. For the past ten days, the whole town had been abuzz about the scientist who had killed herself.

"Yes, that's me," Hope said, defiance lighting up her eyes. "Faith was my sister."

Burton handed Porter the clipboard. Then he took out his handcuffs, grabbed Hope's wrist and shackled her to the bed rail.

"What are you doing?" Hope yanked on the restraints.

"Is that really necessary?" Gage asked, meeting Hope's terrified gaze.

"Yes, sir, it is." Burton pivoted, facing him. "This woman was never to be permitted past the gate. Under *any* circumstances."

"Now that I'm here, I'm not leaving without answers about Faith's death."

"That's where you're wrong, ma'am." Burton shifted his stony gaze back to Hope. "You'll leave as soon as you're medically cleared."

"My sister was murdered. Someone in this town knows why and covered it up."

Danielle rubbed her arms as if a chill had come over her and eased back toward the door.

"Not my area, ma'am. You already submitted a formal request for information, and it will take six to eight weeks to be processed, at which point you will be mailed a formal—"

"Two months," Hope scoffed, cutting off the staff sergeant. "That's ridiculous."

The time frame was generous considering the deliberate technological limitations in Benediction. No internet. No Wi-Fi. Cell phones didn't work, and forget about email. It was like living in the dark ages, which was exactly why Gage loved the town.

Made it the perfect place to hide out under the CIA's radar.

"That's the way it is," Staff Sergeant Burton said. "You won't stay in this town a moment longer than absolutely necessary."

Gage turned to ask Danielle for her medical opinion, but she had slipped out of the room. He stepped into the hallway and barely heard Danielle's voice. She was speaking to someone in a hushed tone. He crept down the hall and peeked around the corner at the front desk.

Danielle was on the phone, rubbing the nape of her neck. As she flicked a glance in his direction, Gage ducked back so she wouldn't spot him and strained to hear the one side of the conversation.

"She has questions," Danielle said. "Thinks her sister was murdered." A short pause. "I don't know. What do you want me to do?"

Burton marched into the hallway, past Gage to the desk, and rapped on it with his knuckles, drawing her attention.

Danielle raised a finger at him. "Okay. If you think so. I'll take care of it. Get some sleep." She hung up the phone. "Yes, Staff Sergeant?"

"When can Ms. Fischer be discharged?" Burton asked.

"We're going to keep her overnight." Danielle folded her arms. "Ms. Fischer is at risk for complications such as hypoxic cerebral injury, acute respiratory distress, pulmonary damage secondary to aspiration and cardiac arrest. I'll have the doc look her over in the morning. If he clears her, she's all yours."

"Gage," Hope called for him. "Gage!"

He hurried back into her room. "Yeah, I'm still here."

"Can you bring me my purse from your truck?" Hope asked. "It's under the front seat."

"I thought you lost it, ma'am," Porter said, evidently more astute than he appeared.

Hope glanced at the specialist. "My wallet was lost. Not my purse."

Porter nodded with a confused look on his face, but he didn't ask any further questions.

"I'll grab it for you." Gage patted her shoulder and left the room. He crossed paths with Burton in the hallway.

"I need a word with you," the staff sergeant said.

"I'll be back in a minute, and then you can have as many words with me as you'd like." Gage kept moving, not waiting for a reply. He didn't want to leave Hope alone with soldiers any longer than he had to.

He ran to his truck and found her purse right where she'd said. Smart of her to hide it if her identity meant she might've been denied medical treatment.

A sleek silver sedan pulled up. Gage recognized it immediately. The vehicle belonged to Ian McCallister, head of security for Nexcellogen.

Had an emergency telephone tree been activated?

Not wanting to get tied up in a conversation, Gage headed back inside and didn't slow down until he was in the examination room. He handed the purse over to Hope, but Burton snatched it.

The staff sergeant unzipped the wet bag and took a quick look. "Sorry, ma'am. I have to check for a weapon." Once he was satisfied, he zipped it and gave her the purse.

Ian McCallister knocked on the door and strode into the room. Always polished and poised, he wore a crisp white shirt and dark slacks. His silver-flecked dark hair was coiffed, and the scruff of late-day stubble over his cheeks and jaw was the only thing to mar the perfection of his appearance. "Good evening, everyone." He turned to Burton. "Do we know who our visitor is?"

"Yes, sir. She's Faith Fischer's sister, Hope."

"Really?" Though the corners of McCallister's eyes crinkled in sympathy, his watchful gaze was appraising everything and everyone in the room. "I'm sorry for your loss and to hear about your accident on the road," he said to Hope.

Unlike other security chiefs Gage had encountered in the past, McCallister didn't have a bulldog personality or menacing persona, but he did have what could only be described as *presence*. That it factor better suited for public relations than his current line of work.

Single women in town fawned over him, along with some not so single. He was that guy other men wanted to be friends with, who paid for a round of drinks after bolstering you up instead of putting you down. He even started the Future Leaders Club at the school, which had impressive attendance because kids liked him, too.

"Thank you," Hope said. "But if you feel an ounce of compassion for my situation, you'll explain to me why my sister's murder wasn't investigated."

McCallister clasped his hands in front of him. "The medical examiner looked at your sister's body. I'm afraid it was ruled a suicide."

"She didn't kill herself," Hope insisted.

"I can see you've been through a lot tonight." McCallister took a deep breath. "How long will our visitor be with us?"

"She'll stay overnight," Burton said.

"Perhaps we can talk in the morning, after you've had breakfast," McCallister said. "Give us a chance to allay your concerns."

"Once the doc discharges you, Ms. Fischer, we're escorting you to the front gate," Burton said.

"How am I supposed to get back to Goode?" Hope asked. "My rental car is in the lake."

"Specialist Porter," Burton said, looking at the young man. "Call a tow truck to have her rental car taken to the next town and make arrangements with a taxi company to have one waiting for her by 0900 sharp at the gate."

"Yes, sir."

"Don't ever *sir* me again, son. I work for a living."

"Yes, Staff Sergeant."

McCallister rolled his eyes at the exchange between the soldiers.

"Best of luck getting a taxi to show in the morning." Gage leveled his gaze on Burton. "The snow is going to start in the wee hours." It didn't snow often in Virginia, but when it did the snowfall could be heavy in this mountainous region, closing schools and shutting down the roads.

"Calling for a cab was merely a courtesy to Ms. Fischer," Burton said. "But taxi or no taxi, at 0900 she will be put out of Benediction."

"If the doctor clears her, you mean," Gage said.

Burton flashed a cold smile. "We'll see to it that he does. At 0900 Ms. Fischer *will* be at the gate."

"Rest assured, Ms. Fischer," McCallister said, "you will not be walking back to Goode. Ms. Lansing and I will both be here to oversee this process. I'm sure she'll want to offer her condolences personally."

Michelle Lansing was the director of Nexcellogen and

the pseudo mayor of the town. Although she had no authority over the military troops or the townspeople, she ensured affairs between all parties remained smooth. She found ways to deepen relations by holding various events that everyone looked forward to—the Easter egg hunt, movie night in the park, the Fourth of July bash. That sort of thing. She was the thread weaving the town, the military and the company closer together into one cohesive group.

"I welcome a face-to-face chat with her," Hope said. "In the meantime, am I supposed to stay handcuffed to the bed all night?"

Burton took the clipboard from Porter and tucked it under his arm. "Yes. You are."

"Surely," McCallister said, "we can remove the handcuffs and allow Ms. Fischer to recuperate in comfort instead of treating her as though she were guilty of a crime."

"I have my orders," Burton said.

McCallister pulled the staff sergeant aside, but Gage was still within earshot. "Her sister just died. She's grieving. We need to show compassion. Besides, this isn't a good PR look for Nexcellogen. I can see the headlines now."

"Not my area," Burton snapped.

McCallister slipped his hands into his pocket. "Ms. Lansing won't be pleased to hear about this."

Burton shrugged. "She'll have to take it up with Captain Finley."

"What if I have to use the bathroom?" Hope asked, drawing everyone's attention.

"You have three choices, ma'am. One," Burton said, actually lifting a finger, "you can hold it. Two, you can soil yourself. Three, PA Varma can insert a catheter." He wagged his three fingers and it was all Gage could do not to sock the guy in the jaw. "I don't care which you choose. What's it going to be?"

Hope narrowed her eyes at him, not the least bit intimidated. "I'll hold it."

McCallister stepped forward. "On behalf of Nexcellogen, I apologize for this deplorable treatment."

"If you need to relieve yourself during the night," Danielle said, coming back into the room, "just press the call button. I can help you with a bedpan."

"Thank you," Hope said. "But I'm sure I'll be fine. I just need some peace and a few hours of sleep."

"Speaking of which." Danielle came closer, extending a medicine cup with two tiny pills and a small drink of water.

"What is it?" Hope asked.

"A sedative. It will help you sleep."

"No, thank you." Hope pulled the blanket up. "I don't take tranquilizers. I don't react well to them."

"Rest is the best thing for you right now." Danielle jiggled the medicine cup, causing the pills to rattle. "I have to insist."

"She's already handcuffed," Gage said, giving Danielle a warning glance to back off but keeping his tone even. "Forcing her to do one more thing that she doesn't want to do can't possibly be good for her. If she changes her mind, she can always use the call button."

"Mr. Graham is quite right," McCallister said.

Danielle nodded and stepped back as Burton gave Porter additional orders.

Gage leaned in toward Danielle. "Hey," he said low, "who were you talking to on the phone a minute ago?"

"Dr. Howland. I wanted to update him on our latest patient."

"Gage." Hope held out her hand. "Can you sit with me for a little until I fall asleep?"

"Let me run home, change my shoes and I'll stay as long as you'd like."

"No, Mr. Graham, you won't." Burton eyed him. "It's time we had those words." The staff sergeant gestured for him to go out into the hall.

"Actually, you should all leave," Danielle said. "Ms. Fischer has been through a traumatic experience. It's vital that she rests."

"Ms. Fischer," McCallister said, "get some rest. Ms. Lansing and I will see you in the morning."

Danielle shooed everyone from the room. "Light on or off?" Danielle asked Hope.

"On. Strange place. Handcuffed to the bed."

"I understand. I'll make sure no one else disturbs you. Try to get some sleep." Danielle closed the door behind her.

McCallister was already headed out the door. Once Danielle and Porter went back to the front, Burton turned on Gage.

"Captain Finley gave me orders that you are not to remain at the clinic."

Not only had Livingston called his supervisor, but apparently Burton had notified his own, as well. Finley must've called McCallister. Gage smothered his annoyance, not letting it leak into his expression.

"She would like to discuss the matter of you bringing an unauthorized, blacklisted person into the town," Burton said. "You're to be in her office in one hour, and she said not to come empty-handed."

The captain was referring to the package Gage owed

her. It was on his list of essentials and was still sitting in Goode. "Tell her I'll be there in two hours."

"The captain said one."

Although it would've been satisfying to knock Burton's lights out, it also would've created more problems than it was worth. "I'm sure your boss doesn't want me getting hypothermia. My boots are wet and freezing, and in case you hadn't noticed my hands are still shaking." A fact he hated. "I'll be there in two hours." Gage still had to go to Goode and pick up his supplies, including the package Captain Finley was expecting.

He swallowed the bitter taste in his mouth from being at the beck and call of the captain, but that was the deal.

"It's your funeral," Burton said.

Gage clenched his hands and headed for the door. The sleek silver sedan was gone. McCallister probably couldn't wait to get back home.

In his truck, Gage tossed his bag of wet clothes in the back and fired up the engine. But instead of going straight home like he should've, he pulled off from under the awning and away from the doors, where Burton was watching him, and drove around to the side of the clinic. He backed up alongside the building, parking the car so it was shielded by an ambulance and killed the engine.

His thoughts kept circling back to Hope. Once the two soldiers left, he would sneak in and check on her. Make sure she'd be okay right for the night.

He stared at her window, the only lit room on that side of the building.

After a few minutes, two cars passed by, taking the service lane back to the main road. Burton and Porter were finally gone. Gage could only imagine how ticked off Captain Finley was going to be once Burton delivered his message.

Hope was major trouble, all right. Bringing her into Benediction had placed him in Finley's crosshairs, and she was a crack shot. Forgetting about Hope and washing his hands of this business was the smart play, but he'd gotten involved the moment he pulled her out of the lake and hustled her into town.

She had been caught in the wrong place at the wrong time and had nearly died. That made him feel for her, especially since she only seemed to want answers about her sister.

Then there was the matter of Faith Fischer. Everyone believed the rumors about the scientist, swallowed the story that she had a nasty breakup with someone, withdrew from social situations, started spending all her free time alone and got depressed around the holidays.

Everyone except Gage. Something was off about the circumstances surrounding her death. Call it professional intuition. He was an expert when it came to death. How to cover one up, to make it disappear, to eliminate every trace from the scene.

At the CIA, that had been his job. His forte. He'd been assigned to a four-person team. Such a small word to describe the people who, over the years and through the close-call ordeals, had become his family. Their covert missions had been to carry out high-value target assassinations. Everyone had a specialty.

He was the cleaner.

Movement inside Hope's room pulled him from his thoughts. Gage straightened, leaning toward the steering wheel. A shadow darted up to the window and raised the blinds.

Hope.

She was free from the handcuffs.

How in the heck had she managed that?

Hope unlocked the window and raised it. Holding the two blankets around her shoulders so that they covered her body, she threw a leg over the side of the windowsill. A long, toned leg followed by the other one.

What in the hell was she doing?

She eased herself down from the sill, holding her purse and shoes. The second her bare feet hit the cold ground the distress on her face turned to shock. Gage could only imagine the pain she must've experienced in that instant. She hopped up, pulling the window closed.

He started the engine, and his headlights blinked on.

Hope's head snapped up, turning in his direction, and she froze. He shut off the lights and waved to her when she looked ready to bolt in the opposite direction.

She ran to the truck and climbed into the passenger's seat.

"You must really have a death wish," he said, "running around with no clothes on in this weather when your body is still fighting hypothermia."

"I need to get answers about what happened to Faith. Tonight. Once they kick me out in the morning, I'll never make it back inside Benediction. I'll never learn the truth."

"In this town, the truth won't set you free and it won't bring your sister back, but it might get you killed." He shifted in his seat toward her. "So, do you?"

Hope tensed. "Do I what?"

"Have a death wish?"

She blew out a heavy breath and lowered her head. "I can't live with not knowing who killed my sister and why."

Not knowing what happened to a loved one could drive a person insane. In his case, it had driven him to the CIA. His father had worked for the Agency. Went out on a mission and never came back. The circumstances had been classified.

Even after he joined, he never uncovered the specifics surrounding his father's death. The details had been above his pay grade.

Every day it ate away at him. A stinging, helpless feeling he wouldn't wish on his worst enemy.

"I won't let a murderer get away," Hope said. "Someone has to be held responsible."

Every person on his team's kill list had been human garbage, and eliminating them had been for the greater good, to make the world a safer place. Justice had been the cornerstone of each assignment.

If someone had taken the life of an innocent woman in Benediction, there was no way Gage could turn a blind eye to it and allow a killer to run loose in the town. His conscience wouldn't let him rest, and Hope looked determined not to stop until she got answers. Without his help, her endeavor could cost her life.

He looked around at the darkness, trying to figure something out. "What's your plan?"

"From here, I'm winging it." She rubbed her hands together, the sound reviving his sense of urgency. "What are you doing out here, sitting in the dark?"

He sensed her watching him and he wanted, no, needed to look at her but dreaded meeting her eyes. The fact that she had become the focal point of his need or dread in less than an hour knocked him off kilter. Left him unbalanced.

"I told you I wouldn't go far," he said. "If nothing

else, I'm a man of my word. I always keep my promises." Gage looked at her, met that intense, piercing gaze, which was searching his as though she could see right through him—or wanted to.

He hadn't been *seen* in a long time, and the thought of it, like everything else about Hope, had a knot of terror tightening inside him and a strange elation unfurling.

Saving her life had roused his protective instincts, but it didn't explain or give a name to what he was feeling.

"Good to know," she said.

"They'll realize you're missing long before morning. I say you have a few hours until Danielle checks on you and reports that you're gone." Without knowing whom else Danielle had called, Hope might have even less than that.

She held her shaking hands up to the vent. "I'm not leaving this town until I find out what really happened to Faith."

"I have an idea that'll buy you time," Gage said, hoping like hell that it'd work. "But you'll need to do exactly what I tell you. Can you follow orders?"

Hope straightened in her seat. Her features hardened with grim determination, and her eyes gleamed with a fierceness that warmed him but also worried him. "I'll do whatever it takes."

That was precisely what concerned him.

Chapter Five

Hope had neglected to confess she wasn't the best at
following orders. The nature of her job required her to
defy authority and toss out the rulebook. Two things that
came effortlessly for her.

Gage turned on the truck's headlights and pulled off.
They cleared the clinic, hitting the main road.

"Where are we going?" she asked, scooting down low
in the seat to ensure that any passersby wouldn't see her.

"My place. You'll be safe there—for a while, anyway." The roads were empty as he went through the
roundabout, taking the turn into the residential section
of town. "But if they find you, they won't show an ounce
of leniency."

Chilled inside and out, Hope leaned in closer to the
vent, staying down low near the dashboard. That helped
warm her, but her feet were blocks of ice.

They drove through the confines of the compact
neighborhood to the far side. All the homes were built
of brick, painted light gray. The lawns were small and
shaded by decades-old trees. American flags hung from
the eaves or mailboxes of every home.

Gage pushed a button on the remote clipped on the
visor as he made a right turn into a driveway. The house

was at the end of a cul-de-sac, tastefully decorated with white string lights and a brightly lit Santa's sleigh complete with reindeer adorning the front lawn. The door of a double garage opened in front of them. A gold SUV was parked inside, and a mountain bike hung on the wall.

"You don't live alone." The possibility of a wife or girlfriend hadn't occurred to her.

"No. I live with my stepsister, Claire, and her son, Jason. I stay in the apartment above the garage." He pulled in, parked and hit the remote-control button, lowering the garage door.

"So you're single?" she asked without thinking. Not that she regretted it. Clarity was a good thing.

"I am. No romantic attachments for me."

At the moment? Or ever? "Why?"

He was smart, brave and attractive. Had chosen to help her when others would've abandoned her. Everything about him was hard but appealing, from the expression on his face to his sculpted body.

"My life is complicated. It wouldn't be fair to ask someone to deal with my baggage." Before Hope had a chance to ask any further questions, he said, "Wait here for me. I'll only be a minute." Gage jumped out of the truck and made his way into the house.

The interior garage light went out, and the ensuing silence was unsettling. Would Gage tell his stepsister about her? Was he the type of man to keep secrets from those closest to him?

A shiver ran through her, more from the quiet and waiting than the cold. She missed the soothing heat blowing from the vents, but the truck cab stayed warm until Gage returned.

As promised, he'd only been gone a couple of minutes.

He came around to her side of the truck with clothes, shoes and a sealed Tupperware container full of food in his hands.

She opened the door and looked down at the floor, dreading the feel of the concrete against her bare feet.

"Don't worry." He thrust the bundle that he was holding into her arms. "You carry that stuff and I'll carry you," he said, as if reading her mind.

Her whole body softened in gratitude while her brain warned, *It'll be a mistake, a big, big mistake!*

In twenty-eight years, no man had ever carried her until Gage, a gorgeous, good citizen who was willing to lift her into his arms for a third time in one night. "You probably shouldn't. It's starting to become a habit and I might get used to it."

"I can think of a lot worse tendencies to get used to."

He had a point, but she needed to use better judgment. "I'm strong enough to walk."

"No doubt about that after your great escape from the clinic." His smile was crooked, playful and had her smiling in return.

It was so unlike her. She never let a sexy grin or an impressive body throw her off stride. Knew better than to be lured in by chivalry and charm. She stayed on track. Took whatever risks were necessary regardless of the danger. She'd do the same with Gage. He was her best option to get answers, but he was also a stranger. Still, something about him kept derailing her focus from the cold and death and had her thinking about ridiculous things, like how warm his eyes became when he smiled.

The way he'd fearlessly endangered himself to save her—twice. His refusal to cave under pressure from the military and willingness to hide her in his home.

The selflessness that became more apparent with each of his actions, and that inclined her to trust him despite the fact that everyone in Benediction was a suspect she had to investigate.

Her instincts regarding him were dangerous.

Kindness was the best disguise when a person had something to hide. She couldn't drop her guard around him.

Not that she had any intention of sharing that. It was hard enough to admit to herself for some reason. "I can handle the cold ground for a little longer."

"No need." He plucked a pair of sweatpants and canvas sneakers from the pile in her hands. "You and Claire are about the same size. I think they'll fit."

She took the pants and shoes, setting the other stuff down. "Thanks."

Gage nodded and went to the front of the truck, putting his back to her, giving her privacy.

The lounge pants were tapered through the leg, fitting like snug pajamas, but they were warm. The sneakers would do, even if they were a little too loose on her feet.

She hopped out of the truck and closed the door gently. "Thank you."

He took the rest of the stuff from her. "Come on. It's this way."

With the two blankets from the hospital wrapped around her shoulders, she followed him. Gage led her through the side door of the garage and up a steep exterior staircase. Glancing behind her, she checked to be sure no neighbors spotted her.

At the landing, she had a clear view behind the house to a one-story building. It looked commercial, at least twice the square footage of any of the residences with plenty of parking in the area. Only an uninterrupted expanse of grass and a footpath ran between the two properties.

Gage quickly unlocked the door, ushering her inside, and switched on the lights. "Feel free to look around."

She took in the simple apartment, not that there was much to see. Three rooms consisting of an eat-in kitchen connected to a living room with a gas fireplace, bedroom with a queen-size bed and a full bathroom.

The walls were white and plain. No paintings, no pictures, not a single personal photograph. The furniture was well-worn and mismatched like pieces picked up from a rummage sale. Though she barely knew Gage, nothing in the apartment seemed to fit him. She imagined his taste would run toward brown leather and dark polished wood.

"How long have you lived here?" she asked, folding both blankets into a neat pile.

He set the container of food and other clothes on the kitchen counter. "Here in this apartment or here in Benediction?"

"Both."

"Well, the answer is one and the same. Nine months."

"What brought you to Benediction?"

He put the Tupperware container in the microwave, setting it for two minutes. "It's complicated."

That was fast becoming his favorite word, she noticed.

He crossed the room, going to the gas fireplace, and turned it on. "Claire has lupus. She had a bad flare-up around the time I needed a major change in my life. They weren't sure if she'd make it. I came and helped her out."

Hope had never met anyone firsthand who had the

autoimmune disease, but she knew it was chronic and triggered the immune system to attack the body's healthy tissue. The disease could affect the skin and joints, cause organ damage. The severity and symptoms varied from person to person. "That was extraordinary of you to put your life on hold like that for her."

"Not really." Looking Hope straight in the eye, he said, "Please don't think I'm noble or anything close to it. Because I'm not."

The more she learned about him, the more *noble* became the perfect word to describe him. Along with modest and brave.

Why downplay his acts of kindness? Humility she understood, respected, but this self-denigration felt like deflection.

His brow creased, and a look of raw vulnerability flashed across his face as she considered him.

"Dumb luck brought Claire and me back together, and we both got something out of it." He held the stare for a beat longer, then he bent down and unlaced his boots. "She's doing much better now, can handle things on her own." Slipping the boots off, he gave a sigh of relief. He set them on the hearth. "Put yours next to mine to dry. Excuse me a sec. I'm dying to get something warm and dry on my feet." Gage went into the bedroom, leaving the door open.

Hope sat on the soft shag rug close to the fire, placing her shoes near his.

All this time, he'd put off his own needs without complaining while looking out for her at the entrance to Benediction, at the clinic, in the garage. Yet another example of how he came across as a good person at the core. Not just for show. Most of the men who had passed through her life had only helped her if they benefited in return.

The microwave beeped.

She was rising from the rug when he came back out wearing socks.

"I've got it. Stay seated and rest. Doc's orders." He tossed her a pair of wool socks.

She caught them and didn't waste a second trading them for the canvas sneakers.

He switched off the main overhead light, leaving the soft glow from the fire to illuminate the room. Her eyes softened and her shoulders relaxed in immediate response. She hadn't realized every muscle had been clenched.

Gage washed his hands and grabbed two spoons from a drawer and bowls from a cabinet. "I hope you're hungry and eat meat."

"I am and I do."

He took the container out of the microwave and removed the lid.

A heavenly aroma wafted through the room, making her stomach rumble. She hadn't realized she was hungry, but it had been hours since she'd last eaten. "That smells delicious."

"Claire is a good cook." He divided the food between the two bowls, then, coming closer, he handed her one along with a spoon and sat beside her in front of the fire.

The stew was thick, with chunks of meat and hearty vegetables bathed in a fragrant broth. The first slightly gamey bite told her it was venison, fixed with carrots, juniper berries, turnips and parsnips rather than potatoes. "This is wonderful. Claire isn't a good cook. She's excellent."

"Hits the spot, doesn't it?"

After almost dying, a ham sandwich would've been ambrosia, but the stew was truly tasty. She nodded to him and finished eating, letting the warmth of the food soak into her body.

"Need something to wash it down?" he asked.

"Yes, please."

He took her bowl from her and stood. "Water or brandy? I have the good stuff."

"Both." Her body had relaxed, but her mind still whirled with thoughts of Faith and the military police and what would happen if they found her. "On second thought, maybe I should stick to water. I only have a few hours before—"

"I promised to buy you time, and I will." Though he neglected to say how. He poured two waters and one brandy, leaving the bottle on the counter. "I'm a man of my word, remember?"

How could she forget? "I guess it's my turn to ask what's your plan."

"Leave that to me." He carried the three glasses to the rug and gave her a water and the brandy. "I want you to focus on resting and getting your strength back."

"No brandy for you?"

"I need a clear head if I'm going to ensure no one comes looking for you, but you should drink up. You've been through a lot tonight. I'm sure there's still too much adrenaline in your system. The sedative Danielle offered was probably a good idea, but I can understand you not wanting to take it. Not knowing how it might affect you. But the brandy will make it easier for you to relax. You'll be safe here."

She wasn't prepared to put her complete trust in him,

but if Gage had wanted the military police to capture her and kick her out of town, he wouldn't have picked her up outside the clinic. It would've been a heck of a lot easier to simply report her. Whatever his motives for helping her, for now, they appeared aligned with her own.

Hope sipped the brandy. Smooth and warm, the amber liquid burst with complex flavors, relieving the vestige of tension in her chest. "The good stuff indeed."

"There's something I need to ask you," he said. "How did you get out of the handcuffs?"

"Let's just say that after being detained by authoritarian governments, taken hostage by a warlord and restrained by a local extremist group, I've learned how to get out of a pair of handcuffs."

The corner of his mouth hitched up in a half grin that was endearing and equally sexy. "You used something from your purse that the staff sergeant overlooked, right? It's the reason you asked me to get your handbag from the truck."

As a matter of fact, he was right. Her handy-dandy Swiss Army knife had a variety of features, including a handcuff key that had gotten her out of more than one pinch. Most people dismissed the multitool because of its glittery, jewel-tone case, not bothering to examine it further. "Thanks for the assist. Without it, I'd still be locked to the bed."

He drank his water. "Authoritarian governments, warlords and extremists. That's an impressive list."

"It comes with the professional territory."

"What profession might that be?"

"I'm a photojournalist." The equipment she used made her easy to spot in a crowd, and her images always drew unfriendly attention. Intimidation, imprisonment, even torture happened to those in her line of work sometimes. Hope had never experienced the extreme end of the spectrum, but she knew of others who had.

"Ah," he said with a touch of a smile on his lips. "That explains the intrepid, won't-back-down air about you. I like a persistent woman who goes after what she wants."

His flattery was comforting in a way it shouldn't have been. A verbal stroke of her ego that made her smile. But it was more than that. There was such warmth to him she wanted to bask in.

She pulled her legs into her chest and rocked slightly, fighting the strange sense of ease that came over her in his presence. "I'm not intrepid." Though she did like the sound of it, almost as much as she enjoyed the idea of him thinking of her as such. "Merely stubborn." She'd learned the difference a long time ago.

Weren't they a pair? He wasn't *noble* and she wasn't *brave*.

Gage leaned in toward her, forcing her to meet his eyes, and everything inside her quieted. "I see real courage when I look at you. And determination. Most people don't have either. Their resolve is born out of fear. Unlike yours."

Not quite knowing how to respond to the best compliment she'd ever received, she looked away from him and sipped the brandy.

The fire provided the only light between them and continued to spread its warmth through the room. The heat eased the stiffness in her body.

A moment later, she found her voice. "Courage is admirable. My tenacity has often been called reckless."

"No doubt. Climbing out of the clinic's window barefoot without any pants on in this weather was reckless, but the truly brave always are. How can I fault you for that?" Gage got up, snatched a heavy blanket from the back of the sofa and dragged it around her until she was encased in a cocoon. "I have to go. Once you feel like sleeping, take the bed. I'll bunk on the sofa."

"Where are you going?"

"To run an important errand to get supplies. Then I have to go see Captain Finley."

"Who's that?"

"The one person in Benediction who can call off the military police."

Chapter Six

Sheriff Ryan Keller didn't think his night could get much worse. But every minute it slid farther downhill from *bad* to *wretched*.

Wearing a black turtleneck and jeans—instead of his uniform, since this was supposed to be his night off—he walked into the station and up to Deputy Owen Finnegan.

He stared at Finn's battered face, black eye and broken nose, and exhaled a string of expletives. "Did that kid do this to you?" Ryan asked, hiking his chin at a male, no older than eighteen, who was locked up in a holding cell, pacing back and forth like a rabid wolf ready to gnaw off a limb.

Finn lowered the ice pack from his bloody nose. "Kid? More like a doped-up punk."

"It took the two of us to subdue him," Deputy Dwight Travers said, pouring himself a cup of coffee.

Ryan took off his black wool beanie and traded it for the stiff ball cap he rarely wore. The front panel of the cap had white block letters that read *Sheriff*. Besides his cuffs and Glock holstered on his hip, the ball cap was the closest he was getting to an official uniform tonight.

Tomorrow it'd be business as usual with his Stetson. "Good thing he didn't have a weapon."

"Still, he did a number on Finn," Dwight said.

"What's he on?" asked Aimee Newsome, his administrative assistant and the heart of the office. She kept things running smoothly and the station stocked, made sure he didn't miss anyone's birthday or anniversary.

Dwight stood next to Finn and put a hand on his shoulder. "Must be Zion."

That was the name of the latest and greatest drug on the streets. There was always something new, but this stuff supposedly made a person feel invincible with no nasty hallucinations.

He'd read reports that it was fast becoming an epidemic in cities like Richmond, Virginia Beach, Arlington, DC.

This sort of thing wasn't expected to happen in a sleepy town where you had to drive two hours for soft-serve frozen yogurt. Granted, the preconceived notion that smaller equaled safer wasn't accurate. Crimes happened across geographical areas. People locked their houses and cars in Goode, but they didn't have junkie dens, meth labs and drug-related assaults there.

At least they weren't supposed to have them.

A long time ago, he'd made peace with the fact that he was stuck in Goode, caring for his ailing dad. Alzheimer's and cirrhosis were slowly eating away at him. Ryan loved his father and didn't mind the thankless task of playing nursemaid in the absence of the home care helper. He'd even convinced himself that he was lucky to have this suffocating job, but the only luck he had was the bad kind.

Now he had to deal with the cons of a big-city life with none of the perks on top of everything else.

Ryan rubbed the metal bump on his sternum under his sweater. A reminder attached to the chain around his neck that this was all his life would ever be.

"Now that I'm here, Dwight, take Finn over to the ER so he can be checked out."

The local tow truck came down the street, hauling a banged-up sky blue sedan. The front end and trunk had been partially crushed, the roof was crumpled and the driver's window was busted.

Ryan's hair stood on end. He knew that car. A rental that belonged to Hope Fischer. The woman hell-bent on getting answers about her dead sister. "Give me a sec," he said.

He shoved through the door and jogged across the street to where the truck waited at a traffic light.

"Hey, Zach, where did you get that car?"

"I pulled it out of Goode Lake on the road to Bene-diction."

Damn it. "Was it completely submerged?"

"May as well have been."

"What about the driver? Do you know what condition she's in? Is she alive?"

"They took her to the medical facility in Benediction for treatment. Can you believe that they let her in? That newcomer must have good mojo. If it had been one of us Goodies, we'd be dead on the side of the road."

The fact that she was receiving medical care meant she was alive. "I'll call over in the morning and see how she's doing."

"No need, Sheriff. I heard the MPs scheduled a taxi to pick her up tomorrow."

Then her condition wasn't serious. *Thank God.* Strangers never understood that it was best to stay away from Benediction. "All right." Ryan patted his door. "Thanks."

As the light changed, he crossed the street.

He'd give it forty-eight hours. If Hope Fischer wasn't back in Goode by then, he'd drive over to Benediction. His sheriff's badge wouldn't get him through the gate, but he'd raise hell until he knew that nothing fishy had happened to her.

SNOW FLURRIES HAD started falling earlier than the forecast had predicted. Luckily, Gage had made it to Goode, picked up the essentials he needed and returned before the snow started to stick.

He parked near the Benediction military police station. The unmarked building was within walking distance of the shops and diner but sat apart from everything else. Glancing at the clock, he saw he had two minutes to make it to Captain Erin Finley's office or he'd face her ire.

The CIA had taught him many harsh lessons, including how to deal with someone who had a gun pointed at your head when you only had a knife.

Taking a deep breath, he prepared for battle. When it came to his personal situation, which was now compounded by the liability of protecting Hope, winning wasn't an option. The best he could hope for was a draw.

Keeping the MPs from conducting a manhunt in town to find Hope would be tricky at best, but the deception was necessary if she was going to stay in town to find answers about her sister's death. And it appeared she had every intention of doing so. Gage understood the feeling and would do likewise in her position.

The woman roused his protective instincts, and there was little he could do to fight nature. But what would he do if that impulse were pitted against his own sense of self-preservation?

In the next sixty seconds, he was going to find out.

Gage grabbed the box from the passenger's seat and hopped out of the truck.

Floodlights bathed the one-story building and surrounding area. At least one guard was always on duty inside. The contingent of MPs in town was small, ten enlisted plus Finley, and they were a tight crew.

As he approached the entrance, the soldier seated at the front desk spotted him and hurried over to assist.

The specialist held the door open for him. "Evening, Mr. Graham. She's waiting. You should hurry."

All the MPs were aware of Gage's regular deliveries, though he suspected none of them knew what they consisted of or had the gumption to question Finley.

Gage quickened his step down the short, narrow hall, passing the evidence room.

Finley's office door was closed.

He peered through the glass insert. Seated behind her desk in uniform, her blond hair in a tight, slick bun, she was working on her computer. No doubt she'd heard his footsteps approaching and was cognizant of his presence, but she didn't acknowledge him.

A silly show of power. Not that he blamed her for being miffed she was there later than normal on his account.

He rapped on the door, balancing the heavy box on his knee, and waited.

Lifting one hand from the keyboard, she beckoned

to him to enter with a wave, still not looking away from her computer.

He strode in, his shoulders squared and his head held high. No slinking in like a dog with its tail between its legs for him. He plopped the box on the desk, causing the glass bottles inside to clatter, and took a seat.

"Cutting it down to the wire, aren't you?" Leaning back in her chair, she finally stopped typing and looked at him. Her amber eyes were cold as frostbite.

"Good evening to you, too, Captain Finley."

She drew her mouth tight in a sour expression and checked the contents of the box.

Ten pounds of imported gold-grade Wagyu steaks, hard-to-come-by bottles of Château Margaux and Lafite Rothschild, and a few hand-rolled Cuban cigars.

Residing in Benediction made it impossible to procure such high-end luxury items online. No internet was one thing. Package delivery companies didn't service the town, and Benediction wasn't a part of the regular postal system. Mail was routed through military channels for security purposes because no civilian postal carriers were allowed inside the town.

Life here was miserable for those unaccustomed to the constraints.

Even under *normal* conditions, Captain Finley couldn't afford the contents of the box.

That was over four grand worth of goods. Paid for with Gage's savings.

Captain Finley closed the flaps of the box and pushed it aside. "When I set a meeting, I expect you to rearrange your schedule to make it." She propped her elbows on the desk and stared at him over the steeple of her fingers. "Never change the time again."

Her expectations had been crystal clear from the beginning, but these were extenuating circumstances. "If I had come earlier, I would've been empty-handed, and I didn't want to disappoint you," he said, his tone casual.

Holding his gaze, Finley hit a button on her keyboard, and the printer spit out a piece of paper. "You disappointed me the moment you brought an uncleared person through my gate."

It wasn't *her* gate, despite the power trip she was on telling herself otherwise, but he wasn't there to quibble. "I'm sorry to disappoint you. Certainly, you were informed that it was a medical emergency."

She gave him a withering glance. "It was wrong for you to manipulate the gate guards, promising they'd be hailed as heroes. They're young and impressionable. The rules keep everyone safe. We're under no legal obligation to assist anyone beyond the boundary of Benediction for good reason."

"What about an ethical responsibility?"

Finley swiveled in her chair, took the paper from the printer and placed it in on her desk in front of her, ignoring his question. "Your actions tonight threaten our agreement," she said, her voice edged with acid.

They had forged a tenuous arrangement when he arrived last spring. One mutually beneficial to all parties.

Gage needed a place to lie low after his CIA team had been disavowed and put on a kill list. The irony of the tables turning—now he was the one being hunted—wasn't lost on him.

Getting into the town had been simple for him. He first became a resident of Benediction briefly as a child. His mother had married Claire's father, a townie who had been born and raised there. But an insulated life in the mountains of Virginia hadn't been for his mom, and the marriage only lasted a few years. Long enough for him to be documented as a former inhabitant and loosely considered a relative of a current native.

All of which had been sufficient to get him through the gates with Claire's dire medical situation and Dr. Steve Howland's support. Doc had been in Benediction forever and had known Gage as a child. Howland had vouched for Gage's character. Something he'd claimed didn't change. He had insisted Claire needed help to recover and the town required someone to manage her family business, which provided a critical service that Gage happened to have the rare qualifications to take over.

The right time, the right place, the right circumstances.

The problem was the background check Captain Finley wanted to send up through her chain of command as part of their security protocol.

There were no digital records connecting Gage to Benediction. He never included the town on his list of prior residences in his disclosure paperwork, and he had never shared the detail with a soul. If his name had been logged into the system, it would've drawn a bull's-eye around his head while giving the CIA his exact coordinates.

Gage had confided in Claire that a background check would be bad. As in disastrous. She told him about Finley's marital problems. Secrets were hard to keep in a small town. Finley was having a difficult time hanging on to her husband. A man of particular tastes, he loathed this remote assignment and the constraints it put on his own career and missed the creature comforts of a big city.

With Gage's connections and his rainy-day fund, he struck a deal for the duration of her assignment. Once Finley moved on from Benediction, she had promised the paperwork would appear as though he'd been properly vetted, so her replacement wouldn't ask questions. Not that Gage trusted her to follow through on her end.

She had two more years on her orders. Two years Gage could count on having sanctuary. For a disavowed CIA operative on the run for his life, two years could feel like twenty.

A feasible trade considering he had virtually no living expenses, even though the arrangement proved an irritating inconvenience.

Escape was not peace, he had discovered.

"These bimonthly deliveries of yours keep my husband happy. Living here is now tolerable for him. You've also found a way to make yourself indispensable to the town while somehow remaining invisible. Takes quite the talent to pull that off."

Well, he worked very hard at it. He'd stepped in for Claire while she was sick and still handled the less desirable aspects of the job for her. When the school's physical education teacher relocated, Gage offered to substitute, the same way he joined the fire department the moment they fell short on a required number of volunteers.

The trick was noticing a need and filling it while keeping everyone at arm's length. The more distance the better.

"I'd hate to dissolve our partnership and file this." Captain Finley slid the paper across the desk to him. "But I will."

Gage took the document and scanned it. A formal request for a background check on him.

He crumpled the paper in his fist but remained silent. Seething, he swallowed the bitterness rising in his throat. The threads of his long-suffering patience were beginning to fray.

"I can always print another and fax it," she said.

"Then how long until your husband leaves?" His tone was matter-of-fact as Gage steered the conversation back to her. "Every time he opens one of those boxes, I bet he feels like a king, relishing the extravagant commodities that didn't cost him a dime. Does he enjoy the surprises I include?"

Sometimes it was a tin of caviar, now and then a bottle of champagne that couldn't be found in a liquor store within a three-hour drive. Whatever Gage chose, it was sure to titillate the taste buds of Mr. Finley.

Apparently, the way to a man's heart was through his stomach. Or rather, his sophisticated palate.

Captain Finley's mouth twisted into an ugly expression that suggested her husband absolutely loved those little surprises.

Gage bit back a smile. It would've been mean to revel. There was no excuse to stoop to such a level, even though he'd been provoked.

"If those boxes stop, I give your marriage six months tops." Gage was treading a fine line. He'd made his point, and now he needed to ease off before he taunted her into lashing out. "Tell me what you want to maintain our accord."

"I want you to remember your place." She stared at him with barely concealed loathing. "I. Own. You."

No one owned him. Not even the CIA while he'd

worked for the Agency. But if letting her believe that he was a harmless peon stuck under her thumb got him what we wanted, which was to stay, then so be it.

"When I say jump, you ask how high." She leaned back in her chair and put her feet up on the corner of the desk. "You stay invisible. You don't cause problems for me, like driving *trouble* through the front gate, making my life harder."

Hope was definitely trouble. On that, he and Captain Finley were in complete agreement.

"Mea culpa." He raised his palms in mock surrender. "But you'll be pleased to know that I have resolved the entire situation."

Finley arched a manicured eyebrow. "Resolved how?"

"I sneaked back into the clinic, got Ms. Fischer out of Staff Sergeant Burton's handcuffs and drove her to Goode," he said, assured that Hope was actually safe at his apartment, where he'd help her get to the bottom of her sister's death.

Finley's eyes narrowed as she studied him closely. "But I gave explicit orders for you to vacate the premises of the clinic."

He nodded with a practiced look of contrition. "Your orders are the law around here, but I realized how upset you were going to be once I learned Ms. Fischer was on your blacklist. It's already snowing. No taxi will show up in the morning to take her to Goode. The roads will be too dangerous by then to travel. Danielle examined her. Ms. Fischer was no longer in immediate danger, and I thought it would be easier for everyone, you most of all, to simply get her out of town quickly and quietly."

"Is that so?"

Not the response he'd expected. An attaboy or pat

on the back would've been more appropriate. "Yes, it is. Problem solved. You're welcome."

Captain Finley swung her legs down and put her feet on the floor with a harsh thud. "You won't mind if I verify that, will you?"

Corporal Livingston would confirm the time Gage left Benediction and when he returned. On the way out of town, vehicles were never searched, much less stopped. His truck had tinted windows, so Livingston wouldn't be able to say one way or the other whether Hope had been inside.

All the corporal could do was corroborate Gage's comings and goings.

"By all means, go right ahead," he said. *Knock yourself out.*

"Then I have your consent?" Her question sounded like a trap being set.

He nodded. "Of course you do."

Finley's face took on the look of a cat poised to catch a succulent canary as she picked up the receiver of the landline phone. "If Corporal Livingston supports your story that you left town after the accident, as I'm sure he will, I'll have Staff Sergeant Burton check the clinic," she said, the words sounding magnanimous, but Gage was no fool. "And since you've given your consent, he'll then search your residence to be a hundred percent certain Ms. Fischer is gone."

The trap snapped shut.

Gage's temper flared at unknowingly giving Finley the upper hand and putting Hope in a vulnerable position. Hope was clever and audacious, but she'd proven that she reacted without thinking things through, examining all the angles.

He filtered his anger, keeping his face relaxed, his posture easy and his eyes soft. "Anything to put your mind at ease, Captain." What else was he supposed to say as a man with nothing to hide?

"If you're lying and she's found, you'll regret playing this game with me. I'll call my commanding officer first thing in the morning and relay my request for a background check on you verbally to expedite the process. Then I'll discover whatever it is you've been hiding out from here in Benediction."

Her smug expression was difficult to tolerate, but he crossed his legs and folded his hands in his lap. "Rest assured, it won't come to that," he said with a soft smile, hoping that was true, for everyone's sake. "Can the specialist make some coffee while we wait? It's been an exhausting evening. I could use something hot and strong to drink."

"Certainly."

This might all backfire on him in a million different ways.

No matter what, he wasn't going to let Finley call her commander to initiate a background check. If she did, all hell would break loose, turning Benediction into a bloodbath.

Under no circumstances would he allow the folks of this town to end up as collateral damage.

Chapter Seven

A combination of the heat from the fire and the brandy worked its magic, making Hope drowsy. By the time her glass was empty, it was hard for her to keep her eyes open. Fatigue had threaded through her, and her limbs had grown heavy.

Gage had encouraged her to sleep in the bed, but she didn't want to impose any further. Taking the sofa was the least she could do after the taxing evening she'd put him through and everything he'd done for her. She could only imagine how exhausted he must be.

As for her, curling up and drifting off was not an option while he was out there still helping her. How were things going with Captain Finley?

A car door slammed closed outside. Hope turned toward the window in the kitchen that faced the street. Blue and red lights were flashing.

The military police were there.

Hope scrambled to her feet. The room spun at the sudden movement. All the blood drained from her head, leaving her dizzy, but there was no time for weakness.

She hurried to the window, taking great care to stay low so her shadow wouldn't be seen. Not wanting to draw attention, she slowly slid the curtain to the side only enough to peek out and chanced a quick look below.

Her nerve endings prickled at the sight of Staff Sergeant Burton crossing behind his patrol car and striding up the walkway toward the front door.

Pulse skyrocketing, she ducked down.

Why was the staff sergeant there? Had Gage given her up?

Almost immediately, she dismissed the idea. Yes, Gage was a stranger, but he was a good person intent on helping her. That much she believed, even if he might have ulterior motives.

Something must have gone wrong during his talk with Captain Finley. It was the only reasonable explanation.

If the soldier was there to look for her, it wouldn't take him long to make his way up to the garage apartment.

Staying crouched, she scurried into the living room. After shoving on the canvas sneakers, she hid the blankets from the clinic and her wet shoes under the sofa.

It was better to leave the gas fireplace alone, so it looked as though Gage had forgotten and left it on. If she turned it off, Burton would be able to tell that it had been done recently.

She glanced around for any other evidence that she'd been there.

Two bowls and three glasses were on the rug. She scooped up the dishes, mindful not to let them clatter, and tucked them in the dishwasher.

The rumble of an electric motor came from below, followed by a soft rattle. The garage door was lifting.

Burton was searching the garage.

She had to get out of there, but she couldn't use the exterior staircase, and where was she supposed to go, anyway? Gage had proven the only friendly in Benediction, and she wasn't familiar with the layout of the town well enough to know a good spot to hide.

Pressure built in her chest as her mind buzzed. She breathed through it. *One step at a time.*

Knowing where to run was the least of worries. First, she had to leave, and then she could figure out the rest.

From the living room it was plain to see there were no windows in the bathroom. The only possibility was the bedroom.

Hope grabbed her purse, throwing the strap across her body, and hurried into the adjacent room. One small window was on the wall to the side of the wrought-iron bed.

Voices came from the exterior staircase. One female, the other male—Burton's.

She shoved the curtain aside and looked to see if there was a way to escape. The window faced the rear of the property. A portion of the sloped lower-level roof ran beneath it. She might be able to use it to reach the ground.

The voices drew closer, coming to the landing. A knock at the apartment door sent her heart pounding. She was out of time.

"Gage, are you home?" asked a woman in a loud voice. It must've been Claire.

"You said no one was here. Why are you knocking?" Burton demanded.

Shutting the bedroom door halfway, Hope blocked the view of most of the bedroom from anyone entering the apartment.

"He's not here," Claire said. "You saw as well as I did that his truck is gone. Force of habit, I suppose. What are you going to do? Arrest me for having manners?"

Hope ran to the window and unlocked it but couldn't

lift it open. It was stuck. Someone had painted over the bottom seam.

A fresh wave of anxiety flooded her system with adrenaline.

Footsteps pounded up the staircase. "Hey, Mom." A teenage voice outside the apartment door. Gage's nephew, Jason. "What's going on?"

Hope unzipped her handbag, fished out her utility knife and started working the blade from one tool across the sealed seam.

"The military police are looking for someone."

"An unauthorized outsider," Burton said. "Where have you been, Jason?"

"Next door, hanging out with Tyler. What do you care?"

"I think you should go wait in the house for your mother while we finish up here."

"The last time I checked, I hadn't enlisted," Jacob said. "So I don't care what you think."

Hope stripped the last of the seal, brushed the bits of scraped paint away from the windowsill and pried it open. She threw her leg over the edge outside and squeezed through the opening. A strange calm kicked in, the way it always did out on assignment whenever she took a risk for the sake of getting the perfect photo to capture a story.

"Open the door. Now!" Burton snapped.

Keys jangled, and the doorknob rattled.

As Hope lowered the window, she prayed it wouldn't squeak and give her away.

Shutting it quietly was easy, but she turned to move from the window and her foot slipped on the slick rooftop.

She grabbed on to the thin ledge of the sill, biting her bottom lip to swallow her scream.

Using her feet, she searched for a safe spot along the shingles, trying to gain purchase so she could crawl to the side. If Burton ventured a glance outside the window, he'd see her instantly.

Snow flurries whirled around her as the wind whipped the air. Hope heard them, inside the apartment now, their voices getting louder, drawing closer.

She had to move, but she was worried about making noise. There was only one choice.

Sucking in a breath, she abandoned her fear of falling and let go of the ledge. She tried to scoot from under the window, scrabbling with elbows and hands and knees. Another slick patch sent her sliding down the slanted roof as her stomach bottomed out.

Desperate, she clawed at the shingles. She caught hold of a vent stack pipe with one hand at the same time that her feet jammed into the rain gutter, breaking her fall.

Her heart was pounding in her throat, and the tangy taste of blood was in her mouth. During the fall, she'd bitten her lip deep, though slipping might have been a blessing.

The only way Burton would see her was if he opened the window and leaned out, which was still a possibility.

Jason yelled something inside the bedroom, but Hope was too far away to hear what he'd said. Burton shouted back. Claire's voice was caught between them, softer yet firm.

A moment later, there was silence.

Hope looked up at the window. She hadn't dropped far, less than four feet, but how was she supposed to get back inside? The roof was too slippery to climb. Was it even safe for her to try yet?

Had Burton been satisfied with his search and left?

"I need you to take me over there so I can search the place," Burton said, somewhere outside on the side of the house.

Guess that bloodhound wasn't satisfied.

"You don't have to do it, Mom! This might be Benediction, but it's still America and we have rights. Don't you need a search warrant?"

Their voices were traveling toward the rear of the house, where Hope was. She pressed against the roof and froze.

"Is this really necessary?" Claire asked.

"It is if you want to get me out of your hair," Burton said, sounding as if he were just below Hope.

"Instead of dragging this out," Claire said, "let's get it over with."

Something moved near Hope's head. Before she could stop herself, she shifted away in reaction. Her foot knocked leaves from the gutter to the ground as an owl flew away.

Hope looked to see if anyone had noticed.

Claire was walking across the yard, away from the house beside Burton, rubbing her arms to fend off the cold since she didn't have on a coat. They were on the path headed to the commercial building.

Where was Jason?

Hope glanced straight down over the side, and her breath snagged in her throat. Jason was staring right up at her.

Oh, no. Putting her finger up to her lips, Hope silently pleaded with him to say nothing.

Their gazes locked, and Jason looked at her for what felt like an endless moment before he turned toward the yard. "Mom!" Jason said, making Hope's heart clench. "Have fun with the Gestapo. I'm going inside."

"All right, sweetie," Claire said, raising her hand in a wave without looking back.

Staff Sergeant Burton was focused straight ahead and didn't bother to glance over his shoulder.

Hope let out a shaky breath. Her teeth chattered, but she wasn't sure if it was from the cold or fear.

Jason took off, disappearing around the side of the house, closest to the staircase, while Claire led Burton to the building several hundred feet away.

Two minutes later, Jason opened the bedroom window and stuck his head out, taking in her situation. "I'll help you up," he whispered.

Jason reached his hand down to her, and she did likewise, reaching up.

Their fingertips touched, but even if he'd managed to grasp her hand, he was no more than fifteen years old and didn't have the strength to lift her up.

"Hang on a second." He ducked back inside. It didn't take long for him to return. Jason draped the blanket from Gage's sofa out the window and held on to the other end. "Climb up. I won't let go."

Hope nodded. She took hold of the blanket and scaled the side of the roof, using the material for traction.

At the window, she grabbed onto the sill. Inside the room, Jason had his feet on the blanket, propped up against the wall, his back to the floor for leverage, and was holding the edge with his hands.

Smart kid.

Hope climbed inside, landing on the floor beside

Jason on her hands and knees. "Thank you for help-ing me."

"You're welcome," Jason said, getting up. He pulled the blanket in, closed the window and, after drawing the curtain, turned to her. Standing taller than her, he was five-ten, maybe five-eleven. His hair was sandy brown and he had intelligent blue eyes behind rimless glasses. "Who are you?"

"My name is Hope." Grabbing on to the bed, she pulled herself up. Her arms shook from the climb, and she regretted not getting into the gym on a consistent basis.

"I know your name. Staff Sergeant Burton mentioned it. But that doesn't tell me who you are." His entire de-meanor shifted. His eyes hardened, and his expression became inscrutable.

"Mind if we talk in front of the fire? I'm freezing." *Again.*

She stalked to the living room without waiting for a response and plopped down in front of the fireplace.

Jason turned off the bedroom light and followed, tak-ing a seat near her rather than beside her.

"Thanks again for not saying anything to Staff Ser-geant Burton," Hope said. "I really appreciate it."

"Why are they looking for you?"

If he already knew Hope's name, then his mother would later explain why she might be in town. Hope would rather tell her own story on her own terms. "My sister was a scientist here. She died. I'm trying to find out what really happened to her, and the military is mak-ing it very hard."

"Faith Fischer was your sister?"

She looked at him in shock, although she shouldn't

have been surprised. It was a small town. Probably reasonable to assume that everyone had heard some version about how Faith had died. "Yes. Did you know her?"

He nodded. "She gave a couple of lectures at the school. Dr. Fischer was so excited about science and sharing what she knew, it made all of us want to learn more." Jason's eyes softened, and a smile tugged at his mouth. He'd obviously been taken with Faith, captivated by her, as everyone who knew her had been. "But how do you know Gage?"

"I'm an acquaintance of your uncle."

"He's my mom's *former* stepbrother. That doesn't make him my uncle."

"I heard Gage put his life on hold and helped your mom when she got sick. Doesn't that make him a family relation of some sort? Even if a distant one."

Jason rolled his eyes. "Did you know that the larvae of monarch butterflies are more likely to survive infection from certain flies if they're also infected by a protozoan?"

Was he calling Gage a parasite? "I bet you learned that in your biology class."

"I learned that from your sister. Regardless, where or how, it doesn't make it any less true."

Hope got the sneaking suspicion that she was treading in a family quagmire better left alone. "I don't know Gage that well or his relationship to your mom. But he saved my life when he didn't have to. At great risk to himself. I'd be dead if it weren't for him. *I owe him*, but he's the one still helping me."

"First my mom, then the fire department and the kids at my school, now you." Jason shook his head, disdain stamped on his young face. "That's his thing. Saving people, making them feel like they owe him, so they end up protecting him instead of the other way around."

Maybe this was worse than she first thought, but she was in no position to dismiss the kid's feelings. Not that Jason sounded like an ordinary teenager. "You saved me a minute ago when you could've turned me in to Staff Sergeant Burton, which would've been easier. Did you help me so that I would owe you?"

Jason shook his head. "No. Never."

"Then why did you help me?" Hope asked gently.

"I don't like the military. Or at least not the military in this town. They're bullies."

Hope was no fan of the MPs in Benediction and was itching to do an exposé on them, but she had seen the United States military do tremendous things, supporting liberty and preserving democracy abroad, too. No entity was entirely one thing, good or bad.

"Yeah, I don't like bullies, either." She'd always been drawn to photography, loved capturing the world through her lens, but when she realized that with her camera she could speak for those who had no voice— the downtrodden and disenfranchised—she'd found her calling. "Gage stood up to the MPs for me when he didn't have to."

Jason shook his head. "Don't believe anything he says. He wants people to feel like they can trust him, to like him, but he's worried that they might see who he really is, because he's hiding something."

Everyone had secrets and scars of one kind or another. Of course there was more to Gage beneath the surface. She would be a fool to think otherwise, but he was the one person she hoped she could trust. This conversation was making her reconsider, and she didn't like the unease stirring in her belly.

"Gage is not what he seems," Jason continued.

"In what way?"

"It's hard to explain." Jason lowered his head as if thinking and then looked at her. "A couple of years ago, my mom took me to a conference in New York City she had to go to for work. She gave me permission to explore around the hotel within a four-block radius. I saw these guys set up with a table doing a card trick. Three-card monte. For hours, people would bet, thinking they knew where the queen was. After a while, even I swore I knew which card it was, but I was wrong, and they kept losing, too. A few times, someone figured out the trick and won once or twice, got confident and bet bigger, only to lose even bigger. That's Gage." Jason looked at her expectantly.

Hope wasn't sure what to make of that, but she was ready for another brandy. "People aren't like card tricks." It was never that simple.

"Gage is." Jason stretched his long legs out and leaned back on his hands. "After my mom insisted that I call him uncle to show appreciation for how he helped us, I do. To his face, he's Uncle Monte. I told him why I call him that, but he's never chastised me or asked me to stop. Because he knows that I know the truth about him. It's the one honest thing between us."

Gage's words replayed in her head. *Please don't think I'm noble or anything close to it. Because I'm not.*

Maybe Gage had been trying to tell her something important about himself. But why would he bother unless he was a decent person?

It wasn't adding up, didn't make any sense.

"I'm sorry you have a difficult relationship with him," she said, being sincere.

Jason exhaled heavily. "You don't believe me. But just you wait, you'll see. Even my mom told me not to get too close to him."

Hope recoiled in surprise. "Really?" If Claire cautioned her son to be wary of Gage, then this was more than a teenage grievance and legitimate cause for Hope to be concerned. "Did your mom say why?"

"She said that she didn't want me to end up getting hurt."

The silence between them was absolute.

Hope couldn't write off the significance of a mother's warning to her child, but if Claire believed that Gage was a danger to her son, why would she allow him to stay?

The low rumble of the garage door opening cut through the quiet, and a vehicle pulled inside.

They exchanged a look. Gage was back.

Instead of feeling relieved, every muscle in her body was tight.

Gage crept up the staircase with the stealth of a thief, not making a sound. She didn't realize he'd reached the landing until the doorknob turned and he walked in.

Hope glanced over her shoulder at him. He hesitated near the door. Either it was her serious expression, Jason seated on the floor staring at the fire or the tension in the room that gave him pause. None of it was good.

"What are you doing up here?" Gage asked, his tone as neutral as his face.

"Saving your girlfriend from discovery," Jason said.

Hope gaped at the young man. Nothing was further from the truth, but she couldn't deny how the suggestion made her chest tingle. "I'm not his girlfriend."

"Whatever. It's none of my business." Jason got up, stuffing his hands in his jacket pockets, and faced Gage. "Aren't you going to thank me?"

Gage stepped deeper into the apartment. "Thank you." The tension in the room swelled. "There are some supplies in the back of the truck. Would you take them into the house? Your mom is expecting that stuff, and I got those comics you wanted."

"Sure, I'll take it in."

"Aren't you going to thank me? For the comics."

The room grew deathly still. Hope held her breath, sensing the delicate peace between them stretching like a rubber band that might snap.

"Thanks, *Uncle Monte*," Jason said with a sarcastic grin.

Gage didn't so much as blink. "Good night."

Jason shot her a look that screamed, *I told you so!* "Night." He strutted past Gage and left. His footsteps pounded against the stairs, fading until they were gone.

Hope let out a shaky breath.

"What happened when Burton searched the place?" Gage knelt beside her and closed a hand on her shoulder.

"Claire made a lot of noise on the way up the stairs and gave me time to sneak out through the bedroom window. Did she know I was here?"

"No, but she does now, or will once Jason tells her. I guess she was playing it safe. I'll talk to her tomorrow about the situation."

"I'm sure Jason will do that, too. I told him about Faith and why I'm here." In hindsight, it was probably risky to tell a temperamental teen the truth, but she didn't have much choice. "Will it cause more problems?"

He shook his head. "They'll both be discreet. For different reasons. How did Jason get involved?"

"I nearly fell off the roof and got stuck outside. He helped me get back in."

"I'm so sorry. The search was my fault." Gage cupped her chin, tilting her face up to his, and when their eyes met, a warm jolt shot through her like static electricity. "Are you all right?"

She swallowed hard, only managing to nod. What was it about Gage that had her nerves dancing in all the right places?

"The good news is Captain Finley believes that you're no longer in Benediction and that I took you back to Goode. Which means you'll have to keep a low profile." He stroked her jawbone with his thumb.

Driven by an impulse she didn't want to analyze, she leaned into his touch.

His fingers inched higher, caressing her cheek. "I'm glad you're okay and that Jason looked out for you," he said. "Grateful, actually."

Jason. The mention of him was enough to start her gut churning again with doubts. "Do you know why he calls you Monte?"

"Yes." Gage dropped his hand, but he didn't look away. "Do you?"

"I do." She waited for him to say something, to move, to do anything, but when he only stared at her like they were playing a game of chicken, she said, "Why haven't you defended yourself, tried to explain who you are to him?"

"Have you met Jason?"

Hope smiled. Teenagers were tough, but she got the impression that Jason was a special breed of difficult.

"Once he makes up his mind about something, there's no changing it," Gage said. "Besides, anything I could say about myself to him would only reinforce what he already thinks of me."

For a second, she was tempted to ask why Claire would warn Jason about Gage, but it had been a long night and they were both exhausted. The conversation could wait.

"You should get some rest," he said.

"I'll sleep out here. I don't want to deprive you—"

"Nonsense. I insist you take the bed. In the morning, you'll be thankful that you did, because I'm an early riser." The gleam in his eyes told her that she wouldn't be able to change his mind, so there was little use in fighting him.

"Fine. If you insist."

"When you wake up, we'll sit down and talk about Faith and the next step."

"Okay."

He gave her a hand up from the floor and walked her to the bedroom.

"Thank you, for everything." She rose on the balls of her feet and kissed him quickly on the cheek. His skin was cold and covered in day-old stubble, and she wanted to know what his lips would feel like against hers. Coming down onto her heels, she avoided eye contact. "Good night."

She hurried into the bedroom and shut the door behind her.

Why did you kiss him?

"Talk about reckless," she whispered to herself. Even if it had only been on the cheek.

Hope sat on the bed near the nightstand that had a

lamp on top of it. Bending over, she took off the sneakers. She rolled her shoulders and stretched her neck. Her gaze settled on the drawer in bedside table.

She grasped the knob and pulled, but the drawer didn't budge. Leaning closer, she spotted a keyhole. It was locked.

Her curiosity was too overwhelming to resist. She pulled out her utility tool—which she loved more and more each minute she spent in Benediction —and tried picking the lock.

If she got it open, Gage would eventually know that she'd broken into it, but she kept fiddling with the locking mechanism, anyway. Everything Jason had told her had sparked doubts. Niggling suspicions crawled in the back of her mind.

Finally, the lock gave way, and the drawer popped open.

Hope pulled it out farther. There was one thing inside. A black badge attached to a lanyard. She picked it up and turned it over.

Written across the top was *Nexcellogen*. There was a bar code in the middle. At the bottom, typed in all caps, was *Fischer, F.*

She stared at her sister's name, shock icing her blood. This couldn't be, but it was.

Why did Gage have Hope's Nexcellogen ID badge? Did he have something to do with her death?

Clenching the badge, she struggled to understand what it could mean.

There was a light knock at the door, and she jumped.

"Do you need anything?" Gage asked.

Hope opened her mouth and then closed it. This was

one of those times when she had to think carefully before she spoke, much less launched a verbal attack.

"No. I'm just really tired."

"I can imagine. Sleep tight."

She stared at the ID badge and shuddered.

Gage had saved her life without knowing who she was, and when he found out, he didn't abandon her to the military police like a killer eager to hide his crime.

But Jason had insisted in no uncertain terms that Gage *was* hiding something, Claire didn't want her son getting close to him, and there was the fact that he had Faith's work badge.

Hope locked the bedroom door and sat back on the bed.

If she was going to get to the bottom of things, she had to strategize. Come up with a plan rather than questioning him impromptu.

She needed to gather her thoughts and emotions and process everything first.

Then she'd find out if Gage had anything to do with her sister's murder, and if he did…so help him God, she'd kill him.

Chapter Eight

"Thanks for being so understanding about everything," Gage said, seated at Claire's kitchen table the next day.

"I knew something was up the second the staff sergeant knocked on the door." Claire poured herself another cup of coffee and sat across from him. "Honestly, I was relieved that it wasn't about Jason getting into trouble. I don't know what I'm going to do with him." She scrubbed a hand across her furrowed brow and ran her fingers through her light brown hair.

Jason was the spitting image of his mother, same hair, same sharp eyes, but the boy got his lean frame and height from his father. Gage had known Calvin from his earlier time in Benediction. They'd all been kids around the same age.

Claire had been in love with Calvin since she was ten, but it took him a few years to feel the same. When Gage heard about the car accident that had claimed Cal's life, Gage regretted missing the funeral, but he'd been away on a CIA mission.

"Just keep doing what you have been," Gage said. "Love him, be patient and tough when you need to."

They kept their voices low since Jason was in his bedroom. The town was so small there was only one snowplow, and it took time to clear the roads. The school had called a snow day.

She held her mug with both hands. "It seems like all I show him is tough love these days. I'm terrified I'll push him away and even more scared of what will become of him if I'm not strict enough."

They'd been through so much. First, Claire's dad and Gage's onetime stepfather had died of a heart attack. Then two years later Cal passed away, and most recently, Claire had had a horrible lupus flare.

"The kid has lost a lot in a short amount of time." Gage took the last swallow of his coffee. "He almost lost you, too. He's grieving, angry and more scared than you are, but he's a fighter."

She sighed. "Don't I know it."

"In this case, that's a good thing. He's strong. As long as you listen to him and love him, he'll be okay. I wish there were more that I could do."

Claire clasped his forearm and patted it. "I'd let you, really, I'd welcome it if…" She lowered her head.

He nodded in understanding and agreement, even though she didn't see it. "It's what's best. If I got involved, I might do more harm than good in the end."

Her gaze lifted, meeting his. Tears filled her eyes. "I know. I just wish things were different."

"Me, too." And he did, more than anything in the world.

Gage was already separated from his team, his surrogate family, wondering if they'd evaded detection, if any one of them was alive or dead.

He couldn't risk forming any attachments in Benediction.

"This woman, Hope Fischer. Is the situation with her going to change things around here for you? For us?"

"It might. I'm going to do everything in my power to prevent that, but I have to help her."

"Of course you do." She gave him a sad smile. "Even as a scrawny kid, you were taking on bullies and fighting for justice. I'd never ask you to change, not that you would. I've always loved that about you."

Gage wanted to hug Claire, tell her that everything would be all right and how much he loved her, but his rules applied to her, as well. He wanted the best for them, to make life easier for her and Jason in the ways he could.

The last thing he desired was to become a source of pain for either of them.

"There's something I want you to remember," Gage said.

"What?"

"It's okay to go easy on Jason. If you ever feel guilty about it or worry that you're doing the wrong thing, remember that Benediction and all the rules are harsh enough. Try giving him mandatory cuddle time and movie night with his mom as punishment."

Claire laughed and wiped the tears from her eyes. "If only he saw how special you are instead of hating you."

Jason's contempt for him was Gage's own doing. Not deliberately, but if Gage could go back in time and handle certain situations differently, he would.

"I'll take his hate over hurting him any day," Gage said.

He got up and washed their coffee mugs while Claire wrapped a plate of food for Hope.

"Tell her I'm sorry about her sister." Claire handed

him the warm meal. "If there was foul play, you find who did it and make them pay."

Gage nodded that he would, not only for Hope, but also to rid Benediction of a murderer.

Outside, the snow had stopped falling, leaving a little less than a foot on the ground. Not that it had prevented him from going through his morning routine of running six miles and doing a hundred push-ups and boxer sit-ups.

He climbed the exterior stairs and went into his apartment. The bathroom door was closed, and the shower was running.

Hope was finally awake.

Not a peep had come from the bedroom all night. Gage was normally a light sleeper, professional habit, but he wanted to be aware if Hope had nightmares, any trouble at all resting.

To avoid disturbing her after his workout, he'd cleaned up down at Claire's. Then he'd shoveled the walkway from the staircase and the sidewalk in front of the house and for the closest neighbors.

He set the covered plate down. The note he'd left explaining he'd be back and the extra clothes that had been on the counter were gone. Last night, he'd haphazardly grabbed what he could from the slim pickings in the dryer, not wanting to alert Claire that he had a woman stashed away upstairs. He should've asked her for a better assortment of things this morning. Sweaters, jeans, anything Hope might be comfortable in.

Once the shower stopped running, he sat down at the counter and waited.

The bathroom door opened, and he swiveled around on the stool and stopped. Stopped thinking. Stopped breathing. Of course he'd seen Hope before, but in the light of day... *Wow*.

Hope stood in the doorway with a towel in her hand drying her hair, which in the sunlight was a rich reddish brown, more brown than red. Her fresh face needed no makeup to accentuate her clear, tanned skin. She was so wholesome, so pretty in a girl-next-door way. Her lips were a rosy pink and kissing her was all he could think of. Until he realized what she was wearing—yoga pants and a white tank top. No bra.

His breath caught in his throat. The clothing molded to devastating curves, cupping breasts that were the perfect size for his palms, and it was hard for him to ignore the slight pucker of her nipples through the fabric. Then he wanted not only to taste her but to touch her, too.

"I didn't realize you were back." She followed his gaze down to her chest. Her cheeks flushed pink, and he lowered his eyes to the floor. "Excuse me a minute," she said, stepping into the bedroom and closing the door.

Way to make her feel comfortable.

He should've thought to call out to her, give her a heads-up that she wasn't alone in the apartment so she wouldn't wander out half-dressed.

The image of the tank top hugging her breasts and flat stomach was stuck in his head, and he couldn't shake the desire to kiss her. Which would be stupid and foolhardy. He was neither.

The bedroom door opened. She came into the kitchen wearing his hooded sweater zipped up over her top and had put on sneakers.

"Sorry for not warning you I was back." He grabbed a fork and set it next to the plate. "You slept through breakfast, but I've got lunch for you."

She sat on one of the stools. "What time is it?"

"A little after two." He studied her face. Up close, her eyes were a light green, soft and subtle as jade. "You must've really been wiped out."

"Took me a while to fall asleep. I had a lot on my mind." Pulling off the aluminum foil, she smelled the food. Meat loaf, mashed potatoes with gravy and green beans.

"It's simple but tasty. Claire made it."

Hope dug into the food. "Is she upset about me being here?"

"No." Gage poured a glass of water and handed it to her as he sat beside her. "She understands. Wishes you, *us*, the best in finding out the truth."

Hope coughed, choking on her food, and dropped the fork.

Watching her closely, Gage patted her back. She flinched and recoiled from his touch. Standing, she put the stool between them.

"Are you okay?" he asked. "What's wrong?"

"I was up half the night, thinking about Faith. After the military police came here looking for me, I couldn't shake the sense that I'm surrounded by danger." She pushed damp hair back behind her ear, avoiding his gaze. "I have no idea who's a threat and might want to hurt me."

Gage came around the stool, standing in front of her. He couldn't help but notice how she leaned back against the counter, away from him. "I'll do my best not to let anything happen to you."

"As much as I want to believe that," she said, finally meeting his eyes, "the truth is that you can't be with me every minute. I'd feel better if I could protect myself. Do you have a gun?"

"Do you know how to use one?" If she didn't, having one wouldn't make her any safer. In fact, it was liable to put her in more danger.

"Yeah, of course."

The pitch of her voice going a little too high and her eyes shifting to the left told him that she didn't. But why lie?

Gage lifted his wool pullover and withdrew the Sig from the holster at the small of his back. He handed her the weapon, handle first.

Hope grabbed the gun, not wasting a second to point it at him and put her finger on the trigger.

"What are you doing?" He slowly raised his palms to his chest.

"Explain this." She reached into the pocket of the sweater and held up the Nexcellogen badge. "Why do you have Faith's ID?"

She'd rummaged through his nightstand. He'd forgotten the badge was in there, but he wouldn't have expected her to pick the lock.

"It's difficult to explain. I think it might be easier if I take you somewhere and show you."

"Show me what? I'm not going anywhere with you until you start talking. And if I suspect that you're lying, for even a second, I'll—"

"What will you do? Shoot me?"

"Yes!" Hot emotions blazed in her eyes—grief, suspicion, anger, fear.

Gage set his feet and leaned into the Sig until the muzzle pressed against his sternum. "The report of the gun will be loud. Have you considered the attention it will draw? Not just from Claire and Jason, but the neighbors. Some of those neighbors are the military police. They only have to walk over to investigate." He stood still, his tone even, and held her wild gaze. "Hope, you're not a murderer. You're scared, and obviously finding Faith's badge has made you think you can't trust me."

"You're right about that. But even Jason told me not to trust you. Claire, the woman you supposedly took care of like some white knight, warned her son not to get too close to you."

White knight? Had she been listening when he'd confessed that he wasn't noble?

"Whose side are you on?" she demanded.

"My own." The truth was plain, and he didn't try to sugarcoat it. "And yours. The two don't have to be mutually exclusive. You can trust me, Hope. On my life, I swear it."

"Prove it, beyond a shadow of a doubt. Right here. Right now. Because I'm not going anywhere with you."

Anything he told her she'd question and doubt without first seeing what he wanted to show her. That left him one option.

Gage snatched the barrel of the gun and twisted it from her hand in a lightning-fast move.

Hope gasped, her eyes going wide.

Gage shuffled back two steps and held the gun up, barrel pointed at the floor. "Only put your finger on the trigger when you're prepared to pull it. And if you are, you had better make damn certain the safety is off and the gun is loaded." It'd also be a good idea to stand far enough away from her target so they couldn't take it from her, but he was confident he'd just taught her that last lesson.

He bent down and took out the sound suppressor he'd shoved into his boot earlier. Best to be prepared for any eventuality, especially with Hope being in Benediction with a killer on the loose. Gage attached the suppressor, screwing it quickly onto the muzzle.

"This is the safety." He pointed to it on the side of the weapon. "Flick it down when you're ready to shoot. The gun has a twelve-round capacity, and a bullet is already chambered. Extra ammo is in a shoebox in my closet and in the truck's glove compartment." He handed her the gun, once again handle first.

If that didn't inspire trust, nothing would.

Hope took the weapon and lowered it to her side. Pressing a hand to her stomach, she dropped down on the stool. "I wasn't going to shoot you."

"I know."

"You don't." She glanced up at him, looking like she might be sick. "Last night, when I thought you might have something to do with Faith's murder, I was going to kill you if I learned that you had. But as I was standing here, staring at you, all I wanted was to believe whatever you said, and I doubted myself."

He put a hand on her back, longing to comfort her, and this time she didn't pull away. When it came to Hope, his rules disappeared—maybe they didn't apply. They were two ships passing in the dark swamp of Benediction. She needed his help, a temporary situation, and beyond that she didn't have any expectations of him.

There was little chance of him letting her down, and if he died or had to take off again, he wouldn't leave a hole in her life. That knowledge was liberating. Freed him to care deeply for another and show it.

Hope took a deep breath, her gaze falling to the gun.

"Ordinary citizens don't carry around silencers. Why do you have one?"

"I'm not ordinary."

"Then what are you?"

"Concerned, about you." Gage didn't trust lightly or easily, and neither did Hope. Her confidence in him had been shaken. Rocked to the core. They couldn't move forward until it had been restored. "Let's make a deal. You share your secrets, starting with why you were on that road last night, and I'll share mine."

She considered him a moment, her hands trembling. "What did you want to show me?"

"There's something you need to see to understand why I have Faith's ID badge," he said. "It's not far. Can I take you?"

"Okay."

Chapter Nine

The temperature had risen at least ten degrees from the previous day. Snow was already melting and wouldn't stick around long. Strange Virginia weather.

Wearing a coat and boots Gage had borrowed from Claire, Hope stared up at the sign hanging in front of the commercial building just yards behind the house.

Ferguson Funeral Home.

"Claire's dad owned and ran this place. Bequeathed it to her." He unlocked the doors that had beautiful stained-glass panels and ushered her inside.

She stomped off the snow from her boots on a mat and pushed back the hood that she'd pulled on so neighbors wouldn't be able to tell she wasn't Claire.

"My mom met her father at an NFDA convention in Washington, DC."

"What's NFDA?" Hope asked.

"National Funeral Directors Association." He led her through the foyer, past a desk and down a side corridor away from the viewing rooms. "They have conventions every year in different cities. Anyway, they clicked immediatcly, discovered that they'd both been widowed and lived in Virginia. He visited us for six months up in

McLean, bringing Claire with him. Next thing I knew, they were married, and we moved to Benediction."

"You work here?"

"I ran the place while Claire was too ill. Now I handle the grunt work for her."

"You're a mortician?"

"I have a degree in mortuary science, but I haven't had an active license for years. No one asked when I took over—they were simply glad that someone could fill in for her."

They went down a flight of stairs to the basement, where he brought her into a large supply room. There were coffins and urns, but it wasn't set up like a showing room.

"After the doctor examined Faith's body, she was brought here. I was the one who cremated her. Nexcellogen handled shipment of her cremains to her next of kin."

Tears welled in Hope's eyes. She'd been Faith's primary emergency contact and listed as her next of kin. Faith had been the same for Hope. They figured if something ever happened to one of them, they wanted to break the news gently to their elderly parents and not shock them into cardiac arrest.

The same day a Nexcellogen representative had called to notify Hope of Faith's death, stating it had been suicide, she'd also received the urn in the mail.

The mail, for God's sake! No letter of condolence. Only Faith's supposed suicide note that had been typed and unsigned and the death certificate, along with a packing slip. Like her sister was an expired product being returned.

Her stomach roiled thinking about it.

Hope followed Gage to a desk at the back of the room.

"Claire turned over Faith's cremains, but she didn't know I had some of her belongings. I took the ID badge and kept it at the apartment."

"Why?"

"No one can get inside the Nexcellogen facility without it. I thought it might come in handy if they neglected to disable it. Small details fall through the cracks around here under ordinary circumstances. When your sister died, there was a lot of chaos." Gage opened the top desk drawer. "This is what I wanted to show you, besides the funeral home itself." He took out a small zip bag and gave it to her. "I wanted to mail it to her next of kin with a letter, but every time I tried to write it, I didn't know what to say."

Inside the bag was a necklace that Hope had given Faith. "As children we'd been joined at the hip, but as adults, both of our careers took us down different paths away from one another. No matter how many miles separated us, nothing weakened our bond. She gave me my favorite camera, the one I take with me everywhere." Hope hated being apart from it now, but she'd left the camera in her room at the B&B in Goode. "I gave her this necklace. She was wearing it when she died?"

Gage nodded. "She had it on when she was brought in."

Tears fell from her eyes. He brought her into his arms, wrapping her in a hug, and she wept.

The thought of Faith terrified with no one to help her as someone took her life tore Hope to pieces. Devastated her in a way she couldn't explain.

"I've got you," he whispered, his mouth against her ear. "It's okay to let it out." Gage tightened his embrace, his body steady and solid as a rock around her.

The kind gesture, the empathy and simple permission, broke her.

Her sobs deepened. Tears ran down her cheeks and dripped onto his shoulder. This was the first time she'd cried since finding out that Faith had died. It was as though her heart had been too congested with shock and denial to feel the agony of the loss.

How could her sister be gone? She was only two years older than Hope.

Faith had planned to take time off from work and fly out to LA for Christmas. Even their parents were going to come from Carmel. But now Faith was gone.

"It's so unfair. Faith was the brilliant one. Our parents swore she'd win the Nobel Peace Prize someday. She had this effortless beauty, glowed, radiated from the inside out. She was patient and caring and would never hurt a soul."

Hope was the reckless one, throwing herself into harm's way, crawling out onto battlefields, standing up to warlords with no fear of consequences, just for a picture. To tell a story.

"Faith was the one trying to make the world a better place. I'm only a stupid photographer. If one of us had to be taken before our time, it should've been me." Even her mother had expressed the same thing over the phone during the height of her own grief.

"Your sister is gone. Leave it alone! Let her rest in peace."

"She can't be at peace, Mom. Not until we figure out who did this to her. That's why I'm going to Virginia to look into it."

"Oh, please. Your conspiracy theories aren't really about Faith. You're going to Virginia because you need

to make this about yourself, like you always do. Your sister is not some story for you to exploit."

"I'd never take advantage of Faith's death."

"Then stop this! Do you hear me? Let her rest and let us mourn. Why do you always have this constant need to be at the center of attention?"

"Don't you care about the truth? Don't you want to know what happened to her?"

"How dare you! It should've been you who died instead of my sweet Faith."

HOPE'S WHOLE BODY SHUDDERED.

"It shouldn't have been you, and it shouldn't have been her, either." Gage pulled her even closer, if that were possible, and swayed back and forth. He consoled her without trying to calm her down or stop her from crying. He let her feel, reassuring her that sorrow was all right. "Grief is like a tunnel," he said. "You have to walk through it to reach the light."

But there would never be any light until she found Faith's murderer.

They stood like that for a long time, with her cocooned in his protective warmth, her chest aching as though her heart might rupture.

Once she stopped sobbing and had gotten the worst of it out, Gage guided her down into the chair behind the desk. He crouched in front of her and peered up at her face. Taking her hands in his, he simply held them. Breathed with her, deep and steady, in and out. Neither of them spoke, their eyes locked. The moment stretched out—her jumping nerves stilled, the chaos inside quieted—thinning until it snapped and passed.

He must've seen or sensed the shift in her. A soft,

sympathetic smile tugged at the corner of his mouth, and he handed her a box of tissues.

"Thanks." She took it from him. "Sorry that I lost it for a moment." As she wiped her eyes and nose, she realized what a wretched mess she must have looked. "Everything just poured out of me." It was good she hadn't been alone, because she might not have been able to stop. She needed his comfort, his kindness. "I wasn't able to cry before, for some reason."

Still squatting in front of her, he rested his hands on her knees. "This may have been the first time you cried, but it won't be the last, and that's okay. I lost my dad when I was seven. I know how hard it can be."

"My parents think I'm a nutcase for coming out here. They don't want to think about it or deal with it. They just want to accept this and move on." Which was bewildering. Her parents should've known better. Unlike Hope, Faith had been a devout Catholic. She was determined to be there for those she cared about. Committing suicide wasn't something she would do.

"They're grieving in their own way, like you."

She nodded. "But it'd be nice if they supported me in this."

He blew out a heavy breath. "The rumor in town is someone broke Faith's heart. Is it possible that she got depressed and—"

"No," Hope spit out, shaking her head, refusing to even consider the preposterous idea. "Faith would never commit suicide." She didn't care what BS story Nexcellogen was pushing.

"I don't mean to come across as insensitive, but why are you so sure your sister was murdered?"

"Faith was happy. She had her dream job and had

fallen in love with a guy in Goode. There was no breakup. Faith wasn't depressed." She was so excited about visiting Hope at Christmas and was planning to bring her boyfriend, too, introduce him to the family. "My sister was the type of person to see something through until the end. She wasn't a quitter, especially not on life. If you believe the rumors about suicide, why are you helping me?"

His fingers slipped through her hair in a soft caress. "I think there's a strong chance that you might be right."

Hope straightened and threw her tissues in a wastebasket. "Why?"

"A couple of reasons." He held her hands again like he was bracing her for what he was going to say next. "They claim Faith sat in her car in the garage and started the engine."

Hope's stomach twisted. The Nexcellogen representative who'd called her didn't have details and advised her to submit an official request for further information.

"Men tend to choose violent, more lethal methods," he said, "such as firearms, hanging and asphyxiation. Whereas women are more likely to overdose."

Hope squeezed her eyes shut, trying to stop her mind from spinning to all kinds of dark places, and breathed through a wave of nausea.

"Do you want to take a break?" he asked.

Opening her eyes, she shook her head. "Continue, please."

"In the case of suicide or suspected foul play—not that there has ever been a proven murder inside Benediction—an autopsy is supposed to be performed. But Dr. Steve Howland signed the death certificate without conducting one. When I cremated her, I only knew the cause of death was asphyxia, but I didn't know how. Later I learned about the carbon monoxide because a neighbor had seen smoke coming from her garage. There should've been a cherry-red or bright pink tint to Faith's skin and red coloration of her fingernail beds because carbon monoxide binds to the hemoglobin, but there wasn't any."

"Do you think that means Dr. Howland was involved in covering it up?"

"It's possible, but not necessarily. I'm the one who cremated her, but I'm not a part of a conspiracy. Nexcellogen might have pressured Doc to wrap things up after a thorough examination. The same way they pushed to have the body cremated immediately, per Faith's instructions."

Wait. What? "Faith never wanted to be cremated. I assumed it was some mix-up in Benediction. She wanted to be buried in our family plot. I spread most of her ashes there."

Gage made his way to a file cabinet and took out a folder. He leafed through it and gave her a document with the Nexcellogen logo.

At the top of the form, the words *In Case of Death Instructions* were printed. It was an employee's declaration of how to handle their remains along with funeral wishes. Under internment request, the option for cremation as soon as possible had been checked, but that wasn't the only problem with the form.

"I'm not sure that's Faith's signature at the bottom," Hope said.

"What's wrong with it?"

Hope stared at the writing. "It's similar, very close, but something about it is off." She shrugged, unable to pinpoint what it was.

"This is an internal Nexcellogen form. Someone there must've forged it. Did Faith ever say anything about having problems at work with anyone in town?"

"No." Hope lowered her head. "Faith suspected the landlines here in Benediction were tapped and her calls monitored."

"Her suspicions were correct. Either Nexcellogen or the military police or both listen in on the lines."

"She never discussed her job on the phone. All I knew was that she worked in a lab with her team. Eventually, she started sending me letters, but there was never any mention of her project or conflicts with anyone." Her gaze fell to her lap. She opened the plastic bag and dumped the necklace into her palm. "Maybe this might be able to tell us something."

Gage picked up necklace by the chain and looked at the tube-shaped dangling pendant. "A mini cryptex."

"Yes. It's designed after the original sketches of Leonardo da Vinci. Faith and I were obsessed with puzzles and codes growing up. This was the best gift I could think of for her. Art, a puzzle and practicality all rolled into one." She spun the five cryptex rings one at a time, aligning them to the five-digit code she'd preset, praying that her sister hadn't changed it.

The mechanical combination lock clicked in place. The container opened, but instead of a secret piece of paper hidden inside, it was a USB flash drive.

"This holds 256 gigabytes of data," Hope said.

"Let's take a look and see what's on it."

Chapter Ten

For hours, Gage sat beside Hope, poring over the contents of the thumb drive. Her fingers flew across the keyboard of the funeral home's laptop, accessing every file.

They took their time reading document after document. There was a mountain of data.

"This is more of the same," Hope said as she stared at the screen. "Results of a compound tested on mice. This is sample 180. Again, a different chemical ratio from the last. Always the same intervals of time. A dose administered to the mice either one month, one week or one hour before *the event*." Hope sighed. "What event?" Most of the markers were color-coded in red, others in yellow, but a few had green bars on the graph. "With so much red, I'm guessing this one didn't work, either." She skipped to the last test marked sample 221. "Looks like progress compared to the others. It's mostly green. But what do you think this long bar of red represents?"

"You've got me. Try this folder." He pointed out one they hadn't opened. "We need to find something that explains what she was testing."

Hope clicked on it. More documents. She opened the most recent one. This time, they weren't test results. "Finally, her notes on the tests and findings. Everything she'd use to write a scientific paper. Here. The drug is a neuro pathway beta-blocker, and the event they subjected the mice to was…a series of small shocks."

Gage skimmed the page Hope indicated. "She was working on a drug to prevent post-traumatic stress disorder in soldiers. Regardless of which war or conflict you look at, there are high rates of PTSD in veterans. Soldiers' lives are completely ravaged by the things they had to do in combat." It happened to CIA operatives, too. "Only a few treatments are effective, and as far as I know there are none that can prevent it. A drug that could block the effects before it took hold, to be used to inoculate soldiers from the devastation of PTSD before they go into combat, would be revolutionary."

"Worth a lot of money. The government would pay any amount for something like that. Probably the closest they could get to creating a super soldier."

"That's why they're working on it here in Benediction instead of the labs at Nexcellogen headquarters."

A confused look crossed Hope's face. "Faith didn't think there was anything strange about the transfer from Herndon out here. She said it was for security reasons."

"This town has a weird history. When I lived here as a boy, I heard stories about government testing on humans, soldiers, not just mice. An endeavor to make the ultimate warrior."

"Oh, come on," Hope said incredulously. "I was kidding a minute ago."

"The townspeople believe the stories. Claire's father did."

"They also believe the story about Faith."

"What I know for a fact is that the military has a stake in whatever that company produces. Years ago, a lot went wrong with their testing on soldiers and Benediction was almost shut down, but then Nexcellogen won the bid for a new contract and replaced whatever pharmaceutical company was here before. A drug like this—" he gestured to the document up on the screen "—would benefit soldiers greatly and falls in line with the mission objective of this town."

"But the drug isn't effective." Blowing out a breath, Hope sank back into the chair and scrolled through the document. "The only one that showed promising signs had been administered one hour before the stressor. Those mice exhibited no freezing when they returned to the test environment, a higher threshold for pain, but some demonstrated violent tendencies. They would need a dose given one week to one month in advance that didn't potentially turn someone homicidal for it to have practical applications for the military."

"Do you think Faith might have been working with another company on this?"

"You mean corporate espionage?"

Gage nodded. They needed to explore every possibility. "If she were, it would be a motive. Maybe someone at Nexcellogen found out and wanted to stop her. Or the rival company received the data and needed to silence her."

"Faith would never spy. She was loyal to a fault."

"She risked sneaking this data out of the facility for a reason. It must be important somehow."

"But I have no idea what to do with it or how it explains why she was murdered. I was hoping for something concrete."

A smoking gun would've been nice, but far from realistic. Few people planned for their own death, lining up dominoes to fall and point to their killer.

Gage did, but no one would miss him other than his disgraced teammates, and no one would seek justice on his behalf.

But maybe he could help Hope find answers. "At least this gives us somewhere to start."

"How? This feels like a dead end."

"Faith was obviously worried about whatever was going on in her lab. We need to find something to help us make sense of why she had this data on her thumb drive."

"Where do we look?" Her gaze drifted, then she straightened and met his eyes like she had an idea. "Nexcellogen. We break in using Faith's ID badge."

"Absolutely not. Getting in would be one thing. Finding evidence of a crime and getting back out undetected is another thing entirely. That should be a last-resort measure. We have to tread with care."

"Do you have a better suggestion?"

"Maybe she smuggled out more than what's on this thumb drive. It's possible she may have kept notes on her personal laptop for her own reference since there was no chance of anyone hacking into it from the outside."

"You think we should search her place." A statement, not a question.

Hope was close.

"They boxed up her all her belongings and removed them from her townhome. Everything is sitting in the evidence room at the MP station," he said, and she grimaced. "I have an idea on how we can get to it. Discreetly."

"I bet you do." Hope eyed him. "Don't take this the wrong way, but I need to know why Jason doesn't trust you. Why Claire is worried about her son around you."

Exhaling, he lowered to a knee and cradled one of her hands in both of his. "I am hiding things. Hiding *from* things. It's the reason I keep him and Claire at a distance. Because I don't want to hurt them when I leave." Or when his past caught up with him and put him six feet under. "Jason has been through a lot. He needs stability, people he can rely on no matter what, like an anchor. That's not me. I can't be that for him and Claire. She understands, though she doesn't know why, and we both agree on this. But I've made mistakes with Jason. I handle sports for the kids at the school. I'm friendly with them in a way I'm not with him. They see me for forty-five minutes once a week. Whereas I live with Jason. I need to be careful not to let him form any attachment to me. For his sake."

"That's why he thinks you're not what you seem."

"I'm one way with others and another with him. To protect him. He believes my compassion toward others is fake because he doesn't think I have any for him. But I love that kid and Claire."

She tangled her fingers with his. Her light green gaze had a gravitational pull all its own, tugging the tide of his focus toward her.

"What about how you are with me?" she asked. "Can I trust it to be genuine?"

More than he cared to admit. "Yes." There was a kinship between them. Not just the fight for justice, the empathy of needing to know what happened to a loved one, but there was mutual recognition of a fire burning in the soul of another.

"Then we should go through my sister's personal belongings."

"We'll eat dinner and wait until things in the town

wind down." Gage unplugged the flash drive. Handed it to Hope for safekeeping. Packed up the laptop to take with them just in case they needed it later.

As they walked up the stairs, their arms brushed. He took her hand, and she interlaced their fingers.

Bringing her to the funeral home had been the right call. She was no longer wary of him.

Being close to her physically came naturally to him, had him craving more. Not fighting it had her opening up on an unexpected level. One he hadn't planned.

One he liked.

Living in Benediction, detached from everyone, his emotions caged, was hollowing him out. Leaving a shell of a man.

Hearing Hope's pain, seeing the rawness of it, comforting her, touching her, soaking in her presence, made him want to stop hiding who he was. One day a kill squad might come for him, and if they did, then he wanted to connect with someone before that happened. To be known. To be seen. To be accepted.

Sounded simple, a small desire, but it was the greatest thing he could imagine.

They walked down the corridor that led to the lobby.

Right before they came to the corner, she stopped him. "Hey, thank you." She cupped his jaw, her thumb caressing his cheek. "I mean it. No one has ever done this, put themselves out there, on the line for me. I couldn't do any of this without you."

The sincerity in her eyes filled him with a bubbling warmth, but her gaze heated in a way that told him this was more than gratitude. Convinced him there was something between them beyond what he imagined in his head—call it chemistry…inevitability.

Her hand slid up into his hair, and she tugged his head down slowly as she rose on her toes. She kissed his jawline, his cheek. Warm, soft lips gently brushed over his, barely touching, almost teasing him with the invitation to do what he'd longed to do since pulling her out of Goode Lake. Needed to do now more than he'd needed anything in a long time.

Wrapping his arms around her, he kissed her, gentle at first, eased into it like sliding into a warm bath. He guided her back to the wall, their bodies pressed together. He breathed her in. Kissed her with growing urgency, more intensity, and Hope made a provocative, needy sound that rocked straight through him.

For one delicious instant, he forgot everything else. His mind went blank; his brain shut right off. His equilibrium was lost, but his center of gravity was found. There was only the sensation of her body moving against him. The feel of her hot tongue. The sweet taste of her mouth. Her scent. His heart thundering in his chest.

Just a heady euphoria that had him leaning into her, yearning for something deeper, more satisfying—until he heard it.

A slight squeak of a hinge that had his eyes flying open.

Hope was oblivious, kissing him, her fingers clenched in his hair.

He stilled. Pulling his head back, he covered her mouth with his palm.

The front door closed. Someone entered the lobby, shuffled to a stop and trod lightly.

Her brow creased with worry, but he pressed his mouth to her ear. "Stay here. Don't make a sound. I'll get rid of whoever it is," he whispered.

After she nodded, he handed her the laptop and rounded the corner into the lobby.

Dr. Howland walked toward him. A sociable man in his seventies with curly gray hair, he waved and smiled, deepening the wrinkles at the corners of his eyes and mouth. "Hey, Gage. I've been trying to track you down."

"Oh, yeah?" Gage walked up to him, keeping the doctor near the door. "Eager to get back the sweats I borrowed? I'll have them washed and delivered tomorrow."

Chuckling, Doc adjusted the tweed flat cap on his head. "No, no rush on that. Take your time."

"So what brings you out in the snow?" On a day like this, Danielle would be running the clinic whether she was scheduled for duty or not, and Doc would be curled up in front of the fire reading a book and sipping whiskey.

"I wanted to get some information regarding the woman you saved. Hope Fischer. I wanted to talk to her."

Gage shoved his hands in his pockets. "Really? About what?"

"Danielle called me last night and told me about her. I think she mentioned it to you," he said in a dismissive way, as though it were no big deal, with a little bob of his head, his eyes cast down.

When someone in Benediction downplayed something, you needed to pay close attention, because the details they didn't want under a spotlight were the ones that mattered.

"I recommended she stay overnight, to be certain she was well. I wanted to follow up with her. See how she's doing. Captain Finley mentioned you took her to Goode. Is that right? Where exactly did you drop her off?"

The question struck Gage as wrong. Howland was

a good doctor and was known for checking up on patients, but Hope hadn't been his patient and tracking Gage down in the snow seemed a tad much.

Gage wanted to give Doc the benefit of the doubt, but this was how people tied up loose ends. Track the person down and finish the job. "Did you also hear she thinks her sister didn't commit suicide?" Gage stepped closer, studying him. "That she was murdered?"

"I did." Doc met his gaze. His gray eyes narrowed a bit, only for a second. "That's also part of the reason I wanted to talk to her. To apologize."

Well, wasn't that interesting? Not the response Gage had been expecting at all. "Apologize for what?"

"Not doing an autopsy on her sister." Howland, the primary physician and medical examiner, was aware a mortician would know whether one had been conducted. "If I had, it would've closed the door on any doubt for her. It's upsetting to think about a young woman wasting time chasing ghosts."

"Why didn't you perform one?"

"For starters, they said she'd been depressed for months. A suicide note was found on the dashboard in her car."

"Signed?" Probably forged the same way the form authorizing cremation had been, Gage was willing to bet.

"No. Typed but not signed." Doc removed his cap and ran a hand over his thinning mop of silver curls. "My preliminary examination of the body confirmed asphyxiation. When they asked me to expedite the process, for the sake of the family, I did. In hindsight, I shouldn't have if her sister has lingering doubts."

The story was good. Even to Gage it sounded plausible. Doc looked believable. But this was Benediction.

Gage needed to push, hard, to get to the truth. "I looked at the body, too. There was no cherry-red lividity to her skin or discoloration to her fingernail beds. I consulted with the coroner in Goode, and Faith Fischer may have died from asphyxia, but not CO. Not in her car." The lie was a bluff, and he had an excellent poker face.

"Oh, please, Gage. I've been a doctor fifty-plus years and you're a mortician still wet behind the ears. The slight flush of the skin was there, but subtle. You must've missed it. Not as if you have an expert eye." He made a waving motion with his hand.

Trying to downplay it. Again.

"I know she didn't die of carbon monoxide poisoning," Gage said. "So why did you lie?"

"That's ridiculous. You don't know what you're talking about."

Gage snatched Doc by the coat collar and spun him, shoving him up against the wall.

Doc's eyes glazed over with panic. "What are you—"

"Who paid you to sign the death certificate as a suicide?"

"Are you crazy?" Howland jutted his sharp chin up in the air. "I'd never do such a thing, accept a bribe!"

"But you did. And I want to know why."

"Benediction is starting to get to you, son. The isolation, the rules, they're messing with your head."

It was time for Gage to mess with Doc's head. "I never cremated Faith," he said. "Her body is downstairs in the mortuary fridge."

Doc's florid face went pale. "I don't understand. You told everyone that you cremated her. Nexcellogen shipped the remains to her family."

"I drove two towns over, had a deer cremated and

those were the remains I handed over." When a body was incinerated, it was reduced to the skeleton. Not ashes. Then the bone matter was pulverized, ground down into a fine, grainy powder. To the naked eye, human and animal cremains looked the same, but the weight had to be right. "Five point seven pounds. How about I take Faith's body to Goode and see what the coroner there has to say about the cause of death?"

"No! Don't."

There was only one reason why he wouldn't want that to happen. Faith had been murdered.

"How could you?" Gage asked, disgusted with Doc. "Sacrifice your principles and integrity?"

"It's not what you think. If you had questions, why didn't you come and talk to me?"

"I knew something about this was wrong." That much was true. He wished like hell he had pushed for the details of how she'd died and questioned the fact that there hadn't been an autopsy. Though it didn't make him complicit like Doc, Gage was ashamed he'd toed the line. His gut burned thinking of it. He had a responsibility to help Hope that he wouldn't ignore, and if he were being completely honest with himself, guilt spurred him on, too. "How much did they pay you?"

Lowering his head, Doc sighed. "Nothing. I wasn't paid one red cent."

"Then why? Tell me the truth."

"The night I examined Faith Fischer's body, I was drunk. I had been in the pub earlier, drinking with some of the guys. Faith had come in, picked up an order for dinner like she often did. One of the boys mentioned how sad she looked, depressed. That it must've been over her breakup. I wasn't too far gone at the point, and it was plain to see that she wasn't herself, had a weight on her shoulders. Something was troubling her. Later, when I examined Faith, it seemed obvious that it was suicide."

"Obvious that a woman who was so depressed she wanted to kill herself that she would bother picking up dinner?"

"Everybody thought it was suicide and said so. We've never had a murder in Benediction."

"Who is everyone?"

"I don't know." Dr. Howland shrugged. "The MPs were there. Captain Finley. Ms. Lansing."

"Who asked you to expedite things?"

"No one. I said that to you now to cover my negligence. I'm so ashamed."

Gage was aware of Howland's fondness for 101-proof Wild Turkey. It packed a mean punch on a modest budget. "Why are you looking for Hope Fischer?"

"I told you. I only wanted to make sure she was okay and convince her to go home. I feel bad that poor woman is out here because of me, because I neglected to be thorough. It's the God's honest truth."

Dropping his hands, Gage stepped back. "If you mean Hope no harm, stop looking for her and leave her alone."

"All right. I will." Doc nodded. "Gage, you're right that the lack of discoloration to Faith Fischer's skin would indicate that she didn't die in the car from carbon monoxide. Though it did look like asphyxiation to me. But that would mean someone wanted it to look like suicide." Doc wrung his hands. "If you take her body to Goode, I'll lose my license. I'll be disgraced." His face was quivering, his eyes moist, near tears. "My job is all I have. I'm a good doctor when I'm sober. You know that. I saved Claire's life. I never drink if I'm going to be at the clinic. Never. Danielle makes sure of it. Please, Gage."

It was despicable that even now, sober and lucid, Howland was more concerned with covering his own tail than helping Faith's family get justice. "Her body isn't here. Her cremains *were* given to her family."

Doc's face twisted in disbelief. "You lied?"

"I bluffed." The gamble had paid off, too. "It was the only way to get you to tell me the truth. I needed to know. For my own sake." And most of all for Hope's.

Doc wiped his brow with the back of his hand. "If you're smart, you'll drop this. It's dangerous. If someone was willing to kill once, they'd do it again." He turned and scurried out the door.

Gage hesitated a minute. Once he was sure the doctor was gone, he went back around the corner and found Hope leaning against the wall. She had the laptop pressed to her chest and her arms curled around it.

"Did you hear everything?" he asked, cupping her cheek.

"Faith was murdered, and the doctor helped cover it up with his negligence."

"Are you okay?"

"I won't be okay until we find out who killed her and why. But there was something the doctor said about Faith's suicide note that got me thinking. It was mailed to me along with her remains, but it wasn't signed." She took out the Nexcellogen document. "If whoever forged her signature on this killed her, then why not sign the note, too?"

Gage considered that, ran through possibilities. "That document," he said, pointing to the one in her hand, "is an internal corporate form that they only share a copy of with the funeral home. We usually shred it when we're done. I only kept it after learning about the carbon monoxide discrepancy. I don't think her killer ever expected you to see it."

"How high do you think the cover-up goes?"

It was hard to tell. "Michelle Lansing has been the director of Nexcellogen operations in Benediction for six years. She's as high as it could possibly go here."

"Tell me more about her as a person."

"Michelle is agreeable, diplomatic, but she's also the corporate type. A bigwig. She has a considerable amount of power and influence and likes it. Works seven days a week. She has white hair but makes fifty look like the new forty. Her hair is the only thing that gives away her age. She's always the center of attention at functions. She even gave the eulogy at the memorial service for Faith."

People were happy with her in charge, and unlike most outsiders, who found it hard to adjust and hated it here, Michelle loved Benediction.

"I think we need to look at everyone who was close to Faith," Gage said. "Who worked with her on her research?"

"Faith was the lead on the project, and she brought in Paul Kudlow. He's been here working in the lab with her from the start. I met him a few years back when they were in Herndon. We all had dinner together a couple of times. They were friends. Last year, she requested that an extra scientist join her team. Neal Underhill. She called him a rising star with lots of potential."

Gage was familiar with both men from a distance. Kudlow was happy-go-lucky, the kind to crack jokes not everyone found funny. Underhill was astute and serious, a bit of a cliché in a geeky way, wearing glasses and MIT Nerd Pride T-shirts.

"Why did she wait until last year to bring on Underhill?"

"She only said that he was going to be a good addition to the team."

He rubbed both her arms. "We have to see if there's anything in your sister's stuff that can shed some light on this."

She agreed. "Do you think Dr. Howland will tell anyone about your conversation?"

Gage shook his head. "I don't have any proof that could hurt him, and I don't see him wanting to unburden his soul to anyone else. But Doc was right."

"About what?"

If they asked more questions, eventually someone was going to take notice.

With this, he couldn't be on his own side and Hope's. The two were mutually exclusive. He was wrong to think otherwise.

Digging around would rile a hornet's nest and make staying in Benediction impossible.

So, now there was only Hope's side.

"This *is* dangerous," he said.

"If you're reconsidering, I understand."

"I swore to see this through with you. To take it as far as you dare go. I stand by that." And by her, because she wasn't going to let anything stop her.

Holding his gaze, Hope straightened. The fierceness he so admired blazed in her eyes. "Then I want to take it all the way."

Chapter Eleven

Benediction was so quiet and serene with an almost idyllic quality at night. But if you peeled back the holiday-themed veneer, beneath the surface this place was rotten, festering with corruption like a disease.

Hope was bent low inside the truck as Gage parked close to the MP building.

Replaying the plan in her mind, she pulled the hood of the zip-front sweatshirt over her head, tucking the strands of her ponytail inside, and tied the draw cord under her chin.

"You mentioned there are cameras inside and that you had a way for me to avoid detection. This feels like a good time to share."

Gage flashed a grin that demanded her full attention. "Take this." He handed her a black device resembling a remote that fit in her palm. There was a small antenna at the top and a single switch in the middle. "It's a hybrid analog/digital video scrambler, a little something I picked up when I knew I was heading back to Benediction."

"Did you get this at the same store where you *picked up* a silencer for your gun?"

"No. I already had the silencer."

His attempt at humor was awful, but he had her smiling nonetheless. "Ha-ha."

"I'm not joking, Hope."

Under different circumstances, with a different man, the statement should've unnerved her. She didn't know Gage's past or the secrets he was hiding from. What she did know was that she could trust him. That was enough.

"What exactly am I supposed to do with it?" She held up the scrambler.

"You have to be within five feet of any video camera for it to blur the feed. You'll be within partial view of the camera on the exterior before that, so you'll have to approach from the side. If you stay as close to the wall as possible, you'll be in the camera's blind spot once the scrambler becomes effective. But to be on the safe side, never look up at the camera and keep your head down."

"Got it. I guess I just flick the switch."

"Yep. You'll need this, too." He unzipped a case the size of a mini manicure kit, revealing instruments she recognized.

"You failed to mention I'd have to pick a lock."

"It's a skill set you already possess. I didn't think it'd be an issue."

She narrowed her eyes at him. "What kind of lock are we talking about?"

"Padlock." Quickly, he pointed out the tools she'd need and explained how to use them. "Got it?"

"Yeah, I think so."

"I'll keep whoever is on duty distracted for as long as I can. Ready?"

"As ready as I'll ever be."

He covered her hand with his and gave her a reassur-

Loyal Readers
FREE BOOKS Voucher

We're giving away **THOUSANDS** of **FREE** **BOOKS**

Suspense

THE SETUP
CAROL ERICSON

HIS TO PROTECT
SHARON C. COOPER

Suspenseful Romance

Get up to 4
FREE FABULOUS BOOKS
You Love!

To thank you for being a loyal reader we'd like to send you up to 4 FREE BOOKS, absolutely free.

Just write "YES" on the Loyal Reader Voucher and we'll send you up to 4 Free Books and Free Mystery Gifts, altogether worth over $20, as a way of saying thank you for being a loyal reader.

Try **Harlequin® Romantic Suspense** books featuring heart-racing page-turners with unexpected plot twists and irresistible chemistry that will keep you guessing to the very end.

Try **Harlequin Intrigue® Larger-Print** books featuring action-packed stories that will keep you on the edge of your seat. Solve the crime and deliver justice at all costs.

Or **TRY BOTH!**

We are so glad you love the books as much as we do and can't wait to send you great new books.

So don't miss out, return your Loyal Reader Voucher Today!

Pam Powers

LOYAL READER
FREE BOOKS VOUCHER

YES! I Love Reading, please send me up to 4 FREE BOOKS and Free Mystery Gifts from the series I select.

Just write in "YES" on the dotted line below then return this card today and we'll send your free books & gifts asap!

➡ YES ⬅
‾ ‾ ‾

Which do you prefer?

☐ **Harlequin® Romantic Suspense**
240/340 HDL GRHP

☐ **Harlequin Intrigue® Larger-Print**
199/399 HDL GRHP

☐ **BOTH**
240/340 & 199/399
HDL GRHZ

FIRST NAME

LAST NAME

ADDRESS

APT.#

CITY

STATE/PROV.

ZIP/POSTAL CODE

EMAIL ☐ Please check this box if you would like to receive newsletters and promotional emails from Harlequin Enterprises ULC and its affiliates. You can unsubscribe anytime.

HI/HRS-520-LR21

ing look. The anxiety dancing in her stomach eased, and she nodded that she was okay.

"On my count," he said. "One." They opened both doors at the same time. "Two." Out of the truck. "Three." They closed the doors in unison.

It needed to sound like one person got out of the truck rather than two in case the guard inside was paying attention.

She scooted around to the rear of the truck while Gage sliced his tire.

They gave it a minute, with her crouched low and him pretending to inspect the flat, before he went inside to ask for assistance.

Hope wanted nothing more than to bounce, pace, work off her nervous energy with movement. Instead she drew in deep, steady breaths, focused on the steps she needed to execute and stayed still.

"Thanks, Specialist Porter," Gage said moments later.

"No problem. I've a got a jack in my vehicle."

"Getting a flat is bad enough, but getting stuck without a jack is the absolute worst. I didn't want to risk driving home and damaging the rim."

Their voices drew closer, and she braced to spring into action.

"We're here to help." The trunk of Porter's car popped open.

That was the cue.

She dashed to the side of the building on the balls of her feet and switched on the scrambler in her pocket.

Gage was chatting up Porter behind the trunk door, where the young man's view was obscured.

A quick look around, then, following Gage's instructions, she made a beeline for the entrance with her back close to the brick wall. She slipped inside the building and pulled the door closed behind her before Gage and Porter headed for the truck.

It'd been a short run, but her heart was slamming against her chest. Air punched in and out of her lungs. She was fit, did more yoga than cardio—still, her shortness of breath was startling.

Adrenaline. It intensified her body's response. Nature's way of fueling her through this.

She looked around the MP station. Gage had drawn a simple diagram of the one-story building. There weren't many rooms, and only one was her concern.

She ran around behind the receptionist desk and checked the camera screens on the monitor. Complete picture degradation, as promised by Gage. She hustled down the main hall. After passing what looked like a supply closet, she came to the evidence room.

Lowering down on one knee, she took out the tool kit. She inserted the bent end of the tension wrench in the lock opening. Applying pressure to hold the opening over the lock hole, she turned the wrench in the direction the key would go in as far as it'd budge. She pushed the rake-shaped tool in with the teeth and ridges against the locking mechanism. Jiggling it, she moved the instrument in and out. A click, and the lock popped open.

Voilà. Not as easy as the nightstand drawer, but she'd managed. Maybe she did have an innate talent for lock picking.

She opened the door and hooked the padlock on the loop of the fastening.

Inside, she disregarded the locked cage of evidence bags and headed to the stacked boxes in the corner. Each one was labeled *F. Fischer* and had been sealed with bright yellow tape.

Anyone checking the boxes later would know someone had been in them. It could draw the MPs to review the videotape. The obscured footage would raise more questions than answers.

Until Porter rehashed the events of the night.

Damn.

But Gage must've considered that. Little to nothing escaped him. He was a man who paid attention to details. If anything went wrong, he had to know everything would lead to him.

With sudden clarity, the magnitude of how much he was risking hit her. Pressure built in her chest. Her thoughts raced. There had to be a way to cover her tracks and protect Gage.

Stop. Focus.

There was no turning back, and time was running out.

She sliced the tape on the first box, removed the lid and riffled through it. Item after item dredged up memories, forced her to think about Faith's life here, her death, brought a wave of grief that she had to push aside.

All the clothing, toiletries and thick science manuals she left. A small flipbook of pictures of her and Faith as children and highlights of her sister's accomplishments Hope set to the side to take. It was sentimental and contrary to why she was there, but she couldn't bear to leave it behind.

Noticeably missing from the boxes was a personal laptop. Gage had thought she'd have one, and so had Hope. Faith liked to work late in bed when she couldn't sleep. But there was no computer and no printouts of additional data.

She opened the last box. Inside she found a copy
of *To Kill a Mockingbird*. It was Hope's favorite book,
not Faith's. She rummaged through the box, looking for
Wuthering Heights, which her sister reread at least once
every year, but there wasn't a single edition. It seemed
odd for some reason.

Her gaze fell to a notebook. Faith wasn't the type to
keep a diary. Hope leafed through the pages, expecting to glance over paragraphs about Faith's boyfriend,
a clue as to how the data on the thumb drive might be
related to her death, but what she stared at instead left
her bewildered.

Pages of gibberish. Random words and numbers
scribbled throughout. Most written in nonsensical pat-
terns. None of it appeared connected. To anyone who
didn't know Faith, they might see this and suspect she
was losing her mind.

But Faith had been sane. Lucid and logical. Not depressed or losing her faculties.

Another dead end?

Cursing her luck, she was ready to scream in frustration and kick one of those boxes across the room,
but then she saw it. Five words that made absolute perfect sense.

One does not love breathing.

Of course. Turning through the pages again, now she
understood, saw the connection. "Thank you, Faith."

Hope grabbed the journal along with the Harper Lee
book and put them on the pile of stuff she was taking.

Spinning around the room, she searched for the one
thing she needed next. Yellow tape with the word *Sealed*
printed across it.

A roll was sitting on a shelf.

Moving like her life depended on it, she threw the lids back on the boxes and only added tape over the seams. She scooped up the items from the floor. Closed the door. Locked it.

Still not a sound in the station. She crept down the hall. At the front door, she peeked outside.

The guys had changed the tire and Gage was talking Porter's ear off while keeping the young man's back to the entrance.

Gage nodded, as though in response to something Porter had said, but she caught the subtle flicker of his gaze in her direction.

Gently, she opened the door and slipped out onto the sidewalk. There was no way for her to make it back to the truck without being seen by Porter. Staying close to the wall, she hurried along the walkway, moving swiftly and softly. She darted around the corner and pressed her back against the side of the building.

Her heart thundered in her ears, and her legs shook.

When Gage pulled up beside her, she couldn't wait to jump in.

As soon as Hope dropped into the passenger seat, Gage took off, headed back to the house.

"Get down," he reminded her. She had done well. But caught in the adrenaline high she must be feeling, it was easy to slip up and make the simplest mistake.

She slid down low in her seat, clutching the things she'd taken from the station. "There was no laptop."

"It was a long shot. Nexcellogen must've confiscated it before packing up her belongings." He slapped the steering wheel as he pulled into the garage. "I thought her personal effects might have been one of those small details they could've overlooked. Guess not." The garage door lowered closed. "They probably took everything of any value to us."

"Not everything."

He stared at her. "I'm on pins and needles. Spill it."

"Upstairs, where it's warm and we can talk."

That was best, and it went without saying that they needed privacy. Not for Claire or Jason to wander into the garage. "All right."

After he made sure the coast was clear by the exterior staircase—no neighbors taking a late-night stroll, no one peeking out their curtains—he ushered her up the stairs and into the apartment.

He turned on the kitchen light and the fireplace.

Hope sat at the counter, laying out the items. Gage came up beside her. Standing with an arm around the back of her stool, his chest brushed against her shoulder, and a ripple of warmth slid through him at the simple contact. He ignored it and tried to focus on what she discovered.

"I think this is important." She opened the journal and flipped through it for him.

Gage stared at the pages. "It looks like a bunch of scribbles, random thoughts. Am I supposed to know what this means?"

"No." Hope smiled like that was a good thing. "I don't think she wanted anyone who stumbled across it to understand. Faith was clever not to use a consistent pattern to hide what she was really doing."

"Why are you happy about that?"

"Because I understand it. When we were little, we use to talk in code around our parents, loved to put together puzzles. We even created our own ciphers."

"Are you saying this is some kind of code?"

"This is evidence that she wrote something *in code*." She handed him a book, *To Kill a Mockingbird*. "That's the cipher she used."

He shook his head, still lost. "Okay. We know how to break the code, but we don't have anything to decipher."

"Not yet." She peered up at him, bring their faces close. A sssssssss apart. "We, um—" She licked her lips, and her gaze dropped to his mouth for a second and bounced back up, meeting his eyes. "We just have to get—"

"Please don't tell me we have to break into Nexcellogen."

"Nothing like that."

"Glad to hear it." When she didn't look relieved, he searched her face. "But I don't like to be kept in the dark. So, tell me what I'm missing."

"You might want to sit down first."

Straightening, he stiffened. "I'm not a take-bad-news-sitting-down type. I prefer standing while drinking. Just spit it out."

"Faith had been here four years, but she didn't start writing to me until a few months ago. I think the code is in the letters she wrote me. They're in my suitcase back in Goode. I brought them on the off chance they might come in handy."

Exhaling, he sat next to her, delighted he didn't need that drink after all. "That's not so bad. I'll go there tomorrow and get them."

Hope grabbed the bottle of brandy on the counter. "While you're there, I need you to speak to the sheriff for me. Ryan Keller."

Gage got a bad vibe. Dealing with Captain Finley had

proven tricky enough. Having a conversation with any more law enforcement was not on his to-do list. "Why?"

Pursing her lips as though she tasted something sour, she poured two fingers of brandy in two glasses. "If you don't tell him that I'm all right, he's going to come here to Benediction looking for me. He'll make a lot of noise, blow this whole thing, and then the MPs will know that you never took me back to Goode."

That bad vide turned into a terrible one. "Why is he going to come looking for you?"

Hope took several deep breaths, like someone standing on the edge of a high board looking down at a ten-meter drop. "There's something I need to tell you, and you're not going to like it." She handed him a glass of brandy and took the plunge. "The reason I was on that road the other night was because it was part of my plan to get inside Benediction. The sheriff helped me…by running me off the road."

Gage's heart throbbed, beating slow but hard, booming in his ears. He gulped the liquor. Let it burn away the sudden cold racing in his veins as he gathered his thoughts. "The accident was deliberately orchestrated?" Saying the words out loud magnified the absurdity of it. The sheer horror of it.

She sipped the brandy. "Yes and no."

"You almost died!"

"That part was a mistake."

"I should hope so."

She gave him a look devoid of humor. "Ryan is a good guy. He fine-tuned my plan. If at any point I changed my mind and wanted to back out, all I had to do was put on my hazard lights as the signal to call it off. But I didn't. Because I was determined to see it through."

"You being a reckless daredevil, I get. A sheriff? Not so much."

"I was supposed to crash into a tree. He had it marked out for me. He even talked me through what I should do if I hit black ice. But I panicked, slammed on the brakes. The car went into a skid and spun out of control. I completely missed the tree and ended up in the lake."

Gage poured himself another drink. "He just left you there. What if I hadn't stopped?"

"The plan was for him to watch in his rearview mirror and make sure someone stopped to help. We timed it. He was watching the gate with binoculars. When he saw someone leave, you, we—"

"How crazy are you? And this sheriff must be even crazier for going along with such an insane, dangerous, reckless plan."

"It wasn't insane. It was clever, and it worked. I'm here." She finished her drink. "And I'm not crazy. I was at my wit's end getting stonewalled by the people here. The desperation inside to find the truth about Faith had taken on a life of its own. Grown into this wild thing, gnawing at me day and night."

Grief wasn't a dark cloud hanging over your head. Grief was animate. A beast with sharp teeth and claws, a predator that devoured. If you didn't conquer it first.

Hope took the bottle. Poured another. "I know it was risky."

He grunted. "That's an understatement."

"I've risked my life for stories. To get the picture that was worth a thousand words. How could I be willing to do that for a job and not for my sister?"

"You were gone." He caressed her cheek. "Unconscious. Water in your lungs. If I had been anyone else, someone who hesitated, someone unable to break your window, someone who didn't know CPR, someone not willing to fight for medical treatment, you would be dead."

She cupped both his cheeks and looked him straight in the eye. "But it wasn't someone else. It was you. A good man, the right man, who at great personal risk is still helping me."

The way she touched him, called him the *right* man, almost took the sting away from everything else. Almost.

"I guess us good men are a dime a dozen. You've got the sheriff. Me. Anybody else I should know about waiting in the wings to assist?"

She recoiled, dropping her hands from his cheeks. "No, and you are not a dime a dozen."

He swiveled in his seat, facing her. "Maybe you're just extremely persuasive. A witch who casts spells on good men." That would explain why he had an uncharacteristic need to get close to her, connect with her.

God, she'd probably done the same with the sheriff. Bewitched them both.

"Maybe I am." She sighed. "Are you trying to imply something else? If you want to ask me something, just ask."

The words danced on his tongue. He hated the pent-up energy whipping around in the pit of his stomach. It was unfamiliar and grating, and if he didn't know any better, he'd call it jealousy. "How close did you get with the sheriff before he agreed to risk his job and reputation to run you off the road, as a favor?"

She threw back her drink, stood up in between his spread legs and brought her face so close they were practically nose to nose. "Ryan is the man Faith was seeing. They were in love. She was going to bring him out to LA to meet the family, because they were serious. Ryan told me he was planning to propose at Christmas, in front of all of us. I even saw the ring. So it didn't take much persuading on my part. I just had to promise to find Faith's killer."

Hope stepped around him and stormed off into the bedroom, slamming the door.

Gage clenched his hands into fists, wanting to throttle himself.

Asking her that had been rude and insulting. He wasn't proud.

He was afraid. Terrified that he cared too much, had feelings unlike anything he'd ever experienced for a woman he'd known less than forty-eight hours.

This was madness.

But it was as though he'd known her far longer. Regardless of time, he could easily end up in love with her. Maybe he already was. He'd made her fight his fight, and there was no noble reason behind it. Hope was the reason.

She was special. He had to hand it to her that although her plan to get inside Benediction had been reckless to the nth degree, it had been smart. And it had worked.

Was he upset because he felt like a sucker?

He growled his frustration.

If his team could see him now, Hunter, Zee and Dean, they would think that he had a screw loose in his head for falling so hard, so fast for any woman. Then they'd have a good laugh at his expense. Then Zee would tell him to apologize.

For calling Hope crazy and her plan insane. For implying things about her and Ryan, the good sheriff who had no problem running Hope off the road. The bit about a witch with a spell was bad, too. It had crossed the line and been over-the-top.

"Yes, Zee, you're always right." He missed them all so much. The only people in the world he'd ever let in and would do anything for.

Gage looked at the bedroom door.

He did owe Hope an apology and reassurance that he'd get the letters *and* alleviate Ryan's worries. If she wanted to slap him and kick him out after that, he deserved it.

Chapter Twelve

Gage's words had sliced deeper than a knife. In all her life, Hope had never met any man so infuriating. Insulting.

But damn hot. Bold. Generous and perceptive.

She unzipped her sweater—his sweater—and took it off. Tossed it across the room. Paced back and forth, needing to get the blood moving in her legs.

The worst part was the attraction to him tugging at her to go back into the living room and hash this out.

She shouldn't have lied to him about Ryan. The sheriff did love Faith, planned to marry her, that was true, but he'd wanted nothing to do with Hope's plan. He'd called her all the things Gage had.

Ryan didn't want her to end up like Faith. Hope had had to guilt-trip him into helping her.

Not her finest moment, but she was so close to avenging her sister now. She just needed those letters.

She'd anticipated Gage would be upset, but after he implied something offensive, she couldn't admit she had roped Ryan into her scheme.

Gage was different. He'd offered her his help, no strings attached, with such conviction and dedication it left her breathless in amazement.

Calling him a good man wasn't meant as a platitude or to butter him up to speak to Ryan. Nor had there ever been the right man under any circumstances. In less than two days, she had come to trust him as she had trusted no one since Faith. She'd never felt so close to a guy. Tethered to something that wouldn't crumble to dust. She knew little about him, but on the other hand, she knew him better than her longest boyfriend or anyone in her life. Understood what was at his core, his character, the nature of his spirit, the essence of his heart that dictated his actions.

To do what he was doing for her, surely, made him exceptional. Singular. The right man for her, and she wanted him so much.

The bedroom door flew open, and Gage stalked in.

"I'm sorry," he said. "For, well, everything. I shouldn't have been such a jerk. You could've lied about the accident and simply said Faith's fiancé would worry, but you were honest. It's just the idea of something happening to you, deliberately, makes me physically sick and—"

Hope threw her arms around his neck and kissed him. No hesitation. No flirting.

Curling his arms around her, he spun her and pressed her against the wall. He kissed her deeper, harder. So completely that heat overwhelmed her.

She lifted her head to get air and smiled. "You had me at sorry."

"Really?"

She nodded, melting against him. "Really."

"Z always said a sincere apology could solve most problems and that men were idiots. Who knew she was right?"

"Who is Z?" An old girlfriend? An ex-wife? Some-one who still meant something to him?

Gage flashed her one of those grins that made her belly quiver. "Unimportant. I'll tell you later."

He lowered his mouth to hers, and she welcomed the touch of his lips. What started out as sweet turned rough, hard and blistering as he pulled her closer.

Every nerve ending sparked to life. She circled her arms around his neck. Opened to him as their tongues came together.

Her insides churned with need. "I want you, Gage."

He looked down at her, and raw yearning gleamed in his eyes. "The feeling is mutual." Pressing his lips to the hollow of her throat, he explored the rest of her body, his hands skimming and groping until she craved more.

All the uncertainty and grief of the past few days evaporated. She might've only known Gage for a short time, but she trusted him, knew she was safe with him. Intimacy was about sharing your heart and soul as well as your body, and if there was anyone on the planet that she was willing to take that risk with, make herself vul-nerable to, it was Gage.

There was only him and this moment. She wanted to touch him, strip his clothes off, have skin on skin. Friction.

The room spun as he lifted her into his arms and car-ried her to the bed. He didn't toss her to the mattress, treat her as if she were a piece of meat. No, it was the opposite of what she'd received in the past.

He lowered her slowly, his eyes never leaving hers, like she was the most precious thing in the world.

He pulled off her tank top and unhooked her bra.

Filling his hands with her breasts, he took a hard tip into his mouth.

Her mind went blank, but her body burned. A soft sound escaped her throat. He kissed his way down her stomach while his hand drifted lower, between her legs, palmed her through the soft sweatpants until she was writhing beneath him.

Every inch of her throbbed and ached from the sensual torture. He peeled the sweatpants off her legs and touched her with no barrier between them.

His skillful fingers teased and played before sliding inside her. Deep but tender, coaxing her to soften to jelly around him. His fingers stroked with the same rhythm as his tongue in her mouth. The pleasure grew so intense she was shaking.

"Hope," he whispered. No man had ever said her name like that. With the reverence of a prayer or a vow. His eyes ran over her, growing darker. Hungrier. "You're so beautiful." His voice was so husky she almost didn't recognize it.

She opened the button at the top of his jeans and lowered his zipper.

"Wait," he said as though he'd remembered something. "I don't have protection."

"I've never been with someone without it. Usually I bring my own." Then she remembered she had her purse and there was probably a prophylactic package in the inner pocket.

He sat back. "I'm not ready to be a father."

No complaints. No cajoling. No trying to convince her that they could do *other things*. Things which were in some ways more intimate because people usually didn't use protection when they did them, and that was the reason she abstained from such acts with strangers. It required a great deal of trust.

She might not know his past or what brought him to Benediction, but she knew his heart.

In that moment, with hunger gleaming in his eyes and his willingness to back off without protest, she was certain—she was falling in love with him.

"I'm not ready to be a mother, either. With all the travel I do, I get a birth control shot every three months. I'm not due for my next one for a few weeks. But I might have a couple of condoms in my purse."

If she was mistaken and didn't have any, then she'd find out whether there was a medical reason they couldn't have unprotected sex since she was on birth control. Gage had saved her life more than once and he was the most trustworthy guy she knew. Making love to him, with nothing between them, being intimate in ways she hadn't with anyone else, felt right.

He grabbed her bag from the nightstand and fished out one.

Part of her wished she didn't have any, but that was another conversation for a different time.

"I want you." She reached for his shirt, and he wrapped his hands around her wrists, stopping her.

"I have scars from my previous line of work. Not as bad as some, but enough to surprise you. To put you off, even." He stared at her, and it was the first time she'd seen him look uncertain. Vulnerable.

This was what she wanted, for them to be unguarded and exposed.

"Let me see you, Gage." She pulled his sweater off over his head. There was another layer, a thin thermal shirt that clung to his body. She removed that, too, along with his jeans, and took in the sight of him.

Sitting up, she traced the marks on his body with her fingers.

Cuts and scars—some she recognized as healed bullet wounds, dozens, were all over his body. She kissed them as she swept her hands across his sleek muscles. He made little sounds of pleasure, and slowly, the tension in him eased.

"Will you tell me about them, later?" she asked, taking him in her hand and stroking his erect shaft. Right now, she didn't want explanations—she only wanted him.

He groaned, his eyes rolling back into his head. "I promise."

Gage drew her back down and kissed her. The weight of his body settled on her, and she loved the heaviness of him, the hard angles, the strength and heat of him. He nipped at her neck, tiny bites that heightened other sensations before licking up her throat.

As he lifted on one forearm, she saw the condom in his hand. Unwilling to wait, she took it and ripped the wrapper with her teeth. Smiling at her, he took it from her hand and rolled it on while she watched. The moment was sensual, intimate, instead of awkward.

Wrapping her legs around his hips, she dragged his mouth back to hers. He pressed inside her wet, aching body and swallowed her moan. He kissed her so long she was lost in her own answering need.

They fit together, snug and perfect, as though they weren't simply joined, but attached. A part of one another.

Sensation bloomed, and that's all there was. His hands

caressing her body. His mouth kissing her, tasting her. The feel of him moving inside her. Thick and hard. The tension building, tightening. Their breaths mingled in a haze of heat and pleasure. Pressure so excruciating and sweet she thought she'd shatter.

HE'D GIVEN HIMSELF permission to love her, thought only of Hope as he had touched her with exquisite care and did his best to make her only think of him. The pleasure of her tight as a glove around him as she'd cried out his name came back to him in a rush. His throat tightened recalling it.

The toilet flushed and the water ran. Seconds later, Hope was back under the covers.

He drew her close against him, and she slid her leg between his thighs. Emotion welled in his chest, threatening to swamp him.

"The scars," she whispered, running her nose up his neck. "Are they related to why you're hiding in Benediction?"

"Yes." He'd never told a soul what he'd done for a living, why he was running. Not even Claire knew, and his work family, his team, didn't count. Though he formed the words in his head, they wouldn't leave his mouth.

"Do you not want to tell me?" she asked in the wake of his silence.

"You can want a thing and fear it at the same time."

She leaned up on an elbow and looked down at him. "I've trusted you with everything, and you've shared the burden of helping me find my sister's killer. To be in something with a person, for them to care enough to share the burden, is beautiful. A small miracle. You've done that for me. Let me do the same for you."

He gave a long exhale and shuttered his eyes. There was no easy way to tell her. "I used to work for the CIA." That was already saying too much. Things never ended well when you confided in people about CIA business.

"Look at me." She pressed a palm to his cheek. "Please."

He opened his eyes and met hers. She stared at him without frustration or disappointment, but with the studious expression of someone trying to sort out a puzzle, put the pieces together.

"You can trust me," she said.

"It's not that." He did trust her. Odd as it might seem, considering she was a photojournalist. "If I tell you anything else, it'll endanger you." To involve her would be unfair. "I want you to have the luxury to walk away, the freedom to go back to your life. Getting too close to me could put a target on your back. I don't want that for you."

"This is a two-way street, Gage. Let me be in it with you, share the burden. Tell me what you're up against and I'll decide for myself. Okay?" After he nodded, she asked, "Is Gage your real name?"

"I was born Gage Graham." Hope was the only person he'd slept with who knew that. "The people I worked with knew, but I had an alias on the job when interacting with others." Using an alias in Benediction would've been impossible. There was Claire and hard-copy records from his childhood as proof of the truth.

"What did you do for the CIA? From all the scars, I take it you weren't an analyst sitting at a desk."

There was no telling what she'd think of him, how she'd react, after he told her, but he'd opened this door based on a gut feeling and instincts about her. "I was a member of a kill team. Our job was to take out the bad guys. Make the world a safer place. We eliminated dictators and terrorists." He swallowed hard and searched her face.

Shock and concern were evident in her eyes. He was waiting for the judgment, but it never came.

"Go on," she said, softly.

"My team's code name was Topaz. We were a close group, solid, tight like family." They'd only had each other to talk to openly, as he was doing now. "Hunter was our team leader. Zee, Zenobia, was our tech guru. A wicked hacker. Dean was the point person." Nice way of saying he was the team assassin.

They each had a specialty but were also skilled operatives, proficient with a variety of weapons and hand-to-hand combat.

"What was your role on the team?"

"I was the cleaner. When a body needed to disappear without a trace, or if we needed to doctor a scene to mislead anyone snooping, I took care of it. Did whatever was necessary to make sure it wasn't tracked back to the CIA."

"So what happened?" she asked, stroking his forehead and running her fingers through his hair.

It was a mystery to him how she could even look at him, much less touch him.

"I wish like hell that I knew. On our last mission something went wrong. We were supposed to take out an extremist, Khayr Faraj, in the mountains of Afghanistan, along with his financial backer, and thought we had."

"Faraj? I've heard of him. He's still alive. They say in a couple of years he'll be more powerful and dangerous than Osama bin Laden ever was."

"That's why we were so eager to get him. There are no pictures of Faraj, but the file we were given had a description. He purportedly had a birthmark on his cheek. The information we had indicated he'd be with a group of other terrorists and meeting with a corrupt Afghan official who was secretly funding him. We were instructed to use explosives. Take everyone out. It was odd, because normally we decide which method of elimination is best."

"If Faraj wasn't there, who did you kill?"

"Turned out to be a tribal leader meeting with the Afghan official."

"How did the mistake happen?"

"I don't know. We never got a chance to ask. Our planned extraction was compromised. A kill team had been waiting for us. We weren't sure at the time if it had been a CIA hit squad. Fortunately, Hunter always has a contingency ready. We camped out for weeks in shipping containers on a freighter until we were back Stateside." Not his fondest or prettiest memory. "Hunter tried to meet with our CIA handler, but everything went sideways. Instead of Kelly Russell showing up, another kill team did. Mercenaries. Ruthless, with no regard for collateral damage. And no interest in asking us questions or taking us in alive. Then we knew for certain that it was the CIA trying to eliminate us. We had to split up. We've been lying low ever since."

She put her hand on his chest. "My goodness. I can't imagine. Losing your career. Your team. Forced to run and hide. With no idea why."

"It's been a living nightmare."

"At least you have Benediction. The CIA isn't looking for you here."

"This is temporary. I trust Captain Finley about as far as I can throw her to keep her end of our bargain."

"What bargain?"

"I procure items for her husband, to keep Mr. Finley happy. This town can be hard on spouses. In return, she conveniently forgets to run a background check on me. When her assignment is close to ending, it'll be time for me to move on. Somewhere."

Finding a safe place to hide out was tough and next to impossible to do on short notice, but he had two years to pinpoint where to go.

"Well, you have me." She brushed her lips over his and caressed his face. "This—us—it doesn't have to be temporary."

This woman was amazing. After everything he'd told her, she wasn't running for the hills or horrified. In fact, he didn't see one drop of fear in her eyes.

As much as he would love to explore a relationship with Hope, the logistics didn't seem feasible. "I'm holed up in a town that you're not allowed to be in. Your life is in LA, a city with a ton of closed-circuit cameras, which isn't conducive to a wanted man staying under the radar."

"I'm a freelance photojournalist. My life, my home base can be anywhere. Except Benediction."

They both laughed.

Hope. That's what she was, his hope, opening him to new possibilities. In a million years, he never would've dreamed this could happen. That he'd meet a woman he wanted to bare his soul to, who made his pulse race every time he touched her.

"I've been on my own," she said, "for a long while. So long I'd convinced myself that I wasn't lonely and that solitude was better. That there's freedom in not getting attached to anyone. Not relying on anyone. I can take care of myself, but in the short time I've known you, I've realized how nice it is not to have to. Nice to be able to depend on someone. To have him hold my hand, let me cry on his shoulder, to help me without asking for anything in return. I've never had that before, and I don't want to lose it." She pressed a kiss to his lips, and he tightened an arm around her.

His heart swelled until his chest tightened, as though his lungs were crowded and fighting for space.

He had to move on from Benediction eventually. Maybe she could stay in a nearby town—preferably not Goode, where she was friendly with local law enforcement—but somewhere within an easy drive, and they could explore this.

Take things slowly, giving them both an opportunity to come to their senses. Who was he kidding? Give her an opportunity.

He didn't need one.

"Spending time with me could be risky," he said. "Life would be easier, simpler for you if you didn't even consider it."

"Haven't you learned who I am by now? Hello." She took his hand and shook it. "I'm Hope Reckless Fischer."

He was well aware of whom he was dealing with. "Nice to meet you, Ms. Fischer. I hear they call you Trouble for short." He cupped the back of her head and brought her mouth to his.

She had no idea what she was suggesting. How dangerous it could be for her. He needed to make her understand. Which wasn't going to happen while their emotions were clouded with all the endorphins running high in their systems.

"I'll make you a deal," he said. "Let's find your sister's killer first, starting with me getting those letters and having a chat with the sheriff. Then we'll talk about us. Outside of the bedroom with clothes on."

"You've got yourself a deal."

"Any idea where I can find the sheriff? Besides the station."

"He has breakfast in a diner on the same street as the B&B I stayed in. Pretty early, before the rush."

"I can work with that."

"Thank you." She gave him a quick kiss. "Since we have to be up early, are you ready to go sleep?"

"Sleep isn't really what I had in mind." He pulled her on top of him and ran his hands down her back and lower. Yes, he wanted her again, but his deeper desire was for what would come after, when she'd ask more questions and he'd give answers, letting her peel back more of his layers.

She smiled. Her direct gaze pierced right through him. "Good, because I'm not tired."

That terrible vibe he had still niggled at him with the irritation of a splinter under the skin. If destiny was whispering to him this time, he couldn't hear what it was saying.

Hope slid down his body, kissing and licking him along the way. Then she took him into her mouth and everything else slipped away.

Chapter Thirteen

At seven o'clock on the dot, Ryan logged off his computer, finished checking emails that might have come in overnight. Sunlight streamed through the wall of windows into the office. At least it wasn't a dismal day. Then he reminded himself that didn't mean it would be a good one.

He put on his jacket and campaign hat, tucking the brim down low.

"You want me to grab you breakfast?" he asked Dwight on his way to the front door.

Aimee wasn't in the office yet, but she would be there by the time Ryan returned.

"I had a big bowl of oatmeal. I'm good." Dwight typed away on his keyboard, completely focused for once. "Thanks for letting me take care of this paperwork this morning instead of last night."

"Yep. I'm just glad Finn is going to be all right."

"He'll be in later, at five o'clock. For the evening shift."

Shaking his head, Ryan took out his sunglasses from his jacket pocket and put them on. "I told him to take the day off." Ryan was prepared to work a double and had already coordinated with the home care helper to spend the night.

"He said he was fine and wanted to come in."

Ryan shrugged. "Suit himself. I'll never complain about having more deputies on hand. Be back in an hour."

Dwight waved and turned back to the computer.

This used to be Ryan's favorite time of day, that brought him a sense of peace. Everyone was just waking up. The streets were clear and quiet, and he could hear himself think as he walked. Once he'd enjoyed that. Before Faith.

They'd met four years ago when she was staying at the B&B until her housing in Benediction was finalized. Like a fool, he'd waited a year to ask her out. Thinking no one that pretty and sophisticated from a large city would have any interest in a simple man who was a bit rough around the edges and the sheriff of a tiny town.

Physically, Hope resembled Faith. Both attractive and slim without being rail thin, but Faith had had a glow about her. She wasn't afraid to eat pasta or pizza or split a piece of pie. Most of the time, she'd stolen his. Hope's brown hair had a hint of red that matched her fiery spirit. Whereas Faith's had natural blond highlights, giving it a golden sheen in the sunlight. She was the kindest, gentlest person and the only one who could get his father to smile. She would read Ryan's thoughts by the expression on his face and finish his sentences.

He'd felt blessed to be in her presence, to have her love, and tried every day to be worthy of it.

How could the universe be so cruel to give him his soul mate and then take her away?

They never had a chance to get married, have a family

and grow old together the way they'd planned. He never should've waited a minute to ask her out.

Now he walked these quiet streets, decorated for the holidays, rubbing the engagement ring resting against his sternum that he had planned to give her at Christmas, his blood boiling and his heart bleeding. After Faith was gone.

He rounded the corner and stopped cold.

A man he'd never seen before came skulking out from the walkway that ran between the bookstore and the B&B, carrying a suitcase. A *blush* Tumi carry-on that sure as hell wasn't his. Not that a dude couldn't own luggage in any shade he desired, but Hope had clarified the color wasn't pink, as Ryan had called it, but blush. When he'd been notified that a woman bearing a striking resemblance to Faith had checked in, he'd gone over to investigate and met her sister.

The stranger hadn't left the B&B through the front door as someone who belonged there would. He put the luggage inside a truck, locked the door and crossed the street, entering the diner. The man had the build of an athlete, nothing soft about him, and walked like he knew how to handle himself.

Not with the swagger of someone looking to advertise what they were to the world. That man was far more subtle. He had the prowess of a mongoose.

Looked so harmless most wouldn't bat a lash at him, but Ryan was certain he was deadly enough to kill.

Ryan hung back, collecting himself, letting the steam of wild ideas burn off in his mind.

Nexcellogen, the military police or some other group inside Benediction had Hope. They'd sent that man to dispose of her things. To tie up loose ends.

So they could make Hope disappear.

Ryan pushed off the wall and headed to the diner. Walking in, he looked around. Folks at two booths, one table. The stranger was at the counter at the far end away from everyone else, reading a newspaper.

"Morning, Sheriff. Bring your usual over?" Sally gestured to the booth where he always sat.

"The usual, yes, but I'll be sitting at the counter. Change things up a bit."

She appeared flustered a moment, but she nodded. "Okay. Change is good in Goode." She smiled.

"I like that. Sounds like a campaign slogan." Ryan headed to the back of the diner. Tipped his hat to patrons acknowledging him with a smile or a wave. Everyone he recognized, knew by name, but he didn't want to get bogged down in idle prattle, so he kept moving.

He sat next to the stranger, though every other seat at the counter was empty. The gesture would speak volumes.

Mongooses were territorial.

Ryan took off his Stetson, placed his sunglasses inside and dropped it on the stool on the other side of him. Sally brought him an orange juice and hurried back into the kitchen.

The stranger picked up the glass of water in front of him, took a healthy gulp, set it down. "How's it going, Sheriff?"

He was a smart mongoose. Those were even deadlier.

"Good. The snow is melting, and the sun is shining." Ryan drummed his fingers against the orange juice. "No complaints."

"I heard differently," the stranger said dryly.

"Come again?" Ryan looked at the man, but the

stranger didn't meet his eyes, still pretending to read the paper.

"Heard you were worried about a woman in Benediction."

A tingling sensation crept up Ryan's spine. He pushed his orange juice away and turned to him. "Did you? Who did you hear that from?"

"Hope Fischer." The stranger's voice was low, barely audible.

"Do you know her?" Ryan leaned toward him, his heart pelting in his chest. "Have you seen her? Is she all right?"

"Hope is in Benediction." The man turned the page and flicked the newspaper. "She's okay. Trying to track down the person you both want to find."

Sucking in a deep breath of relief, Ryan regained his composure. "Does she know who did it? Who killed Faith?"

The man looked around as if concerned others might notice them talking.

Ryan faced forward and drank his orange juice.

"No, she doesn't know yet," the stranger said. "But we know it was murder. The death certificate was falsified."

We. Ryan hung on to that word. "Is there anything I can do?"

The stranger finished his water. "No."

"When will I hear from her?" Ryan needed to talk to her firsthand to be sure she was all right and put his mind at ease. If something suspicious happened to Hope while she was in Benediction, no one would be the wiser.

Sally came out of the kitchen, carrying a white paper bag of food. She set it down in front of the stranger.

"There you go. Two Goode special breakfast sandwiches."

Faith's favorite. Hope's, too. Was the order coincidence or did it mean Hope was okay?

"Enjoy." Smiling, Sally left to greet new customers—the boy with the paper route and his mom.

"I don't know when you'll hear from her." The stranger glanced at Ryan, his gaze steady. Cool? Detached? "Once she's ready to leave Benediction. She can't contact you until then."

Convenient. That could be days, weeks, plenty of time to dispose of Hope and erase any trace that she'd been there. The sort of tactic he'd expect from Benediction.

Everyone in that town was shady, and none of them could be trusted.

Ryan clenched his hands. "Who are you? How do I know you haven't hurt her?"

"Me?" The man folded the newspaper, laid it on the counter and swiveled in his seat, facing him. "You're the one who almost got her killed," he said, his voice low and tight. Razor-sharp. But his face remained impassive, like they were having a conversation about something as interesting as the weather. "Rammed her car and sent it into the lake, where she almost drowned."

Drowned?

Nausea washed over Ryan. He'd sworn to look out for Hope as a brother would, and he'd let her down. From the moment he agreed to help her carry out her plan, he'd regretted it, but it was the only way to find out what really happened to Faith.

"I never meant for that to happen," Ryan said.

The stranger cleared his throat. "The road to hell is paved with good intentions, Sheriff."

"Don't talk to me that way." Ryan spun toward him but kept his tone hushed. "You don't have the right to lecture me."

"Why not? Because Hope didn't die?"

Ryan pulled out the engagement ring from his sweater and pointed to it. "Because I've been in hell ever since I lost the woman I love. Because I've been hanging on to find Faith's killer. Who the hell are you?"

The stranger's eyes narrowed, burning with anger. "I'm the one who stopped on the side of the road to help. I'm the one who gave Hope mouth-to-mouth, saved her and took her to the Benediction clinic." Lowering his head, he turned toward the counter and tossed two twenty-dollar bills next to his glass. "The way I see it, you're the one who needs to be lectured, because you've got lousy judgment. You couldn't protect Faith, and you almost killed Hope yourself."

"Bastard!" Ryan jumped up, his fists clenched, hanging on to his self-control by a fraying thread. "How dare you!"

A hush fell over the diner, and he knew everyone was staring even though his back was to them.

Grabbing the bag, the man stood. "If you want to keep her safe, stay away from Benediction. Don't ask questions about her." Then the stranger was gone.

Ryan did want to keep Hope safe. He owed Faith that much. But he didn't take kindly to condescension, arrogance or disrespect.

If that man had been telling the truth, Ryan would stay away from Benediction, but he didn't know that guy from Adam and had no proof of what he'd claimed.

Not asking questions about Hope didn't mean he couldn't ask questions about other things.

Sally wiped down the counter and went to take the stranger's glass.

"Wait." Ryan held out his palm, stopping her. "Grab a plastic bag from the kitchen. I want to take that glass with me."

"Why, Sheriff?"

"Get the bag."

Sally spun around, shuffled to the kitchen and returned with a resealable plastic bag.

Picking up the edge of the glass with a napkin, he dropped it into the bag she held open for him. "Thanks, Sally," he said, standing.

"What about breakfast?"

"Wrap it to go. Have that kid, the one with the paper route, deliver it." It was another snow day for school. "I'll pay him ten bucks."

"I'm sure he'll get a kick out of it," she said, grinning from ear to ear, her plump cheeks rosy. "That's more than he makes in a week."

Ryan left the diner, holding the bag with the glass, and headed back to the station.

There was something about the stranger he didn't trust. And a whole lot about him that he didn't like. The shifty eyes. The smart mouth. The contemptuous tone. The cocky, I-can-kick-your-butt demeanor. Giving the sheriff orders and telling him what to do in Ryan's town. Pretty slick for Benediction. The stranger might be security for Nexcellogen trying to throw him off Hope's trail. Ryan wouldn't believe everything was all right until he heard from Hope firsthand.

He walked into the station and handed Dwight the bag. "Run the prints on that glass. As soon as you have something, I want to know."

"Will do. I'll get to it as soon as I'm done with my paperwork. How deep do you want me to dig?"

"Every database. Even if there's no criminal record, I want to know about any arrests. Leave no stone unturned."

A NEW FRISSON of amazement ran through her when the door to the apartment opened and Gage walked in. He'd been gone for so long she'd started to worry.

As he set her suitcase on the rug, she uncrossed her legs and got up.

Hope ran her hands over his chest. "I thought it might have been too conspicuous for you to bring my whole bag."

"You're right, but I figured you'd want your own clothes and other stuff. I mean, what's a photojournalist without a camera?"

Even without asking, he'd brought all her things, knew she'd miss her camera.

Cupping his face, she pressed her mouth to his and kissed him. Hard.

It occurred to her she'd never tire of this, even if she kissed him every moment of every day.

Smiling, she had thought the romantic in her had been lost, missing in action, years ago. So nice that it wasn't. "You taste like bacon and avocado."

He lifted the white paper bag in his other hand. "Ate mine on the way back. Yours is cold. Sorry it took me a while, but the pharmacy in Goode didn't open until nine, and I needed to pick up a refill for Claire's prescription. Do you want me to pop the sandwich in the microwave for you?"

"Thanks, but I'm too anxious to eat." Hope dropped

to her knees and unzipped her bag. She grabbed her small jewelry case beside her camera and took out the cremation urn necklace. A heart surrounded by silver angel wings. "Inside are the last of Faith's ashes," she said, holding it up. "I got it so that I'd always have a piece of her with me. I left it in my bag for safekeeping."

"Do you want me to help you put it on?"

"Thanks."

Hope pulled her hair out of the way while Gage draped the chain around her neck and clasped it for her. She put it inside her top. The silver was cool against her skin but quickly warmed.

The heart and wings rested beside Faith's cryptex pendant, which Hope also wore.

She turned back to the carryon. The four letters, bundled and tied together with a white silk ribbon, were in the top left corner.

"We should begin in chronological order," he said, sitting next to her. "See what made her start writing to you."

Hope opened the first letter, dated August 23. "Take a look." She handed it to him. "Faith deliberately mentioned she was reading *To Kill a Mockingbird*. At the time, I didn't think anything of it that she'd specified mass market paperback and the fiftieth anniversary edition."

"She wanted to make sure that you two would be on the same page. Literally."

"Exactly." Hope leaned over and pointed to the bottom of the letter. "After she signed it, she put a quote from the book."

"Hey, I think I see the difference in Faith's signature. Can you grab the Nexcellogen form?"

Hope reached for the jacket on the sofa and pulled it out, handing it to him.

"Now that I'm looking at the real deal in comparison, it's obvious. Faith was left-handed?"

"Yeah. Why?"

"Whoever forged her signature was right-handed. A leftie makes strokes in a right-to-left direction, and the slope of letters has an inclination in a backward direction. But when you compare it, on the forgery, the person did come close, but the letters want to slope in a forward direction, which is the natural inclination for a right-handed writer."

"It was hard for me to pinpoint what it was about the other signature. But now that you say it, I can see what you mean. It's so subtle."

Fortunately, he knew what to look for. Did he ever have to make someone's death look like a suicide, forge letters?

One day she'd ask, but at the moment, there was too much for her to think about.

"With the quote at the bottom of the letter, do you think it corresponds to a page number?" Gage asked.

"I doubt it." Hope opened the book and found the first quote on page 112. "It's the fourth line down on the page. Let's circle every fourth word in the letter. If that doesn't get us anywhere, we'll go by paragraph."

As Gage got her a pencil, her pulse kicked up a notch. With any luck, this would get them one step closer. She began the process, counting and circling. An eerie tingle raced down her spine as the words came together. The message was simple and clear.

"'No success at work. Only failure. Pressure. Don't know what to do. May have a bigger problem. Sidekick is up to something,'" she said, reading the coded message aloud.

"Who is sidekick supposed to be?" Gage asked.

"A sidekick is a buddy, a friend. It must be Paul. She liked Neal and I'm sure they became sociable in this small town, but she never talked about him as if they were buddies."

He stared at her with an analytical frown, as though he was working out an equation in his head. "Look up the next quote."

The letter was dated October 1.

Thank goodness Faith had chosen this particular book and quotes that stood out. Hope had read it so many times, she knew where to pinpoint them without much effort. "Six."

Gage highlighted each word this time. "'Higher-ups in big city expect results that I can't give. Worried I'll be transferred. Forced to move. Can't leave my love now.'"

"We didn't speak on the phone every day," Hope said, "but a few times a month at least, unless I was overseas. She never mentioned anything about the possibility of having to move back to Herndon. Why wouldn't she come right out and say that to me?"

"Remember, she suspected the phone line was tapped, and obviously, she was worried that someone might even check her mail. Maybe she wasn't allowed to talk about the project at all. To admit that she might be kicked off the project meant something was wrong with the drug testing. But I'd like to know why she wouldn't say anything to Ryan if they were in love and on the verge of getting engaged. I didn't think highly of him before, and after meeting him my opinion hasn't changed."

She understood he was upset with Ryan for going

along with her plan, but she needed Gage to look at the facts without bias.

"Faith would never want a boyfriend to feel forced or manipulated into proposing. If Ryan thought there was a chance she might have to leave, then he might've felt compelled to pop the question or lose her. She believed in fairy tales and wanted things to progress in their own time. I could see her not telling him outright."

"I'm sure Faith had her reasons, but I don't trust Sheriff Ryan Keller. He has poor judgment. I don't understand how he could endanger you like that."

Setting the letter down, she scooted closer to Gage. "I wasn't totally honest last night. Ryan didn't want to help me with my, and I quote, harebrained plan. He called me foolhardy, truth be told, but I guilted him into doing it. I shouldn't have misled you, and I don't want it to skew the way you see him."

Gage put his fists on his thighs and shook his head. "You didn't force him. He had a choice and made the wrong one."

They weren't going to see eye to eye on this.

Hope put her left hand on his right fist.

A ghost of a smile touched his lips. He opened his hand, turning it palm up, and enfolded hers. "Moving on."

A small laugh escaped her, and she nodded in agreement.

Hope found the third quote in a letter dated October 27. "Ninth line down."

Gage made quick work of piecing together the message. "'Unbelievable. Brutus wants my job. Promises better results. Lies. Merlin without magic.'"

"This doesn't sound like the Paul I met in Herndon. Perhaps this is about Neal."

"We should read the last message."

"The letter was dated four days after Thanksgiving."

Gage looked over at it. "She was killed the next day."

Hope shivered from a sudden chill, and Gage wrapped his arm around her shoulder.

"I was in Syria when she wrote this. She'd called, left a message, sounded upbeat, ecstatic. Said Ryan was coming for Christmas and everything was falling into place."

"Something must've happened. What's the number for the last quote?"

Pushing aside the grief welling in her chest, she looked it up. It took her a minute, but she found the line. "Five."

She tried to picture Faith happy and smiling, excited to introduce Ryan to the family. That was the one thing Hope could take comfort in.

"'Had it wrong,'" Gage said, reading the message. "'No one can be trusted. Think crony is misusing drug. Selling. Recreational. Horrible. Need proof.'"

"That's definitely about Paul. I can't believe he was using their research to make recreational drugs. But why?"

"Money?" He rubbed her back. "Money, power, passion, revenge—those are always the biggest motives for murder when the victim and perpetrator know each other."

"Paul is nice, the life of the party. Not a scumbag drug dealer."

"How many of those have you met?"

"I see your point. Do you think Paul could also be

Brutus? Taking her job and overseeing the lab would have given him more control and leeway to do what he wanted."

"It's possible," Gage said. "Hang on a minute." He read the letter in its entirety. "She talked about a new illegal drug flooding the area called Zion. How Ryan was trying to find the person distributing it in the area and she wished she could help him."

"I had no idea she thought the source might be coming from her lab." She pushed her hair back behind her ears and grunted her frustration. "I feel like such an idiot. Faith handed me all these breadcrumbs with quotes from my favorite book, and I never put it together."

"You are now."

"But what if I had done it sooner, while she was still alive? Maybe I could've come out here and helped her. Saved her." Regrets spiraled in her mind as her chest tightened, making it hard to breathe.

Gage stroked her cheek with the back of his fingers. "You can't beat yourself up with what-ifs. They'll get you nowhere useful and only make you miserable."

When he flattened his palm against her cheek, she nuzzled into it, allowing herself a moment to absorb the comfort he gave her. She knew he was right, but it was hard to forgive herself for the oversight.

He lowered his hand and pressed a soft kiss to her temple.

"We have to question Paul," she said. "Do you know where he lives?"

"Next door to Faith's old townhome. Near the entrance of the residential area. His place backs up to the woods."

"It's a Saturday. The odds are good he won't be at

work. He might be at home." Hope got to her feet. "What are we waiting for?"

Gage stood, meeting her gaze head-on, and closed his hands on her arms. "We should wait until it's dark."

"We finally have a motive and a suspect. I don't want to wait."

"Listen, you haven't eaten today. It's already lunchtime, and I'm hungry. Let's have a bite and talk this through with clear heads."

"Fine. I'll eat, but if you think I'm going to sit here and stew for several hours, you're the one who's crazy."

Chapter Fourteen

"This is a bad idea," Gage said to Hope an hour later, dressed in all black with a wool hat and gloves, even though it was warmer today than it had been yesterday. He crept through the woods adjacent to one of the running trails that butted up against the rear of Kudlow's property.

He'd gone insane. That thought spun in his head over and over again.

The snow was practically gone, making their trek relatively quiet, and there were plenty of evergreens for great concealment. But it was still broad daylight. This kind of operation was supposed to be conducted under the cover of darkness.

"This is happening." Jogging beside him, she wore blue jeans, winter booties, a dark turtleneck and his black zip-up with the hood covering her hair. She nearly fell when her boot got caught on a gnarled tree branch, but she pressed on through the underbrush. "We do this now," she said, determination sharpening her tone, "and we get answers, no matter what it takes."

Gage hadn't spent his life looking for a partner, trying to find someone like Hope, but now that he was with her, he didn't want to imagine being without her.

Years of retreat and evasion had ended last night when he opened up and revealed himself to her. Told her things only his team—the family of his choosing—knew about him. Told her things they didn't know. There was no one reason that could explain why he'd broken down his carefully erected walls, or why with her. Though he'd given it considerable thought on the drive to and from Goode.

This wasn't love at first sight. He didn't believe in such nonsense.

Maybe it was a series of events that made real the cost of his choices. How her survival and safety hinged on his actions that bound them together.

In her face, he saw his own vulnerability. And his strength, too.

He never wanted to stop looking at her.

"It's this one," he whispered, stopping and crouching low in the thick trees. He scanned the area.

There was twenty feet of lawn and some trimmed hedgerows between the woods and the back door of the townhome. The unit to the right had been Faith's and was vacant. They only needed to worry about the neighbors on the other side possibly hearing anything.

All was quiet in this pristine section of the residential area, apart from the voices of children, probably unsupervised, enjoying their Saturday afternoon on the playground. No movement in Kudlow's kitchen or the bedroom that faced the rear. It was the same next door. A dog barked somewhere down the block, too far to be of any concern, but then it quickly stopped. Silence settled once more.

Considerate neighbors didn't allow their pets or their kids to be a nuisance. Didn't play their music too loud, didn't throw noisy parties and most certainly didn't break in. Everyone in Benediction was a considerate neighbor.

But once again, Gage was about to become the exception to the rule.

He scanned the area one more time, since it was the middle of the day. "All clear," he said. "Ready?"

Hope pulled out the Kylo Ren mask he'd given her and slipped it on. He did likewise, wearing Darth Vader's. They were from costumes he'd bought for him and Jason, so they could dress up as characters from Jason's favorite movie franchise. The kid had had an incident with the military police the week before Halloween. Gage had thought while handing out candy together to a handful of trick-or-treaters, he'd talk some sense into him. But Jason had flat out refused the gesture.

Too little, too late on Gage's part.

The masks had gone unused until now.

"Remember, let me do the talking," he said, not sounding like himself thanks to the voice changer inside the mask. A fortuitous purchase since he was about to break into the house of someone who knew him.

"Got it." Hope's voice was distorted, as well, but he wanted her to take a back seat on the interrogation, worried she might get emotional and deviate from the plan.

He darted through the trees. Took a knee by the back door.

No home security system to worry about, and if he was in luck, he wouldn't even need the lock-picking tools in his hand. Given that the town was so insulated with high-level security, most homes had either unlocked windows or doors or both. It was usually the MPs or some of the Nexcellogen outsiders who bothered to lock up, more so out of habit.

Gage tried the knob—it turned, and the door opened. He gestured for Hope to hurry over.

She looked around before dashing from the tree line. She entered the house and he followed, closing the door softly and swiftly behind him.

Gage handed her the kit to hang on to and crept through the kitchen toward the living room, where a television was on.

From the sound of it, Kudlow was playing a video game. Alone. A shoot-'em-up game with aliens.

Gage drew his gun and swept into the living room.

Kudlow was sitting in a recliner chair, wearing a robe, boxers and a plain tee underneath, and slippers. It took a second for him to catch the movement and notice Gage because he was so involved in the game.

His eyes flared wide, and his lips parted with soundless shock.

"Get up," Gage said over the television.

Finally, Kudlow blinked and raised his hands, dropping the game controller. "What's going on? Is this some kind of prank?"

"Up! Now!"

Shaking, Kudlow rose from the chair and then froze. "Neal? Is that you? This isn't funny."

Gage stalked up to him and pushed Kudlow into the hall, away from the front of the house, where there was street traffic and a passerby might overhear something. Even though there was little chance of that with the volume of the video game.

Kudlow scurried down the hall with his hands up by his ears. "What's happening?"

"Shut up," Gage said in a tight voice.

"Who are you?"

"A concerned citizen." Gage shoved him into the kitchen. "Sit."

Kudlow dropped into a chair at the dining table. "What do you want?"

"Answers." Gage nodded for Hope to restrain his hands with zip ties the way he'd shown her earlier— behind him and attached to the lattice-back chair that came standard in the furnished places. She did so without hesitation.

"Ouch." Kudlow grimaced as she secured the restraint. "That hurts."

Good. Better for it to be too tight than too loose.

Gage lowered the weapon. "Tell me about the illegal drug you're selling."

"Wh-what?" Kudlow's terrified gaze bounced between them. "I don't know what you're talking about."

"I'm talking about Zion," Gage said.

"I've got nothing to do with that." Kudlow paused. His Adam's apple moved and up and down as he swallowed hard. "You've got the wrong guy."

"Either you cooperate and talk, or we do this the hard way." Gage aimed the Sig at the man's knee. "I induce cooperation, which will be very painful, and in the end, you'll still talk."

"What do you want to know?"

That was more like it. Gage lowered the gun. "Where does Zion come from?"

"I—I—I make it."

"Why?" Gage asked.

Kudlow looked perplexed by the question.

"You're a scientist," Gage said. "You're supposed to be making the world better. Why are you selling drugs?"

"Because I can. For the money." An edge of panic

shook his voice, rushed his words. "You think I want to rake in five figures a year while corporations like Nexcellogen make billions off my work?"

"Off Faith Fischer's work," Hope said.

Gage had warned her not to speak. Leave the interrogation to him. It would be quicker and more efficient that way.

"Yeah." Kudlow looked between them. "So what?"

"So you killed her over it," Gage said.

"Me? No, no, no," Kudlow sputtered. "I would never hurt Faith."

"Liar," Hope said, coming up next to Kudlow. "You killed her because she found out the truth about what you were doing and was going to expose you."

"How do you know that?" Kudlow asked, his face contorted with fear.

The man was too unnerved to deny it. "Doesn't matter how we know." Gage stepped forward and eased Hope to the side. "Tell us exactly how you did it."

"She committed suicide. I didn't kill her! I wouldn't, couldn't. Never. She was my friend."

"You would for money." Gage bent over and got in Kudlow's face. "To save your reputation and your career. To keep your drug enterprise running."

"No, that's not what happened!"

The guy was scared and flustered, but he needed a push. "Then tell us," Gage demanded, slamming a fist down on the dining table.

"Yes, I wanted her out of the way in the lab, okay, but for her to go back to Herndon!" Kudlow was sweating and shaking. "Neal stumbled upon what I was doing long before Faith. He promised to keep it quiet if I helped him take her job. It would be a win-win for both of us." His wide eyes were starting to tear, his gaze everywhere, not settling on one spot for more than a second. "I'd get to continue manufacturing my drug and he'd get the glory once we had a breakthrough. Neal would be able to write his own ticket then. But something happened over the Thanksgiving weekend she spent in Goode to make her connect Zion with the drug we were working on in the lab."

"Do you have any idea what it was?" Gage asked.

"No. She didn't say."

Gage studied him, assessing more than his words for the truth. "What was she doing Thanksgiving weekend?"

Kudlow shrugged. "Spending it with her boyfriend, I think. Faith was private. She didn't really talk about that stuff. I just assumed she was seeing someone since she went to Goode so often. After her suicide, there was talk she'd gone through a bad breakup."

"She didn't commit suicide," Hope snapped.

Gage raised a palm to her, needing to keep things on track.

She huffed, folded her arms and crossed to the other side of the kitchen.

"So, Faith came back to work after Thanksgiving and suspected that Zion was being produced in her lab," Gage said. "She learned it was you, and you killed her to keep her quiet."

Kudlow shook his head. "I didn't lay a finger on Faith."

"But she did know you were producing Zion," Gage said.

"Faith started snooping around and suspected me, but she couldn't prove it. She needed a sample of Zion to test and compare to the ones in the lab. But she figured out that Neal must've known what I was doing and that was the reason I was supporting him to take over the project."

"Faith trusted you!" Hope said. "She thought you were loyal, that you were her friend."

"I remember the look on her face." Paul was crying now, tears streaming down his cheeks, white spittle gathering at the corner of his mouth. "Faith said I was a contemptible weasel and called Neal Brutus. She was so mad. So hurt. She was going to disclose the truth about the failing drug trials in the annual report. That meant corporate would shut us down. Everything would end."

The words shocked Gage. He was a man who kept his ear to the ground and hadn't heard anything close to that. "What do you mean, shut you down? Aren't there several ongoing projects?"

Kudlow nodded, with tears spilling from his eyes. "But ours was the shining star, the great hope for Nexcellogen. We had to meet a certain benchmark in the annual report. Show we were ready for human clinical trials. But if we couldn't pull off what we promised, this miracle PTSD vaccine, they were going to pull the plug on funding. That meant us, the company, leaving Benediction by springtime."

Interesting. That was a big statement with even bigger repercussions for the whole town. It meant the death of Benediction if what he said was true.

Then again, the town had been close to dying before and always pulled through.

Gage must've been silent for a moment too long, thinking, because Hope prowled up to Kudlow.

"When you couldn't get Faith replaced and she discovered what you were doing, you decided to kill her," she said. "Admit it and we might let you live."

"Stop," Gage warned her. It'd only muddy the waters if Kudlow admitted to a crime he hadn't committed out of fear, thinking it was the only way to survive. The guilty always wanted to convince you of their innocence. Better to let them talk, dig their own grave.

Invariably they'd say something that could be proven or disproven or get caught in a lie.

"Why should I stop?" Hope asked. "He had every reason to kill her. He had a motive, probably opportunity, too, and no alibi."

"That's not true!" Kudlow said frantic. "I do have an alibi. The night Faith died, I wasn't in town. I was with my distributor. We negotiated new terms. Talked about expansion. Ways to increase production outside the lab, so Faith would never get proof. We ended up partying and I got drunk, wasted. I couldn't drive, crashed at his place."

"Who is your distributor?" Gage asked.

Kudlow squeezed his eyes shut and lowered his head, like he regretted mentioning the alibi and wanted to suck the words back into his mouth.

"Who?" Gage pressed.

"He, uh…" Kudlow hesitated, his bottom lip quivering as though he were more terrified of his accomplice than them. "He'll kill me if I tell you. Please."

This was the part of the interrogation where threatening death worked. "*We'll* kill you if you don't."

Kudlow raised his head. Tears and snot glistened on his face. "He's in the sheriff's department."

Hope's gaze flickered to Gage. The same question he had was evident in her shocked eyes.

If the distributor was Ryan Keller, Gage was driving back to Goode to shoot the man himself. "Give us a name. Now." He put the tip of the silencer to Kudlow's leg. "A bullet in the knee is excruciating."

"Dwight!" Kudlow snapped up. "Dwight Travers. One of the deputies. The MPs, they can verify that I left Benediction after work at five and didn't come back through the gates until the next morning, around, um, nine or so. Faith had already been found by then. The whole town was abuzz about it."

Kudlow was right. Faith had been brought to the funeral home shortly before midnight. According to Dr. Howland's report, the time of death was between seven and eight, and a neighbor whose account of being out for a jog and seeing smoke coming from Faith's garage substantiated at least that part of the doctor's findings.

"Then are you saying Neal killed her?" Gage asked.

Kudlow shrugged. "I don't know who did it," he said, looking as though he truly had no clue who had murdered Faith. "Neal wanted her job and, eventually, he got it, but that doesn't make him a killer."

"But it does make it convenient for both of you now that she's gone." Gage crouched down in front of him. "Maybe Neal killed her and you knew about it. Helped him cover it up. Spread the rumors about a breakup."

"No. That's nuts!"

Hope paced in the kitchen. Gage could feel the rage and tension emanating from her. She was barely holding it together, but he admired the fact that she was.

"Sounds plausible to me," Gage said. "Maybe I should shoot you and Neal, too."

"Please," Kudlow pleaded, sobbing. "Don't."

"Give me one good reason to believe you and Neal didn't do this together."

Kudlow looked up and around as if searching the

room for a way to escape. "Wait. Uh, Neal told me that he was working late in the lab the night Faith died. We have to badge in and out of the building. There's an access log in security. I wasn't in Benediction that night. I have an alibi. If you can get the records in Nexcellogen, you'll know if Neal was in the building or not."

"If it turns out that Neal was in the building that night, who else would have benefited from Faith's death?" Gage asked.

"The whole town. Right? I mean, if Nexcellogen pulled out, Benediction would shut down. These townies are crazy about this place. They'd do anything to keep it thriving."

They would. They were fiercely protective of this place, as if it were a family member.

"But the possibility of the company leaving wasn't common knowledge," Gage said, thinking it through aloud. The townies were gossipy. Something of this magnitude would've spread like wildfire if even one permanent resident had known. "None of the townsfolks knew. I'm guessing they wouldn't have heard about it until after the annual report came out and the company made their decision public." Which brought everything full circle back to the perpetrator being someone inside Nexcellogen. Only an employee would've been able to change and forge Faith's In Case of Death form.

"That's not going to happen now," Kudlow said.

"Why not?" Hope asked, breaking her silence.

"Neal altered the annual report. Made the results look far more promising than they really were to buy us time. We're close to a breakthrough on that drug. I just know it and so does he. We can make it work."

"Did Michelle Lansing know the report was falsified?" Gage asked.

"Are you kidding me? She would've fired both of us on the spot for even suggesting anything so unethical."

Gage believed him about Michelle, who'd always struck him as ethical and reasonable, and it was possible that Kudlow was also right about Neal Underhill. But they needed more than gut instinct. They needed proof.

"Pen and paper," Gage said. "Where can I find it?"

"Top left drawer." Kudlow gestured with his chin.

Gage grabbed it and sat. "You're going to give us the names of all the project team leaders." All of them had something lose if Nexcellogen pulled out of Benediction. "And I want to know the layout of the building and exactly what to expect inside. Any security protocols, how many people typically work on a Saturday. No detail is too small. Do you understand?"

Time spent in reconnaissance was seldom wasted.

"Okay." Kudlow nodded. "Yeah."

Kudlow spilled his guts, describing every inch of the building that he'd seen.

It took over an hour, but Gage wanted to be thorough, going over every aspect several times. Gage listened for any changes or slipups, to be sure the information was credible. While he did that, Hope searched Kudlow's things for any clues they might have overlooked.

She came back into the kitchen, holding two white lab coats and other items with the Nexcellogen logo on it. Catching Gage's eye, she shook her head. There was nothing else useful.

Once Gage was satisfied with the details of the building, he folded the paper and slipped it into his pocket. "How many guards on duty?"

"Four, Monday through Friday. Two on the weekend. One in the lobby and the other in the security room."

"What time is shift change?"

"Seven. Always at seven."

According to the security procedure, every individual had to scan their ID badge to get through the gate turnstile in the lobby that was designed to make piggybacking impossible. Which was a good thing. The access records would be accurate, reliable, and anyone who had been inside the building at the time of death could be eliminated as a suspect.

It also meant they'd need two badges, and both had to work. "Where's your badge?" Gage asked.

"On the counter, next to my wallet."

Gage grabbed it and then nodded again to Hope. This time she took out duct tape and placed it over the scientist's mouth.

Kudlow's eyes widened with renewed alarm as he shook his head.

"Sorry, but we can't have you screaming for help," Gage said. "You'll be set free later. But if you've lied about anything, conveniently forgot to tell us something about security protocols, no one will look for you until Monday." He'd figure out a discreet way to have someone stumble upon Kudlow and release him without it leading back to Gage.

Getting their hands on the Nexcellogen entry and exit log was imperative, and they couldn't risk Kudlow notifying someone beforehand.

It looked like his last-resort measure was their next step.

Chapter Fifteen

Dwight knocked on Ryan's office door and poked his head inside. "Nothing came back on those fingerprints, Sheriff."

"Really? Nothing?" Ryan leaned back in his chair, more than a little disappointed to hear the news. But just because the stranger from Benediction didn't have a record that didn't mean Ryan was wrong about him. Simply meant he hadn't been caught. Yet.

"Yeah," Dwight said. "There were two sets, but I only got a hit on Sally's prints."

Ryan shot him an incredulous look. "Sweet Sally who wants to put a smile on everyone's face?"

"She recently got her real estate license. Remember?"

"Oh, okay," Ryan said, recalling the party for her at the diner. Part of the process of obtaining your real estate license was submitting your prints to the Virginia Central Criminal Records Exchange for a state and national fingerprint-based criminal history check. "You checked all the databases?"

"Yep. FBI, Department of Defense, Department of Homeland Security and even the Foreign Biometric Exchange," Dwight said, referring to the database that was a collection of high-value biometrics on persons of interest from foreign law enforcement in partner countries. *"Nada."*

"All right. Thanks." Ryan turned to his computer.

"One more thing." Dwight leaned on the door frame and crossed his arms. "We got a call from Gary Metsos about ten minutes ago."

Ryan looked back at him. "What about this time? Old man Metsos see another UFO?"

Dwight chuckled. "No, he only sees those late at night. But it was the strangest thing. He said a helicopter landed on his farm."

"Emergency landing? Do some people need help?"

"I don't think so. He said that he was going to talk to them, find out what was going on, but a big black SUV pulled up alongside the state road, in front of his property. Those men loaded in, drove off, going east, and the chopper left."

"That is odd. Did Gary say what they looked like?"

"Yep. Tactical."

"As in armed?"

Dwight nodded.

Terrific.

"Assault weapons," Dwight said. "You want me to check it out?"

Swearing under his breath, Ryan drummed his fingers on his desk. It was going to be another wretched day in Goode.

Firearms with magazines capable of holding more than twenty rounds were classified as assault weapons, but they were legal here. Unless those men had fully automatic machine guns or sound suppressors—silencers— there wasn't much the sheriff's department could do in this county. "If those men are on the state road going east, then they're headed our way and we'll…" Ryan glanced out the window as a black Chevrolet Suburban SUV with dark-tinted windows parked right outside the station. "Well, well. What do we have here?"

"I guess that answers my question," Dwight said.

Only the front passenger door of the vehicle opened. A man with slicked-back hair, dressed in a black suit and wearing sunglasses—despite the fact that the sun was already low on the horizon and it'd be dark soon — got out and closed the door.

"You think they're govvie?" Dwight asked, frowning, and sucked his teeth.

Government preferred this type of vehicle. The suit screamed three-letter alphabet agency—take your pick, FBI, DOJ, DOD, DHS. Not that it mattered, because no local sheriff was going to trust them until they proved their worth.

Fastening the top button on his suit jacket, the man proceeded inside the station. He stopped at the reception-ist desk and spoke to Aimee. She picked up the phone, presumably to notify Ryan that someone wanted to speak with him. But the man stopped her, offering a tight smile that played closer to a grimace, and waltzed across the open floor space, past Dwight into Ryan's office.

Still wearing his sunglasses.

What nerve.

"Boss, you want me to stick around?" Dwight asked, scrutinizing their visitor from head to toe.

Ryan waved him off. "I've got this."

"Okay," Dwight said. "Holler if you need me."

As Dwight's determined footsteps drifted away to-ward his desk, the man took it upon himself to take a seat across from Ryan.

"Hello, Sheriff. I'm Agent Joe Smith." He reached into the inner pocket of his jacket, but instead of taking out a business card as Ryan had expected, he pulled out his cell phone. "It's come to our attention that this man might be in the area." He turned the screen toward Ryan, and on it was a picture of the stranger from Benediction. Shorter hair. Same shifty eyes and severe expression. But without a doubt, it was the same man.

A fine sweat chilled the back of Ryan's neck.

"Have you or anyone in this office seen him?" Smith asked.

"Who is that man?"

"A fugitive. Real menace to society wherever he goes. He's wanted for several crimes. Do you or your deputies know his current whereabouts?"

"What did you say his name was?"

"I didn't." Smith lowered the phone. "Sheriff, I'm all for quid pro quo, but it's rude to answer a question with a question."

"And it's rude to wear sunglasses indoors and just plain stupid to do so at night. I guess we could both use etiquette lessons."

Smith flashed another tight smile and removed his glasses. "The man we're looking for has used many aliases. The last one known was Taggert Jenner. He should be considered armed and dangerous."

"Sort of like your posse in that vehicle?" Ryan pointed to the SUV. "Do you have a permit for open carry?"

"In a vehicle, a firearm isn't considered openly carried unless it's openly visible. Ours are not."

"Mr. Gary Metsos saw you boys on his property with weapons. That would be open."

Smith sat back and crossed his legs. "Unless I'm mistaken, in this county open carry is allowed without a permit for people eighteen years of age and older. And I'm never mistaken."

"I see you've done your research." Which was rather disquieting. "What exactly are y'all armed with?"

"Assault weapons. Semiautomatic. Would you care to see?"

Okay, he'd bite. "Sure." Ryan stood, grabbing his hat.

But Smith stayed seated, punched in a number on his phone, speed dial, and put it to his ear. "The sheriff wants to see what the boys are carrying. Come on in." He disconnected.

Three doors opened, and three men stepped out of the SUV. The lot of them were dressed in tactical gear with bulletproof vests. They all looked grim. Had holstered sidearms on their hips. Assault weapons in their hands.

"Hey, boss, what's up?" Dwight asked in a loud voice, crossing the open space of the station while staring outside.

"They've agreed to show me what they're armed with," Ryan said. "Go back to your desk."

The men entered the station, poured into his office single file and stood around the periphery while Aimee watched like it was any other day.

People carrying assault weapons wasn't anything new. This was Virginia—most folks in the area supported the Second Amendment and proudly showed it.

Smith pointed to one of his men.

The guy stepped forward, holding up the assault weapon to the side, muzzle pointed toward the wall. "This is an MP5K in nine-millimeter semiauto. Magazine capacity is fifteen rounds. Would you like to inspect further, sir?" He offered the firearm, handle first.

"No, that won't be necessary," Ryan said, noting the muzzles were all threaded so you could screw on a suppressor. He'd bet dollars to doughnuts those men were carrying silencers in their cargo pockets or had left them in the vehicle.

This was a good show. Appeared cooperative.

Ryan might be guilty of answering a question with a question, but Joe Smith—and no, Ryan did not think his name was really Joe Smith—responded to questions with a whole lot of baloney without ever giving a legitimate answer.

In the past fifteen minutes, Ryan still hadn't learned the name of the stranger from the diner. Joe had only shared the last known alias used.

Ryan looked around at the tactical contingent in his office. Their bulletproof vests were plain, devoid of any words like Police, SWAT, FBI. "What agency did you say you were with, *Joe Smith*?"

The rubbery smile loosened. "Sheriff, this is a matter of homeland security." Joe held up the phone, showing Ryan the picture again. "Where's the man we're looking for?"

"Homeland security, huh? I'd love to see some DHS credentials. Preferably a badge with your real name on it."

Smith leaned forward. His pupils were dilated such that the black pool at the center of each iris appeared to equal the area of surrounding color. Two black holes in space. "You could save us all a lot of time and energy by cooperating. Because before I leave your station, you're going to answer all my questions to my satisfaction, and once I am gone, you still won't know my real name."

Ryan chuckled, interlacing his fingers and pressing his palms to his stomach. Two Yankees in one day who wanted to be cowboys. "You're a funny man, Joe."

The other men remained stony-faced and silent.

Smith dialed another number. A pause. "It's me. I'm sitting in Sheriff Ryan Keller's office in the Podunk town of Goode. He's refusing to cooperate." He listened a moment, his gaze never wavering from Ryan's. "Thank you." Smith hit the end button and put the phone back in his pocket. "My men and I are going to grab a cup of coffee. You are going to receive a phone call shortly. After you do, I'll sit back down in this chair, and then we'll see who's laughing."

Smith stood and strolled out. His men followed, leaving the door open. They asked Aimee a question. She jumped up and hurried to the break area, since it wasn't a large enough station for a break room, and started pouring cups of coffee.

Ryan had assumed they'd leave, make their way to the café or to the diner while he received this mystery call.

Anxiety rippled through him. He signaled to Dwight, discreetly, urging him to get his tail in there.

Dwight hurried over without looking like he was rushing. "Yes, boss?"

"You said that nothing came back on those prints, right?" Ryan whispered.

"Yeah, boss. No results found in any of the databases."

How in the hell did these guys know to show up here? "Okay, thanks."

Their visitors gathered in the entrance, sipping coffee.

Aimee sat back down as the phone rang. A second later, she buzzed Ryan. "It's the governor on the line for you."

Holy. Hell. Ryan hadn't known who to expect a call from, but it sure as heck wasn't the governor.

Standing near Aimee's desk, Joe Smith looked right at Ryan. Satisfaction gleamed in his eyes as he gave Ryan a two-finger salute, then lowered his index finger, leaving his middle one up.

Ryan looked away and cleared his throat before

picking up the phone. "Hello, Governor. This is Sheriff Keller."

"Before today, I never knew the town of Goode or you, for that matter, Ryan Keller, existed. The only reason I care is because I don't like it when I receive phone calls from people who have the power to make my life difficult. The reason you should care I'm on the phone now is because I can make your life very difficult. Do you understand?"

"Yes, sir, I do." Ryan straightened in his seat.

"There is a gentleman in your office who wants to ask you questions. I want you to answer him. Fully. Truthfully. The more information the better."

Joe Smith would ask questions to connect the dots. Why had the stranger been in Goode? Had he committed a crime? Why had his fingerprints been run since no crime had been committed? What had the stranger discussed with Ryan in the diner?

Those dots would lead to Hope.

Ryan had almost gotten her killed. Throwing Faith's sister to the wolves—who were armed with assault weapons and most likely had sound suppressors—wasn't going to happen without a legitimate reason.

Who were these men? Why were they looking for the stranger? Could Hope be implicated in some crime due to her association with him?

Ryan had no idea what Hope knew about that man or her connection to him. But when Smith and his men found the stranger, Hope would be with him, and she might get caught in the crossfire.

"With all due respect, Governor, I don't answer to you. I was elected by the people of Goode and answer to them. You have no authority over me." The governor could not fire him, nor officially reprimand him, and had no direct control over any funds for his department. It would take effort on the part of the governor to make his life difficult, but Ryan had been polite earlier, allowing him to flex his muscles. "Unless I know where these men came from, I don't have any answers for them."

"I'll spell it out for you in language you'll understand. Their business concerns national security and is above both of our positions and pay grades." There was a long, uncomfortable pause. "Now, you're going to be a patriot and answer Mr. Joe Smith's questions, so I don't have to field any more calls from government spooks or, heaven forbid, the White House. Are we on the same page?"

Smith and his men must have been CIA, which would explain a lot. For starters, how Ryan's office could run prints that turned up zero results but triggered the arrival of a tactical unit. The CIA had absolutely no authority to act on American soil, making this a sticky situation. But if Smith had reached out and touched someone who in turn had touched the governor in five minutes, then this was official. It was serious.

It was big.

Bigger maybe than him, Hope or Faith. What he wouldn't give to know.

"Yes, sir," Ryan said. "We're on the same page."

The line went dead. Ryan hung up and drew in a breath.

After Smith sent his men back to the SUV, he tossed his coffee cup in the trash and stalked into the office. Taking a seat, he said, without sarcasm or gloating and getting straight to business, "Let's try this again." He held up the phone with the picture of the stranger on the screen once more. "Someone in this office ran this man's prints today. Who and why?"

"I ran them after talking to him earlier this morning in a diner. Something about him bothered me." Much in the same way Smith bothered Ryan. But Smith was worse. If the stranger was a mongoose, Smith was a shark. "That's why."

"This man doesn't draw attention," Smith said. "He's adept at blending in. If he caught your interest during a conversation, there's an extraordinary reason. What did you two discuss?"

Ryan shifted in his chair. Crossed his legs and uncrossed them. Leaned back and sat forward. Nothing he did changed the boxed-in feeling he had. "Not what, who. We talked about a woman."

"I want to know exactly what was said, word for word, and please, Sheriff, don't insult my intelligence or waste any more of my precious time by trying to lie."

Ryan's palms itched. "This woman is innocent of any wrongdoing. I need your word, your assurance, that she won't be hurt as you go after your target."

"We're both professionals and know there are no such guarantees. If I gave one, you wouldn't trust it," Smith said, and Ryan had to agree. "What I can say is that she is in imminent danger right now if she's with that man. You want to protect her, save her from herself? Then tell me about the discussion you had, starting with the name of the woman."

The itching worsened. Ryan scrubbed his palms on his pants. He was caught between a rock and a proverbial hard place. Between national security and loyalty to the woman who should've been his sister-in-law. Loyalty to Faith.

His stomach twisted, but there was no way around it. "We talked about...Hope Fischer."

Chapter Sixteen

Hope watched the sun set against the backdrop of the lake and the mountains. Faith had loved this town. The picturesque setting that had made her feel like she was on vacation every day. The quiet, low-key lifestyle. No time wasted stuck in traffic. No hustle and bustle. Making caramel apples for the kids at Halloween, confident parents would let their children eat them without fretting that they might be poisoned. Getting to know her neighbors. The sense of community that her sister had called a blessing.

Turned out that it was also a curse. One of those neighbors had killed Faith.

The alarm on Gage's watch buzzed. It was five o'clock.

Although the scientists at Nexcellogen tended to be workaholics given their dedication and isolation in Benediction, Kudlow had assured them the foot traffic in the facility would be at a bare minimum and practically empty by four on a Saturday. Gage had wanted to give it an extra hour to be on the safe side.

"It's time," Hope said, more out of anxiousness than the need to inform Gage.

She could tell he was cognizant of everything. The time. Which way the wind was blowing. Her eagerness to break inside Nexcellogen that wrestled with her desire to hang on to this moment of calm. The temporary sense of peace dancing in her heart.

Seated on the sofa beside her, Gage hadn't dragged his gaze from her for the past few minutes. The air between them vibrated with an almost palpable awareness. They were in this together. Of that she was certain. But there was something he wasn't saying.

She rested her hand on his leg. "What is it?"

"After they question Kudlow, they'll suspect me. Suspicion I can handle, divert. But once we're inside that facility, the security guard in the lobby will be able to identify me. So might the one in the security room if I can't subdue him without him seeing my face. Then they'll know for certain it was me."

"Gage, I don't want to ruin your life in my pursuit of justice for Faith."

"The CIA destroyed my life long before you came along." He placed his hand over hers. "It's just being on the run is hard. The hardest thing I've ever done. If they know it's me, my back will be up against the wall and I'll be forced to leave. Running unprepared with no safe place to go is…" His gaze fell.

"Dangerous."

Gage looked up at her. "It's suicide." He released a long, heavy breath. "Being on the run, staying at a random place, even for a night, is like flying aboard a tin can that could fall apart at any minute. Crash and burn like that." He snapped his fingers. "So I need to make damn sure that my next hiding place is certified safe. That takes time and preparation, and while I'm looking, I risk exposure."

She got the gist of the metaphor. Gage was a formidable man, but his situation was as fragile as glass. "Who says they have to see your face?"

"I can't go inside Nexcellogen wearing a Halloween mask. Neither can you."

"Why not?" When he made an incredulous face, she said, "Hear me out. Waltzing in together after five on a Saturday would draw too much attention from the guard in the lobby, anyway. We go in separately. We'll both wear Nexcellogen ball caps. Once I'm in range of the cameras outside the building, I'll tip my head low, keep my face down." Just like he'd taught her to do at the military police station. "Kudlow said the guard on duty in the lobby is a formality for visitors. The guard doesn't even check employee ID since the gate turnstiles ensure secure entry and exit. I'll go in first, but as I do, you create a distraction to lure him out. That way he's focused on the diversion instead of what I look like. While the guard is busy outside, you slip in without him seeing you. You keep the video scrambler with you the entire time. As for the guard in the security room, that's when you use the mask. No one will have a good description of either of us."

"That all sounds good in theory, but there is a guard in the security room monitoring the feeds of the surveillance cameras throughout the facility. All it takes is for him to see one fuzzy camera screen followed by another and he'll sound the alarm before I have a chance to restrain him."

In her short time in this town, she'd come to learn something important. This was Benediction, where no one expected murders, robberies or coups d'état in science labs. It was slow, quiet, predictable. "The odds are extremely high the guard will be reading a book, doing Sudoku or a crossword puzzle. Not watching the hallways. On the slim chance that he is, his first assumption will be technical difficulties. Not that someone is breaking in."

"That's a huge gamble. Someone in Nexcellogen killed Faith. The logs will help us narrow down who, but we've got one shot at this."

"It's worth the risk." He was worth the risk.

She wanted to take a chance on him, though the stakes were incredibly high. When she thought about what she wanted tomorrow to look like for herself, she pictured Gage in it. She was holding tight to that vision now.

"All right. We can try it," he said. "But this time, I'll bring my ski mask if I need it."

"What do we use as a distraction?"

Gage thought for a moment. "I've got some leftover fireworks from the Fourth of July in the garage. I think I can make it work. But you can't hang around in the lobby waiting for me. It'll look suspicious." He took out the map of the building and looked at it. "Think you can meet me near the security office by the east stairwell? There's a restroom." He pointed it out. "You can wait inside for me."

"It's not far from the lobby. I don't see why not."

He stood, pulling her up with him, and hauled her into his arms. "We'll be separated for a short time inside. While we are, be safe. Be smart." He withdrew his gun with the sound suppressor attached and handed it to her. "I doubt you'll need it. The Nexcellogen security guards are only armed with Tasers."

She nodded and glanced down at the weapon. It felt heavy in her hand, but she wouldn't need to use it. The gun would never leave her bag.

They grabbed the items they needed—lab coats, ball caps and messenger bags. Kudlow had had a ton of stuff with Nexcellogen logos in his closet, as though the company were constantly handing out things. Or, in addition to being a drug dealer, he was a kleptomaniac, too.

In the garage, she climbed into the truck while Gage loaded the box of old fireworks into the back.

He hopped in behind the wheel. "Provided the details about the security protocols are correct, you won't have any problems. If you do run into a major issue, shoot to injure, not kill. For anything minor, bide your time. I'll be there."

Three words she trusted and believed in, that meant more to her than *I love you.*

I'll be there.

Because he would. No matter what.

Her job had taken her to ugly places, and through the lens of her camera she'd captured terrible things, making her cynical. She had come to see the world as a place in which corruption and greed reigned supreme, promises were broken, trust was betrayed and integrity no longer mattered.

Then Faith had fallen in love with an honorable man and inspired Hope to dream. To imagine.

To hope.

But it was Gage who had proven to her that there was still goodness in the world. Promises that would be kept. Trust that would be treasured.

There were people who would stand with you and not let you down.

She cupped Gage's face and caressed his cheek. "I know you will."

WATCHING JOE SMITH walk out of his office and climb into his black Suburban, Ryan felt sick to his stomach. He'd answered all Smith's questions, and now Ryan wanted to take a shower and scrub off the experience.

Something wasn't right about this situation.

Not for a minute did he doubt that the stranger was a fugitive, but why wasn't he in the database?

Ryan had cooperated fully, as instructed by the governor, and he hadn't received one straight answer in return for his effort.

Hope was in imminent danger. From Joe Smith and his men. Ryan sensed it in his gut. Smith was the type to cut through a human shield to get to his target and call it collateral damage.

The thought of Hope being a casualty in the crossfire because Ryan had been forthcoming made something inside him crumble.

He sat behind his desk, second-guessing everything, itching to do something, anything. But what could he do to help Hope?

Damn. Too bad he didn't know the stranger's name. Otherwise he could call Benediction, give the man a heads-up about Smith. That way, the stranger could watch out for Hope and ensure she wasn't inadvertently in the line of fire that was about to come flying his way.

Then again, maybe Ryan didn't need to know his name.

He buzzed Aimee, and when she picked up, he said, "Get me the number to the clinic in Benediction."

"Benediction?" She spun in her seat and stared at him through the glass.

"You heard me."

The stranger had given essential details that Ryan could use to track him down. The man had been the one to bring Hope to the clinic. Someone there must know who he was. Ryan could probe until he got contact information without letting on that Hope was in Benediction. Those townies didn't have cell phones, but they sure as heck had landlines.

Dwight got up, passing Finn—who had trudged in late, after five, looking worse than warmed-over dog food—and made a beeline to the office. "Hey, boss, what did those yahoos want?"

"They're looking for someone. A man. You ran his prints today. We still don't know who he is, but Joe Smith and his merry band of men do."

"Anything for us to do on this matter?"

"Us? No." Ryan grabbed his Stetson. "Me, yes." He slipped on his jacket and left his office. "Aimee, you got it?"

She tore off a slip of paper with a phone number on it. "Here you go."

"I'm heading out to check on the boys that were just in here," Ryan said.

"You want me to ride along?" Dwight asked.

"Nope. Sit tight." Ryan made his way to his SUV and sped off after Joe Smith. Catching up to them was unlikely and not what Ryan desired, anyway. Getting them in his sights and keeping them there was. He'd have cell phone reception for the next fifteen miles, then he'd lose it on that blasted road to Benediction.

Time was a-wasting, so he'd better get to it. He dialed the number Aimee had given him.

"Benediction Clinic. PA Varma speaking."

"Evening. This Sheriff Ryan Keller from Goode. I'm trying to get in contact with someone in Benediction. A man, early thirties, dark hair, about six feet tall. I don't know his name, but he saved the life of Hope Fischer. I believe he brought her to the clinic for medical treatment. It's important I speak with him. I'd like to thank him for being a good Samaritan, but I also have some urgent news for him. Can you help me?"

Chapter Seventeen

Hope threw on a lab coat and ball cap identical to what Gage was wearing. Her hair hung loose, framing her face. Faith's badge was already around her neck, hanging from a lanyard.

Gage hit the remote button, opening the garage door, started the truck and backed out.

She ducked down and stayed low as he drove until he parked behind the church. It was the closest building to the Nexcellogen facility.

"Maintain a steady pace as you approach the building," he said. "Leisurely, not too brisk. That'll give me a chance to set up and time it for when you enter."

She put the gun in the messenger bag. "Will you be all right without a weapon?"

"Don't worry about me." He smiled, but his eyes remained deadly serious. His gaze dropped to her chest, and his expression changed. "Switch badges with me."

"Why?"

"In case they deactivated Faith's. Take Kudlow's instead."

They exchanged ID badges. "What are you going to do if Faith's doesn't work?"

"Improvise," Gage said. "I'll get in."

Three more words she trusted. "I'm sure you will."

"Focus. Keep your head in the game."

She slipped a hand around the back of his neck and kissed him. "Keep your head attached."

"I'm pretty good at that."

Hope slipped out of the vehicle, walked around the church and crossed the main road. There were only a few scattered light posts. Enough to make a person who was out for a stroll or jogging at night feel comfortable without lighting up the area like a football stadium.

There was no gate around the facility. Not that they needed one, when there was an electrified fence and wide buffer of trees between the entire town and the outside world.

She walked through the parking lot. There were plenty of spots, which would've been a dream in LA or NYC. Along the side of the facility she noticed bicycle storage racks and a dumpster.

Getting closer to the guard and cameras posted at the main entrance, she tilted her head slightly down, in a casual way but not so much that it would appear suspicious.

She passed one row of parking about three hundred feet from the door.

Still no distraction from Gage. She wondered how he was supposed to time his diversion without having a visual of her approaching the entrance, but she had confidence in his plan. As long as she followed his instructions and didn't walk too fast, his timing would work.

Crossing the last of the parking spots, she was two hundred feet from the building. The pavement between her, the cameras and the front door shrank with each step she took.

One hundred fifty feet.

She sauntered at an easy pace as her palms grew clammy and her stomach rolled.

One hundred feet.

The thick rubber soles of her ankle boots were quiet. The air was crisp, cool. There was barely a breeze.

Fifty feet.

Twenty.

A loud pop shattered the night. The sound had come from the east side of the building. If she hadn't known better, she would've thought it was gunfire.

She hurried through the front door. Once inside the atrium that featured a large skylight, she hesitated.

Most lobbies were designed with aesthetics and convenience in mind. This one was the opposite. Security had been the primary concern. A physical wall separated the vestibule from the secured portion of the building. Within the wall were two full-body turnstiles that controlled access to the facility.

Kudlow had described it in detail, but hearing about it and seeing it were two different things.

Hope kicked her brain into gear. She dared to wave at the guard posted at the desk. "There's something going on outside," she said, holding up Kudlow's badge to the card reader.

Another bang echoed. The guard shifted in his seat as if trying to pinpoint the direction of the noise and stood.

The light on the turnstile reader stayed red. Her heart lurched.

Why didn't it work?

If Kudlow had gotten loose or someone had found him early, he would've warned the folks at Nexcellogen. His badge wouldn't have simply been deactivated. Guards would be waiting to apprehend her and Gage.

Bang.

Bang.

Hope's throat grew dry as sandpaper. Staring at the bar code facing her, she flipped the badge to the other side. Tried again.

The security light winked green and beeped. Hope exhaled in relief, pushing through the turnstile. "Walking through the parking lot it sounded pretty loud and scary," she said to the guard.

"It's probably just some kids messing around. Bored teenagers." The guard came around the desk and made his way toward the turnstile. "I'll go check it out. Scare them off."

As they passed each other, Hope lowered her head, pretending to search for something inside her messenger bag.

The guard stepped up to the turnstile with his badge in hand. A second later, the card reader beeped, and he pushed through into the vestibule and went outside.

Cautious to keep her head angled away from the cameras, she bypassed the elevators and took the corridor that led to security. She used her hair and the bill of the cap to shield her face.

She spotted the door to the east stairwell first, then the restroom, which was next to the security office. It was unisex, single occupancy. *Perfect.* The one detail that Gage hadn't grilled Kudlow about had been the type of bathrooms.

Hope tried the knob.

The door was locked.

Her heart skipped.

"Be out in a second," the guy inside the bathroom said.

Hope shuffled backward, shifting a glance down either end of the hall. It wasn't as if she could stand there and wait. She turned and ducked into the stairwell, shoving the door closed behind her.

Pressing her back against the wall, she looked through the glass panel in the top of the door and waited.

The bathroom door opened. She ducked down a second to give the man time to pass.

Once she thought it was clear, she got up, inching her way along the wall, and peeked through the small window.

The guard entered the security office, but the door didn't close. Another man came out and stood on the threshold, holding a bottle of rum.

His dark hair was coiffed. Black pants. White shirt. Red sports coat with Nexcellogen Head of Security printed across the chest.

Hope had met him briefly in the clinic. Ian McCallister.

"Leave the camera in Ms. Lansing's office disabled," Ian said.

"I have no interest in spying on you two," the guy replied. "Why don't you go to her place or take her to yours?"

"She prefers discretion, and I'm a gentleman. The residential area is like living in a fishbowl. She doesn't want anyone to see me coming and going from her house or vice versa. Besides, she ordered an extremely comfortable sofa for her office."

"I understand. Gossip spreads fast around here. A lit match through dry brush."

"Tell me about it." Ian chuckled. "I'm going to head up."

Up?

Her heart drummed in her chest. What if he planned to take the stairs instead of the elevator?

Hope raced up the stairwell on the balls of her feet.

The messenger bag, hanging from her shoulder, flapped against her hip. She held it to her stomach to keep the bag from making noise.

On the second floor, she pressed the badge to the card reader. The light didn't change, and the handle wouldn't turn.

Damn it.

She recalled Paul saying that the two upper floors contained the labs. But a person could only access a floor or lab if they worked there. The only badges that opened every door were Michelle Lansing's and the security guards'.

Hope bolted up the next flight of stairs.

The door creaked open on the bottom floor. "Yeah, okay," Ian said. "Don't leave any beer cans in there this time."

At the top landing, Hope put the badge to the card reader. The light flashed green. No beep. *Thank God.* She eased the door open, slipped into the hall and gently pulled it closed.

Lansing's office was also on the top floor. Ian would be up there in no time.

Hope looked around and spotted the elevator on the right. Michelle Lansing's office was down that end of the hall. According to Paul, the lab he'd worked in with Faith was on the other side closer to the break room, which was across from a conference room.

Six labs were on the third floor. The one she needed to hide in should be two doors down on the left.

Turning, Hope took off.

There were no lights on in any of the labs. This section of the hall appeared deserted. She found the room, the only one her badge would open.

A light tap to the scanner. The door slid open with the softest whisper that shrieked of money. She ducked inside and shuffled backward, deeper into the room.

The lab took up six to seven hundred square feet of space. Like the others she'd passed, it had an open plan and floor-to-ceiling windows treated with privacy screening to provide natural daylight and to prevent the scientists from going stir-crazy. Every wall was transparent. Most likely to enhance collaboration, sustainability and safety.

Perhaps the glass walls were the reason some scientists worked late. To have privacy. To plot. To produce illegal drugs.

But this lab had been Faith's, where she'd spent countless hours, working side by side with Paul Kudlow and Neal Underhill, surrounded by traitors and a murderer.

Hope wandered through the room—glancing at computers, microscopes, petri dishes, a centrifuge, test tubes, pipettes, forceps—wondering which workstation had been her sister's.

All Faith's bread crumbs had led Hope here.

Emotion clogged her throat as she spotted a gift that she'd given Faith for her thirtieth birthday.

Newton's cradle. Such a cliché thing to give a scientist, but Faith had claimed to adore it. Hope drifted closer to the desk and ran her fingers across the upper bar of the toy.

The contraption was simple. Five small silver balls hung in a perfectly straight line, just barely touching one another, suspended by thin wires that connected them to two parallel horizontal bars attached to a base. When a ball on one end of the cradle was pulled from the others and released, it struck the next ball with a click, but instead of the four remaining balls swinging, only the ball on the opposite end of the row was thrown into the air. Then the metal ball swung back to strike the others, causing a chain reaction again in reverse.

Despite its simple design, Faith thought the gift had been perfect. To her, it represented the most fundamental laws of physics and mechanics.

A conservation of energy, momentum and friction.

Hope sat down and pulled one ball on the end of the cradle and let it go.

Watching it in action after so much had happened, it was easy to see that same principle reenacted in life.

Faith had been the first ball to be pulled, colliding with the others. Hope had been the second. Gage the third. A serious of chain reactions. Energy, momentum and friction carried on.

But what or who would be the next ball to strike back?

GAGE RELEASED THE last firecracker on the east side of the building in a blind spot of the cameras.

Knowing the security guard would come from the south, where the entrance was located, he raced to the north side. Just as he rounded the corner and peeked back, he caught sight of the guard coming around the bend.

Gage sprinted along the north wall and down the west side, passing a dumpster and bike rack.

To be sure the guard hadn't simply doubled back without further investigation after discovering no one, Gage sneaked a glance.

The entrance was all clear. He dashed for the front door.

Inside, he glossed over the atrium while catching his breath and went to the turnstile. *Centurion* was printed on the top of the security pad. Just as he was about to put Faith's badge up to the scanner, he stopped.

Deactivation was a possibility he'd considered, and he had a Band-Aid solution in that event. But what if using the badge triggered an alarm?

Or worse, a silent alarm that he wouldn't be aware of until it was too late.

Then it would be game over. With Hope trapped inside.

That was unacceptable. He spun on his heel and pushed through the front door outside.

The security guard was already headed back to the entrance.

Gage strategized his options like in a game of blitz chess. Less than ten seconds to make his next move. He lowered his head and beckoned to the guard with a hand. "I was looking for you. Some kids are spraying graffiti on the other side of the building," he said, deepening his voice with a slight Southern twang and looking toward the west side, away from the man. "Come on. If we hurry, you can catch them."

The guard swore and took off, running past Gage, determined to catch those troublemakers.

Gage was right behind.

After they turned the corner, the guard stumbled to halt beside the dumpster and stared. No doubt perplexed.

Gage swept up behind him and locked his right forearm around the guard's neck in a chokehold. They were roughly the same size, but the man's neck was thick, and he was putting up a struggle. Fortunately, the element of surprise helped, and the guy was panicking instead of thinking, which was always a mistake. Gage tightened the hold with all the strength he had, pinching the man's neck in the crook of his elbow until the guard's body went limp, rendered unconscious.

Not slowing for a beat, Gage checked his surroundings. Then he wrapped duct tape around the man's wrists, ankles and over his mouth. He removed the guard's ID badge, pocketed his Taser and opened the lid of the dumpster. Hauling the body up and tossing the man inside left Gage huffing and puffing, but he made speedy work of it.

He flipped the lid down and strolled to the entrance, winded. Another check of the area and he was confident no one had seen him.

Once he cleared the turnstile in the lobby, he activated the scrambler and hustled down to the restroom next to security. Three light raps of his knuckle on the door and he waited, listened.

Nothing.

Gage tried the knob and opened the door. The bathroom was empty.

Hope, where are you?

Gage reached into the messenger bag for his ski mask and pulled on one made of a breathable polyester fiber that covered his face, save for the band of his eyes.

Leaving the bathroom, he darted a couple of feet down the corridor. On the wall beside the door to the security office was a card reader—one presumably only a guard could access.

Kudlow hadn't mentioned that.

Not that it mattered, since Gage was wearing the badge that belonged to the front guard. He put the ID to the scanner, opened the security room door and swept inside with the Taser in his other hand, low by his side.

The security guard was glued to a paperback, holding a beer and oblivious to the monitors.

Gage recognized him.

Sylvester Faliveno. Laid-back and not the sort to make a fuss.

Probably no need to tase him.

Chuckling at something on the page, Sylvester glanced up from the book. "What's up—"

"Get down on your knees, facing the wall, hands behind your head and I won't hurt you," Gage said in the same fake voice he'd used outside.

With a placid expression, Sylvester closed the book, set his beer down and complied.

Gage trussed him up and sealed his mouth with duct tape. To make things easier on them both, he put Sylvester down on his side, still facing the wall.

Spinning one of the stools on its wheels, Gage sat in front of the large monitor with six rotating screenshots from every camera. Two minutes for them to cycle through all the surveillance feeds: exterior angles, lobby, offices, labs, conference rooms. One screen was dark, but before he investigated it, he found Hope. She was upstairs in Faith's lab, sitting at a desk.

He had no idea what had possessed her to deviate from the plan.

But she was safe.

Gage scooted the stool a foot to the side and turned ninety degrees to face the other computer that was already logged in. He glanced at the icons on the screen. Grabbing the mouse, he double-tapped on the app labeled Centurion.

Sure enough, it was the entry and exit records.

Time to check the log on the night Faith was murdered.

Chapter Eighteen

Hope stared at Faith's computer, listening to the click of the metal balls from Newton's cradle.

During her sister's last days, Faith had taken the risk of copying clinical tests and reports. Hours of documents saved to the concealed thumb drive. Gage had insisted the information must be important. There had been a reason Faith had copied them.

But none of the bread crumbs had spelled out why.

The single word repeated in her head slowly to the rhythm of the clicking. *Why...why...why?* Like a prayer begging for an answer.

Hope stilled the metal balls in the device, and in the silence, it came to her, loud and clear as a clap of thunder.

She realized how Faith had planned to use the data.

"Faith?" The smooth female voice was like an electric shock jolting through Hope.

She looked up, her heart throbbing in her throat.

An attractive woman with soft white hair that framed a face that looked fortysomething stood in the lab holding an ice bucket with a plastic liner. In the moonlight coming in through the windows, her narrowed eyes shone blue. She wore dark slacks, tailored with a meticulously pressed crease, and a light blue silk blouse. There was an unmistakable air of authority to her.

Hope recognized the woman from Gage's description. She was Michelle Lansing.

The woman drew closer. "Who are you?"

"I'm Hope." She rose and edged back from the desk. "Faith's sister."

"For a moment, I didn't know what to think. Maybe I was seeing a ghost. I was going to get ice from the break room." Michelle sat the bucket down on a table and stepped deeper into the space with bare feet. "And I saw you." She shook her head. "You look so much like her. *Faith.*" Michelle's face changed as if she were waking from a dream. The surprise knitting her brow lifted, the lines of confusion across her forehead smoothed. Her bewildered gaze turned to a sword-sharp stare, but her voice softened. "I heard you were at the clinic the other day, dear."

Michelle eased toward the desk.

Hope backed away, skirting around the other side of the workstation in the opposite direction, keeping her eyes on the woman.

"How did you get into the building?" Michelle's gaze flickered down to the computer, as though she were checking to make sure it hadn't been accessed, and then bounced back up. "What are you doing here?"

"I'm here to find out who murdered my sister," Hope said, lifting the flap of the messenger bag and stepping back in the direction of the door. "So she can finally rest."

"Murder?" Michelle recoiled. "I'm sorry, dear, but Faith took her own life. It's horrible, terrible, I know, but I saw her body myself."

"I don't care what you saw. What I know is that

Faith was happy and in love and not rebounding from a breakup or whatever story you all have been spreading."

"Why on earth would anyone want to harm her?" Michelle stepped forward. "She was a lovely person. Bright and warm. Everyone who knew her liked her."

Hope pulled the gun from the bag and aimed.

Michelle stopped walking, but she didn't flinch. Didn't even blink.

"Her project was the *shining star* for Nexcellogen," Hope said. "But if it continued to fail, the company was going to give up on the research and pull out of Benediction."

Michelle stiffened. "How do you know that?"

"It's true, isn't it?"

"It *was* true, but that's no longer relevant," Michelle said, her voice gentle yet firm, her composure unflappable. "We've had a breakthrough and we're staying. If only Faith could've held on long enough to see it, maybe things would've turned out differently."

"Nothing has changed," Hope said. "Your clinical trials are still failures, and I think you know that."

"Dear—"

"Think carefully before you speak. Because if you lie to me about this, then I won't believe you when you try to convince me you didn't murder my sister." Hope slid the safety off and put her finger on the trigger. "You know the report Neal Underhill gave you is fraudulent, don't you?"

"The trials aren't failures. They simply haven't been a complete success. And yes, I'm aware the data was made to look more promising than it is."

"How could you go along with falsifying data?"

"Our contract with the government is worth billions.

Once we're able to inoculate soldiers against PTSD, the civilian applications will be endless. This project is too important and lucrative to have it scrapped when we're this close."

"That's why you killed her?" Hope asked. "Over money?"

"I admit, dear, there's no way I would've made it this far without being a cutthroat in business, but I am not a murderer. Your sister had a choice. She could either play the game or be transferred back to Herndon and Neal would replace her. I'm a civilized woman. The only weapon I use is negotiation."

"Faith would've rejected going along with your scheme outright. There's no way she'd let you pass off false data."

"Your sister was considering my offer, which would've come with a nice bonus and excellent terms that would've allowed her stay in Benediction the way she wanted."

Was that possible, that Faith had contemplated this deal with the devil?

It would've given her what she wanted. To stay in Benediction, close to Ryan. To continue on the project, committed to helping soldiers. To work. Even if she had quit and stayed in Goode, her career as a scientist would've been over. The best she could've gotten in this area was a job as a high school science teacher. Provided there was an opening.

"She was supposed to give me her answer sometime after the Thanksgiving break," Michelle said. "That's when she must've gotten her heart broken and went into a tailspin of depression."

No, that's when something happened to make her connect Zion to the drug in her lab. She must've confronted Paul and Neal, and Faith must've drawn a line in the sand.

Hope shook her head. "After the Thanksgiving break, Faith did make a decision, but it wasn't to play your game or to go to Herndon."

Michelle's gaze shifted over Hope's shoulder.

Hope pivoted as she redirected the gun.

Ian entered the lab, blocking the door. "Michelle, are you all right?"

"I'm fine, but this young woman is crazy," Michelle said.

"Move over there—" Hope gestured to Ian "—away from the door." Hope and Ian both turned in a half circle, so that Hope was closer to the door and facing them. "The annual report you submitted to headquarters is as bogus as my sister's death certificate. I have the evidence to prove your data is falsified." That's why Faith made a copy. To serve as proof. "I'm going to do what Faith would've wanted. What she would've done if she was still alive. I'm going to expose the fraud going on here, but before I do, one of you is going to tell me what really happened to my sister."

Ian clenched his hands.

That's when Hope heard it, the creak of leather. Then she saw it. He'd put on gloves before he came into the lab.

Ian grabbed the ice bucket from the table and lunged. Faster than a blink. He swung. The hard plastic collided with Hope's hand, knocking the gun loose.

The weapon clattered to the floor.

Michelle's hand fluttered near her mouth, her eyes wide, as Ian kept swinging.

The next blow struck Hope on the shoulder and sent her spinning.

Ian dropped the bucket but kept hold of the plastic liner. In one fell swoop, he slipped the bag over her head. Ian was behind her now, tightening the plastic around her neck.

Hope gasped for air, sucking the plastic over her mouth. She scratched and clawed at his hands. Her nails scraped thick leather. Not skin.

That's why he'd worn the gloves.

"Ian!" Michelle said. "What are you doing?"

"Protecting you, as I always have." Ian jerked Hope from side to side, keeping her off balance as she struggled to breathe. "You want to know what happened to Faith. I'll tell you. I happened. I killed her just like this and then dumped her in her car."

Michelle reeled back. "Ian, let her go."

"I can't. For you, I have to kill her. That's what I do, sweetheart. I watch, I listen, I do whatever is necessary to protect you."

Hope fought against her instinct to scratch at her throat to get the bag off. His hold was too tight. Too absolute. She clawed at the plastic over her face instead. Punctured a hole in it near her mouth. Gasped for air.

She shredded the plastic covering and widened the hole with her fingers and breathed.

"Why?" Michelle asked, clutching her chest. "Why kill Faith?"

"Because she fought with Neal and Paul and wanted to send the true results to headquarters, your deal with her be damned. Faith didn't care about the repercussions to anyone else. She was selfish. Shortsighted. She needed to go. Just like her sister."

Hope reached out to grab something. Desperate for anything that might help her. She desperately sucked in gulps of oxygen through her mouth. Her nose was still covered by the bag.

"With Faith, I didn't have this problem, because I used a tear-proof trash bag." Ian tightened the remnants of the bag around Hope's throat to strangle her.

Her windpipe closed, sealing off her airway.

THE ENTRY AND exit logs didn't lie.

Gage looked over everyone who'd been working the night Faith died. Neal Underhill, Michelle Lansing and four of the other nine team leaders had been in the building during the time of her death.

But one thing stuck out.

Ian McCallister had exited the building at five but swiped back in at seven thirty. He was gone during the window when Faith had been killed, sometime between seven and eight. Thirty minutes was plenty of time to commit the murder and get back in the building.

Looking farther down the log, Gage noticed that Ian had left Nexcellogen again later at nine, right after Michelle Lansing. Mostly likely in response to the call notifying them about Faith.

But what was he doing for two hours between five and seven, and why did he kill Faith at all?

He needed to tell Hope.

Gage turned, glancing at the monitor with the surveillance feeds. He waited for the screens to cycle through, to be sure she wasn't on her way down. Still, one camera was out and the screen black.

Finally, the lab that Hope was in popped up on the monitor.

Gage's heart plummeted, and he bolted out of the office.

HOPE CLUTCHED AT Ian's hand, struggling to pry his fingers loose. Spots danced in front of her eyes as he jerked her from side to side.

"My God." Michelle shuffled backward. "How could you, Ian?"

"I got Doc hammered at the bar. Bought lots of rounds, knowing that lush couldn't resist. Planted the seeds about Faith's depression and a breakup. In a bar, nobody cares about the truth, but they all love a good story. I whispered to the MPs, even you, Michelle, that it must've been suicide. Poor brokenhearted Faith took her life. You all agreed, regurgitated it back to Doc. That boozer believed it, signed the certificate. None the wiser I was playing him like a fiddle."

Hope reached out with her right hand. Groped the table for something heavy, sharp.

"Oh, Ian. Please, let her go!"

"I'm doing this for you. For us. In Benediction, we found everything we've both wanted. A second chance at love. Greatness," he said, panting. "We run this town, you and I. Together. You did say reigning in hell is better than serving in heaven."

Hope knocked over test tubes. Glass shattered.

Ian danced her body away from the desk.

She kicked backward. Her heel struck bone. Ian grunted in pain and stumbled, sending their weight skittering, and her hip slammed into another table.

"I never wanted you to kill anyone," Michelle said. "You have to stop, do you understand? Let her go!"

Pressure built in Hope's chest, too familiar, too painful. Breath backed up in her lungs. Her legs grew rubbery. She swept her hand over the table. Frantic. Out of air. Choking.

"No, sweetheart," Ian said. "We're too close now to stop. The annual report has been filed. This empire is ours. Just one more loose end and everything will go back to normal. Then you'll thank me."

It was so hard for Hope to hang on. To fight. Darkness clouded her vision. Her fingers closed around a piece of cold steel. Forceps. She jabbed the sharp, pointed end backward into Ian's leg.

Ian howled, but he held on to her.

She stabbed him again and again.

His hands opened, and he shoved her away as he cursed and screamed. Coughing and gasping, Hope tore off the plastic bag and moved, needing distance from Ian.

The door opened. Gage stormed into the lab like a madman, wearing a black mask over his face. At the same time, Ian dived for the floor. Toward something that glinted in the moonlight.

The gun.

Gage charged, tackling him.

The two men rolled on the floor, fighting over the gun for a long, terrifying moment that twisted Hope's stomach in a knot. Ian clutched the gun, the barrel pointed down between their bodies, as Gage tried to wrest it away from him.

A whisper of a bullet.

Hope froze as Michelle gasped.

Neither man moved.

Not Gage. Please, don't let it be Gage.

Chapter Nineteen

Gage waited for pain to pierce him. But it never came. For a split second, he prayed a stray bullet hadn't hit Hope.

He looked up.

Ian was on top of him. The man's eyes were open and still, his lips parted in a gasp.

Gage rolled the dead body off him to the floor, grabbed the gun and sat up.

A red spot on Ian's shirt grew as the blood from his wound spread. There was blood on Gage's lab coat and some on his sweater, but the wool was dark.

Hope rushed to his side and threw her arms around his neck, holding him. "Thank God, you're all right."

His heart squeezed. "Ditto." If they'd been alone, he would've allowed himself to feel the relief that was just out of reach, would've told her what he was thinking, feeling, but he had to keep it bottled up.

"I don't know what I would've done if I lost you," she whispered in his ear. "Like this. Because of me." She sat back on her heels and stared in his eyes. "Or if I lost you at all."

Gage wrapped an arm around her, the sentiment echoing deep inside him. The prospect of losing Hope had held him hostage from the nanosecond he'd seen the plastic bag over her head until the moment he realized that he hadn't been shot.

He wanted a day, a week, a month with her, as much time as fate would let him have to just be together without these other…distractions. To unwrap this rare gift he'd been given. To know her. Love her.

Be loved in return. If such a thing were possible for a man like him.

They climbed to their feet.

Michelle crept over to Ian, without making a sound, and looked down at him. "Why, you fool? We didn't need everything. Not when we had each other," she said low, under her breath.

"Were they in this together?" Gage asked Hope, referring to Michelle.

"I don't think she knew he killed Faith. Or maybe she didn't want to know. Easier to stick her head in the sand for plausible deniability. But Ian was responsible. He took her life." Hope looked at Michelle. "I'm going to release all the data that Faith downloaded, proving your annual report is bogus. Your headquarters and any news outlet that wants the story is going to know what you did, what your boyfriend did, and how my sister lost her life over a contract."

Michelle straightened, holding her head up high. "If you think I'm going to apologize, you're wrong."

Hope stepped closer to Michelle and slapped her in the face. The sound sliced through the room like a machete. "You're not going to reign in hell. You're going to burn in it."

A flare went off in the dark sky outside the window, soaring in a blazing arc. A second one. Then a third.

That signal meant doomsday.

Gage had given Claire the 26.5-millimeter flare gun. It resembled a snub-nosed revolver with a fat barrel. He'd told her that if there was danger, the-sky-was-falling kind of danger, to fire the flare from the woods across the street from the house three times. "We have to go. Now."

"Good luck," Michelle said, rubbing her cheek. "You won't make it to the lobby before I lock this building down."

They didn't have time for this. There was no telling what was happening beyond the walls of Nexcellogen to make Claire use the flare gun.

Gage took the Taser from his pocket, turned it on and jammed it into Michelle's side. Her eyes rolled up into the back of her head as her body shook violently. Pulling it away, he turned it off.

Michelle dropped like a sack of potatoes.

Gage grabbed Hope's hand, and they made a beeline for the stairs.

They were out of the building in less than a minute flat.

"What's going on?" Hope asked as they ran through the parking lot.

"I don't know. But those flares were for me."

"How can you be sure?"

Besides the fact that they'd been fired in the vicinity of the house and there were three in short succession, as he'd instructed in case of an emergency, he said, "I never leave Benediction without telling Claire or leaving her a note, since we don't have cell phones. She knows I'm here, somewhere. And she just used the signal I gave her."

They crossed the road and got in the truck. Both of them removed the white lab coats.

"Are we going to the house?" Hope asked.

Gage tugged the ski mask off and shoved it into his pocket. "No. In case of an emergency, the rally point is the funeral home."

RYAN SHUT OFF his headlights and pulled over on the side of the road a half a mile from Benediction's gates. He grabbed his binoculars and hopped out.

The Suburban with Joe Smith and his men had stopped at the gate. All four doors opened.

But five men climbed out the Suburban. *Five.*

One must've stayed back in the vehicle when the others had come into Ryan's office for some reason. Dwight hadn't asked Mr. Metsos how many guys got out of the helicopter and into the SUV, and Ryan had assumed it had been only the four.

The two military guards drew their weapons, but Smith and his men attacked them. Bright flashes came from muzzles with attached sound suppressors. Both MPs dropped.

"Dear Lord," Ryan muttered.

Smith's men picked up the bodies and hauled them into the guardhouse.

They'd killed those innocent boys in cold blood when they could've wounded them or disarmed them instead.

There was no telling what they'd do if Hope came in between them and their target.

What have I done?

He crossed his fingers the call he'd made earlier would help.

PA Varma had given Ryan two phone numbers. One

for Gage Graham and the other for his stepsister. Gage hadn't answered, but Claire had. Ryan had told her everything he could without mentioning Hope was in Benediction. The stepsister, Claire Ferguson Coughlin, had thanked him and promised to relay the message, right before his cell stopped working.

Ryan looked back through the binoculars.

Three flares shot up into the night sky, one right after the other, somewhere in Benediction. Near trees.

It could be a coincidence, the timing of those flares, but Ryan didn't think so. He didn't believe in coincidence.

He refocused on what was happening at the guardhouse.

The gate was now open.

Smith removed his suit jacket, threw on a bulletproof vest and got back in the vehicle along with the other men.

Not a bad idea. Ryan dumped his jacket in the trunk, trading it for a vest, and added his sheriff's star to the front.

Another peek through the binoculars.

Smith was inside Benediction.

GAGE THREW THE truck in Park beside the funeral home. Claire and Jason were standing outside by the entrance. Worry was stamped on his stepsister's face. Jason had his hands shoved into his jacket pockets and yawned.

If Claire had set off the flares, then something awful—something awful in particular to Gage—had happened. But seeing Claire and Jason, standing, breathing, and having Hope healthy by his side were all that really mattered. The people he cared about were alive.

He'd work through the rest.

Gage and Hope made their way to them.

"Are you okay?" Claire asked, looking him over.

"Yeah, what's happened?"

"Sheriff Ryan Keller from Goode tracked you down."

Gage and Hope exchanged a glance.

"He had a message for you," Claire said. "He owed you two apologies. First, he never thanked you for saving Hope's life. For that he's sorry."

"Was that all?" Gage asked. If so, the flares were overkill. Then he remembered. Two apologies.

Claire shot him an exasperated look that told him she wasn't finished. "Four men were in his office today, led by a man called Joe Smith. They were looking for you."

"Did he say why?" Gage asked.

"Yes, and it's the reason for the second apology. He took your water glass from the diner this morning and ran your prints."

The sudden noise in Gage's head, filling his ears, the hiss and grinding whir, weren't his imagination. That was the sound of his sanctuary being flushed down the garbage disposal.

Jason snickered. "Are you a criminal, Uncle Monte? Running from the law?"

Claire shushed her son and turned back to Gage. "Ryan wanted you to know that Joe Smith knows you're here with a friend and is on his way. They might even be here already. Benediction isn't safe."

Time slowed, stood still for one perfect second. Where he could breathe and think.

Then he moved. "Come with me." He unlocked the door and led the way into the funeral home.

Jason went to turn on the light.

"No," Gage said, using a tone that discouraged questions. "I'll turn on the light in the basement." He locked the door behind them this time, not wanting anyone sneaking in and creeping up on them. Once was enough with Dr. Howland.

In the basement, Gage flicked on the lights. "Jason, go to the supply closet and grab the sledgehammer."

"But we don't have one."

"Yes. We do." Gage had purchased one in preparation just in case this day came.

Jason dashed down the hall as if he understood the urgency, even if he didn't respect the fact that Gage was at the epicenter of the situation.

Gage hustled to the desk and shoved it to the side.

Jason ran back and handed Gage the sledgehammer. "Wouldn't a gun be more useful?"

Gage withdrew the Sig from the holster at his back. "Like this? That's sort of the idea." He handed Hope the gun so it wouldn't restrict his movement. "Stand back."

Everyone shuffled a few feet away.

Gage swung the sledgehammer at the wall, punching a hole through it. Battered the spot until it was roughly twenty-five inches in diameter. Throwing the sledgehammer to the side, he reached into the hole and pulled out a duffel bag that he'd hidden there his first week in Benediction. He unzipped it, revealing the contents.

Everyone stepped forward and peered inside his go-bag.

"Oh, snap!" Jason said, staring at bundles of cash in different currencies, passports, weapons and other essentials.

Going through the gates of Benediction wasn't like crossing the border of a foreign country, where customs searched your belongings. Besides, firearms and his other items were legal.

"I'm not a criminal," Gage said. "All I have ever done is serve my country. I can't explain why there are men coming here to find me. Or why I have to run. What I can say is that when I am put six feet under, it will be with a clear conscience. If those men survive and I don't and they question you, renounce me as family. Say you know nothing about me or where I came from."

"Oh, my God," Claire said, clutching her chest.

Gage clasped both of her arms. "Even though we didn't stay in constant touch over the years, you've been the best sister that I could ask for. You've helped me without question, and it means more to me than you'll ever know."

Claire dragged him into a hug. "I want you to be safe. I want you to be happy."

At this point, Gage was just looking to survive the night. "I love you. Since the day you called me your little brother and dared any kid in Benediction to treat me like an outsider."

Claire tightened her embrace, squeezed and let him go.

Gage dug in the bag and offered her a bundle of US dollars. Ten thousand.

"I can't accept this," she said.

Better for it to go to her than the Finley family. "My contribution to Jason's college fund." He shoved the money into her hands. She stuffed it in the inner pocket of her coat. Then he turned to his nephew. "You were right that I was hiding something I didn't want anyone to figure out. That's why I let you call me Uncle Monte. I knew this day would come, and I couldn't let you get close to me because of that. You've lost too many people you've loved. I didn't want to be one more person on that list. But you blow me away, kid, in the best way. Your brains. Your spunk. Your courage. But most of all, your big heart. Be nice to your mom and listen to her. She'd do anything for you."

For once, Jason was speechless, but he nodded.

Gage turned to Hope.

"If you try to say goodbye to me," Hope said, "I'll slap you, too."

What was it about this woman? He couldn't help but smile.

"You told me the risks," she said. "I'm willing to take them. After everything…let me help you. Let me go with you."

Gage drew a deep breath, debating, but in the end, he said, "Okay." He'd learned there was little use in fighting Hope on an issue once she'd made up her mind, and there was no time to waste arguing. Once he dealt with the immediate threat, he'd give her a chance to come to her senses. Gage looked at Claire. "Take Jason to the fire station. Stay there until this is finished." There were two full-time firefighters at the station, though one was probably out checking to see who'd fired flares. "Tell them to call the volunteers for backup and that there are violent men in Benediction. They won't let anything happen to you."

"Be careful." Tears glistened in Claire's eyes. "I love you, too, little brother."

"One last thing," Gage said. "Paul Kudlow is tied up in his house and needs to be cut loose. Along with a couple of guards at the Nexcellogen facility, in the dumpster and security room."

Claire's brow creased with concern again. "I'll have someone check on them. After." She kissed his cheek, then she wrapped an arm around Jason and hurried up the stairs.

"How can I help?" Hope asked.

"You need to understand what we'll be up against. The CIA sends operatives like me and my team after international targets. But they contract cold-blooded mercenaries for an op such as this. Going after their own people, especially on American soil. It provides a layer of distance and deniability. They're not here to capture me. They have one objective. To kill me."

"What do you want me to do?" she asked without hesitation.

Tenacity ran through this woman hot as a live wire.

"Your job will be a two for one." He passed her the one bulletproof vest that he had, and she put it on. "The first part is facilitating our exit out of Benediction."

"What's the second part?"

He hooked the sheath of his Venom knife on the back of his belt. "Well, the first will draw attention."

"Wait. Am I supposed to be bait as the second part of my job?"

"It's unavoidable. But I'm the top priority for Joe Smith or whatever his real name is, not the bait. Anyone who helps me, anyone near me out there, they'll try to use as leverage." But once they no longer had any use for her…

There was no way in hell he was going to let that happen.

He removed the sound suppressor from the Sig Sauer Hope had and screwed it onto his HK MP5K. A weapon of choice in his line of work. Extra magazines he stuffed in his pocket.

"If I use this," Hope said, glancing down at the gun in her hand, "they'll hear it."

"Not if. You *will* use it. With what I need you to do, they're going to hear it, anyway." Gage cupped her cheek, held her gaze. "I won't let anything happen to you. Follow my instructions. No deviations like earlier."

Going off script had almost gotten her killed.

"Understood," Hope said. "Tell me what to do. I'll do it."

"Remember where we entered the woods, on our way to Kudlow's?"

"Yes."

"That's the area where Claire set off the flares. The men that are mostly likely already here in Benediction will start there. Or close to that spot. We're going to go there together."

The flares were as much a signal to Gage as they were a lure for anyone hunting him. He knew those woods, every tree, every berm, every shrub, every inch. Ran through them in the day and in the dark. Walked them, too. He was outmanned and outgunned, but in war, like in business, it was the terrain that mattered.

"Why are we going toward them instead of away?" Hope asked. "We don't need to leap into a bonfire to know it's hot."

The analogy was fitting. "In that area of the woods, we took a left and ran parallel to the hiking trail to go to Kudlow's house," he said, and she nodded, listening. "I need you to go straight instead, all the way to the fence line. There's a standing unit that powers the electric fence. You're going to shoot the power source. Disable the fence and cut through it."

"With what?"

He pointed out the bolt cutters and a screwdriver in the bag. "The handle of the screwdriver is solid plastic. Use the metal part to test the fence and make sure it's down before you use the bolt cutters."

"What if I run into trouble?"

"Once again, not if. You will." He picked up the bag and slung the strap over his shoulder. "All you have to do is follow my instructions. Do you trust me?"

"I trust you with my life."

Gage stared into her eyes, fiery, determined, so beautiful. All he wanted to do was kiss her, wrap her up in his arms and hold her there forever, but there was no time. He had to act now.

He put on the ski mask to better help him blend in with the woods. Next, he grabbed his monocular night-vision headgear and unfolded the unit. It fit securely, hugging his scalp, and the high-resolution lens was positioned over one eye.

Unless the men who came for him were wearing a set of their own, they wouldn't be able to see more than ten feet away in the woods at night. No doubt they were well-trained specialists, but the probability was high that they were also a bit cocky. Four against one, thinking they had the drop on Gage and that he was completely unaware. Ego got the best of lots of men.

Guess Ryan was good for something after all.

Taking Hope's hand, he described her part in the plan as they left the funeral home. The explanation was short and simple, and when he was finished, she didn't have questions.

Outside, it was quiet, and all was still.

The calm before the storm.

They took off for the woods on foot, headed toward the section that was far from any of the houses or other buildings. This was his favorite spot to enter, where there was no danger of anyone seeing him.

The snow had almost all melted and there were only a few scattered patches to reflect the light.

Stopping at a large evergreen, he took a knee, and she dropped down beside him. He passed her the watch she'd need to keep track of time and a screwdriver with a plastic handle that she'd need later, and he stowed the duffel bag carefully and quietly under a shrub.

Hope looked to him for the signal for her to take off for the power unit.

But he held up a palm for her to wait as he scanned the woods.

Gage's father had been a hunter, or so his mother had told him. His stepfather had been one, too, and used to take him and Claire hunting beyond the gates of Benediction.

In the woods. In the mountains.

This was in his blood. He preferred hunting predators. What he wasn't fond of were his chances tonight.

So, he needed to even the odds.

Movement at his nine and eleven o'clock. Two men spaced thirty feet apart. They were sweeping the area. In a minute, they'd pass by, headed in the direction of Gage's three o'clock.

Gage signaled her to get down low behind the shrub and to not make a peep.

The four men had probably started in the middle of

the woods, estimating where the flares had been shot, and spread out in twos, going in opposite directions.

Them working in pairs made Gage's task harder. If he fired a gun, outdoors in the quiet, sure, he'd kill one, but the other man would hear it. A silencer didn't suppress all sound.

Still, this was better than an urban environment, where that team would've had an even bigger advantage on busy streets with lots of CCTV for them to tap into.

Gage slung the strap of his weapon across his body, leaving his hands free.

Once the men had passed them, Gage held up a palm to Hope, gesturing for her to stay put.

He drew his double-action knife from the sheath at his back and prowled into the woods. If he could've subdued and restrained them, quickly and quietly, then he would've. Even though those men were there to kill him, Gage did not enjoy taking a human life.

But the circumstances dictated his options.

Gage crept up behind one of the armed men, avoiding the patches of snow that would crunch underfoot. He was nearly on him when a twig snapped beneath his boot and gave him away.

The man spun, raising a HP.

Gage stepped in and drove the blade into his side, between the man's ribs, angling it upward at the heart. Moving his left hand, Gage covered the man's mouth before he had a chance to utter a sound.

The man twitched, but the strike had been fatal and there was no struggle.

Bulletproof vests weren't knife resistant. A stab-resistant vest was made of different kind of fiber and weave. But the sides of a vest were particularly vulnerable. There were two protective panels, one in the front covering the chest, the other covering the back. Gaps along the sides ranged in degree, but they were always there.

Gage lowered the corpse to the ground.

Then he went after the second man, who had altered his course, drawing closer. Gage moved toward the man, head-on. But once the distance between them hit about fifteen feet, Gage ducked behind a large oak. Pressed his back to the trunk. Breathed. Waited. Judged the man's proximity by the subtle sounds the guy made.

The adrenaline moving through his veins quickened.

Branches moved close by. Footsteps through the underbrush shifted from Gage's left to right.

Hold.

Hold.

Gage forced himself not to rush it. To hold still as he coiled with readiness. The knife was tight in his grip.

The man came up alongside the tree.

Gage spun out to face the operative. He knocked the barrel of the assault weapon up with his forearm as he drove the blade of his knife into the man's throat with his other hand, cutting off the yell before it was voiced.

The mercenary gurgled. Clutched at his throat as he fell, dying before he hit the ground.

Gage sheathed his knife and raced back to Hope.

"You got them both?" she whispered.

"Two down. Two to go."

"That was fast, and the way you took out the first guy was…so brutal. And you did that to two of them," she said with an air of awe.

No one had ever him seen him work before—his team didn't count—and it surprised him to hear her sound impressed. "I thought you would've been, I don't know, shocked, horrified."

"That monster Ian shocked and horrified me. You never could."

If he wasn't wearing a ski mask, he would've taken ten seconds and kissed her.

"We're not in the clear yet," Gage said. "Let's go."

Grabbing the bag, he guided her through the woods to the spot where they needed to separate. He checked the path ahead that led to the fence for her, using the NVG monocular. No movement in that direction.

"You're good," he said. "Five minutes. Then you know what to do."

She flicked a glance at the watch on her wrist and nodded.

He handed her the bag. "Sorry that it's heavier than it looks."

Hope held the bag with both hands. "I'll manage." She took off toward the fence in a crouch.

Gage had five minutes to find the next man and eliminate him from the playing field.

He combed through the woods, skulking forward, sweeping 180 degrees.

The other two men would come his way. It was possible that they were both closer to the fence, but they'd want to search near the tree line adjacent to the houses, too.

His internal clock told him the minutes were flying by. At least two, if not more, were already gone. He had to get at least one more before Hope started her part, because his plan wouldn't work if he had to take on two at once.

Gage picked up his pace, keeping his body low. An instant later, he spotted one.

The man stumbled over something but quickly regained his balance.

Gage went all the way to the perimeter, passed the guy and doubled back around to come up behind him.

Time was almost up. Maybe a minute left. He'd have to risk firing his weapon.

Dropping to a knee, Gage slid the weapon off his shoulder, steadied his breathing and raised his MP5K. He lined up the sights through his NVG. A head shot would be quick. Clean. He put his finger on the trigger. Waited for the man to walk around a tree. Back in his sights.

On an exhale, he fired, and the man dropped.

One left.

Chapter Twenty

As Hope had run for the fence, the bulletproof vest had grown heavier, and the bag in her hands weighed her down. Once she'd reached the tree line, saw the fence and the power unit, Goode Lake black and ominous beyond it, she'd dropped by a shrub and caught her breath.

Five minutes passed in a flash.

Time was up. Hope prayed that Gage had had long enough to take out another man.

Standing up from her hiding position, she aimed the gun at the power unit, dead center. She'd never fired a gun before, but she was so close it would be impossible to miss.

To be certain she fried the unit, she pulled the trigger twice.

The unit exploded in a thunderous boom, shooting sparks and sizzling. A plume of smoke wafted into the air.

No wonder everyone was about to make a beeline to her position.

Hope hadn't noticed the hum the power unit had been making until it had stopped.

She lugged the duffel bag over to the fence and dropped it. Panting, she dived into the bag and found the screwdriver. She touched the metal part to the chain link while holding the thick plastic handle.

There was no electric arc or sparks, but she ran the screwdriver back and forth across the fence for a few seconds.

Still, nothing.

Next was the part she was dreading. She had to set the screwdriver and gun down since she needed both hands to use the bolt cutter. Unarmed, with her back to the trees.

The vulnerability and the exposure made her skin prickle.

Holding the bolt cutter, she snipped links close to where they were intertwined, going in a vertical line from the bottom up. Each strand gave way with an audible snap.

Her spine tingled with the creepy sensation of being watched. But she stopped herself from turning around.

She'd cut three feet high when someone pressed the muzzle of a gun to the back of her head.

GAGE DASHED THROUGH the woods, cutting toward the fence and the promise of a collision with the enemy.

Through the tree line he caught sight of Hope.

A man in all-black tactical gear like the others held Hope by the back of her neck with a gun pointed to her head. Their backs were to the fence, and they faced the woods. The man was waiting for him, to exploit Hope as leverage.

Just as Gage had anticipated. He walked to the tree line with his gun at the ready. Not giving the operative a clear shot, he used the trunk of an oak for cover.

"Drop your weapon and come out with your hands up," the man said. "Do it now and I'll let the woman live."

Even if Gage cooperated, did as he had been told so he could be executed, there was no guarantee that man would let Hope live. Not if the operative suspected Gage had confided in her.

There was an order out on Team Topaz because they knew something, saw something or were simply someone else's loose end. His association with Hope made her unfinished business, as well.

"All right." Gage took a step to the side from behind the tree. "Don't hurt her."

"Come closer and drop your weapon."

Hope's hands were up in the air, high, above her head, the way he'd told her.

The second the man moved the gun from her head to refocus the aim at Gage, then she could act, sending an elbow crashing back and down into the guy and dive to the ground to get out of the line of fire.

Gage edged forward, inching closer, and hoisted his weapon up in the air.

A whispered rustle in the undergrowth to the side betrayed movement.

Years of training, pure instinct had Gage ducking. He dropped and rolled. Bullets bit into bark mere inches were his head had been. More live fire. Dirt spit from the ground beside him.

Adrenaline surged, powering Gage as he raced for cover. A trajectory of gunfire tracked his every move. He scrambled behind a tree, cursing the unexpected fifth man with every ragged, dogged breath.

A fast-moving shadow darted between the trees.

Gage got a glimpse of the fifth man.

White shirt, dark slacks, vest. Must be the team leader, call sign Prime.

Where did he come from?

"Come out!" Prime said. "If you don't, my man will put a bullet in the woman. Hope Fischer. I understand you're concerned about her well-being and don't want anything to happen to her. So, you've got until the count of three."

Gage peeked out and assessed the situation.

The guy in all black had the gun pressed to Hope's skull.

If Gage came out, they'd both have a clear shot at him. He'd only be able to take out one man before the other got him. The scenario might have been different if he had also had his Sig, but it was on the ground behind Hope near the fence.

He glanced at Hope, her gaze meeting his, and the steely courage he saw in her eyes skewered him. She wasn't afraid…because she *trusted* him to get her out of this.

"One," Prime said.

Sweat gathered at the nape of Gage's neck. There was no choice. None. Only one thing he could do.

"Two."

Delayed realization kicked hard at Gage. He loved Hope. Without question, he'd sacrifice himself to protect an innocent. But the fear twisting up his legs and winding along his spine—gut-wrenching fear—was about losing Hope.

Keeping her alive was everything to him.

"Three."

"Sheriff's department, drop your gun! Let the woman go," Ryan Keller called from somewhere in the woods, not too far away.

Gage jumped out from behind the tree, aiming in Prime's direction.

Gage's first bullet smacked into a tree as Prime's line of fire barely missed him.

At the same time, the man in all black shifted Hope like a human shield in front of him, keeping his back to the fence, and fired at the sheriff.

No way Keller would get the shot.

Gage maneuvered forward, closing in on Prime's position. Squeezed off two shots. Took up a new position behind another tree.

A barrage of suppressed fire tore into the trunk, vibrating through Gage. Prime was also on the move, tightening the distance between them, as well. Peppering sound from the steady stream of bullets grew louder as the enemy grew closer.

But the man was almost out of ammo.

Off to the side, the other operative was edging away from the fence, trying to get to the woods with Hope in front of him, but she was dragging her feet, slowing him down.

Two more shots were fired at Gage. *Click. Click.* The sound came, signaling the magazine was empty. Prime would have to reload.

Gage spun around, leaving the coverage of the tree, barrel poised to fire back. But Prime tossed his assault weapon, and two hundred pounds of angry muscle charged into Gage, knocking his gun skyward from his hand and smashing his back into hard bark. Pain ratcheted through him.

Prime was on him. They exchanged kicks and punches. Prime threw a fist to Gage's solar plexus—a meshwork of nerves just below the chest.

It was ridiculously painful, knocking the wind from him in one long whoosh and dropping him to his knees.

Doubled over, he blinked through the agony, struggling to regain his bearings and his breath. But another blow hammered his face.

Prime ripped off the NVG monocular and ski mask. Then he grabbed Gage by his hair and tugged back, jerking his head upward. "I want to look you in the eyes as you die." Prime reached for the sidearm on his hip.

Gage couldn't stand. Couldn't fight. He could barely breathe.

But he slipped the knife from the sheath at his back, and with one swift move, he drove the blade into Prime's femoral artery and twisted it.

Anguish exploded on the man's face. The wound was fatal. He'd bleed out within seconds, but the man wasn't dead yet. He drew the gun from the holster, and as he aimed at Gage's head, Gage withdrew the knife and jammed it right up into the portion of his lower belly that was exposed from the vest.

The man's whole body tensed. His face contorted again. The gun slipped from his hand, and he keeled over to the ground.

Gage crawled to his weapon and struggled to his feet to help Hope.

Ten yards away, the man was trying to get her from the fence and into the woods.

But Hope went deadweight, her body going slack, throwing him off balance and leaving him exposed. He tossed her to the side, throwing her into the fence, and shot at the sheriff.

Hope climbed to her hands and knees and picked up the gun. Her fist rose, clenched around the Sig. The barrel flashed, and the man spun in a 180 and hit the ground.

Sweet relief spilled through Gage.

Hope was alive. She was unharmed.

Gage rushed to her, taking her elbow and helping her stand. He pulled her close, her head coming to rest under his chin against his chest.

"Thank God you're all right," the sheriff said, running from the woods toward them.

"It's over," Hope said, holding Gage tighter. "It's over."

"Almost." Gage rubbed a hand up and down her back. "But not yet. The MPs will be here soon."

Hope looked up at him.

"I'm going to have to take you in," Ryan said, pointing the gun at Gage. "You're wanted for something. Those CIA spooks went about it the wrong way, but it doesn't change the fact that you're a fugitive."

"I am wanted." Gage nodded. "But I've committed no crime. I've done nothing wrong."

"I wish I had proof of that," Ryan said.

"Did you see me commit a crime here tonight?"

"No. I didn't."

"Then what am I charged with? Why am I wanted?"

"Those are good questions." Ryan nodded. "Your prints came back with no hits. But those men showed up."

"If you arrest me and take me into custody, it would be like putting a gun to my head and pulling the trigger yourself. The CIA doesn't want me charged. They don't want me on trial. They just want me dead."

Hope went up to Ryan, standing in front of the gun, put her hand on his raised arm and lowered it. "Everything he said is true. Arrest him and you would be killing him. Those men that showed up are proof of that."

Ryan holstered his weapon, but he didn't look convinced.

"Ian McCallister," Hope said, "the head of security at Nexcellogen, killed Faith and made it look like suicide. They were worried about losing a lucrative contract and wanted to keep her quiet."

Ryan shook his head. "About what?"

Hope took off the necklace with the cryptex pendant. "The true test results from her clinical trials. Michelle Lansing, the director here, Neal Underhill and Paul Kudlow all conspired and submitted a false annual report to headquarters. Faith was going to blow the whole thing."

The sheriff's face was a mix of relief and anguish.

Hope put the necklace in Ryan's hands. "Nineteen eight twenty-five. That's the code to open the cryptex. Inside you'll find a thumb drive with all the real data. Nineteen eight twenty-five. Lansing. Underhill. Kudlow. Repeat it."

"Nineteen eight twenty-five. Lansing. Underhill. Kudlow. But what about McCallister? I want the bastard behind bars."

"He's dead. He tried to kill me, too. But Gage stopped him. I owe him my life, again."

Ryan clenched his hands and lowered his head. "First Faith, then almost you."

"There's something else," Hope said. "Faith found out that Paul Kudlow was using the drug she was working on to synthesize Zion."

"What?" Ryan rocked back on his heels, his mouth agape.

"Paul was using someone in the sheriff's department to distribute it," Hope said.

Ryan froze. "Who?"

"Dwight Travers. Paul Kudlow admitted it."

Ryan swore and shook his head in disbelief.

"Go back to Goode," Hope said. "Arrest Dwight. Get a warrant for Kudlow's arrest. Publish the data on that thumb drive through multiple news outlets. Be sure that Nexcellogen headquarters gets a copy, and tell them that Michelle Lansing is a lying parasite."

"I will. You can count on that."

"I never would've found out the truth about who killed Faith and why if weren't for this man." Hope pointed back at Gage. "If you care about me at all, about what Faith would want for me, walk away, Ryan. Tell the MPs you don't know what happened to us."

Ryan rubbed a hand across his chin, deliberating.

"We don't have much time." Gage stepped forward. "Are you going to help us or hurt us?"

Stuffing the cryptex necklace in his pocket, Ryan looked up and said, "I already owed you two apologies. Let's not make it a third. Thank you for finding Faith's murderer. I wanted that more than anything. Justice for the woman I loved." He extended his hand. "Thanks for watching out for Hope, too."

Gage shook it. "If you could buy us ten minutes with the MPs, we'd appreciate it."

"Sure. But then what?"

"I've got that covered."

Ryan nodded and jogged off into the woods.

"Last chance," Gage said. "You can still go back to your life. If that team reported in before they came to Benediction, I'm sure they passed along your name. They'll find you, question you, but if we're no longer together, they'd think you weren't important to me. Just stick to the story that you don't know anything about me."

Hope pressed a hand to his cheek. "But I do know

things about you, and I only want to know more. I think we'd be better off together than apart."

He couldn't agree more. "We have to hurry. Did you cut the fence?"

She took his hand and showed him where.

He pulled a portion of the chain link up and ushered her through to the other side. Grabbing the bag, he followed.

Gage unzipped the duffel and took out the box with the inflatable boat. He handed her the pieces for the oars so she could connect them, putting them together while he inflated the two-person boat with the quick-fill hand pump. He'd timed the inflation before and clocked it at three minutes, thirty seconds. The pump filled the boat with air on each up and down stroke, cutting the time to blow it up in half.

His body ached and his limbs were a bit fatigued, but he got the boat inflated in under four minutes. He set the boat in the water, and they climbed in.

Gage put the bag in the middle between him. Then he rowed with all his might. He pushed aside all thoughts of exhaustion, Captain Finley and the MPs headed down to the fence, Claire, Jason, Benediction. The oars dipped into the water and skimmed the surface. Picking up the pace, he powered through each stroke. He found a demanding rhythm and dug deep for strength.

Once he reached the middle of the lake, far from the shore of Benediction, he took a break and caught his breath.

"Where are we going?"

"A town on the other side." He panted. "Called Riverton. I have another car stashed."

"I meant beyond that. You said that being on the run was like flying in a tin can that could crash and burn."

Good memory, but the imagery was chilling. "I have

a parachute. But using it means that wherever we land, we might have to stay for good."

"I don't understand. Will we be together?"

"Yes."

"Wherever we *land*, will it be safe?"

"Yes."

"Then use it."

Gage dug deep in the duffel bag and fished out his satellite phone. He dialed the emergency number that he knew by heart. Onetime use. The line trilled.

Someone picked up. "Parachute."

Per protocol, Gage had to give the correct response to the challenge for authentication. "Rip cord."

The person on the other line gave him a set of co-ordinates.

Gage repeated them in his head, committed them to memory.

"Do you have them?" The voice was Hunter Wright's.

"Yes."

"A man wearing a blue hat will meet you there. He'll ask you about the weather. You tell him you hate hurricanes. Do you understand?"

"Yes."

The line disconnected.

Gage threw the phone into the lake. The one sanctuary he'd fought to find and keep was gone. He'd pulled the rip cord on the only parachute that he'd ever have. He should've been on edge, or at the very least upset.

But sitting across from Hope, staring at her beautiful face, all he could do was smile. This extraordinary, smart, sexy woman had decided to take the plunge into the unknown with him. That made him the luckiest man on the planet.

Epilogue

Hope sat beside Gage on another boat. This one was little more than a motorized dinghy.

After they'd left Virginia, a man with a blue hat had met them at a port in Wilmington, North Carolina. He'd gotten them passage on a cargo ship bound for South America. The crew had asked them no questions, and no one had requested to see their passports. They were given a cabin. The quarters were cramped, but they'd made it cozy, savoring the time to decompress and connect in more ways than one. They'd shared everything with each other, including their clean bills of health, and made love with nothing between them.

The world could be cold, dark and treacherous, but with each other they'd both found a warm place of light, where they were safe.

Before the ship had docked, a woman also wearing a blue hat picked them up, off the coast of Venezuela, in the small, motorized boat they were in now.

The sun was warm on their faces, and the water was an enchanting light green. "Like the color of your eyes," Gage had said to her.

The woman took them to a small island and let them off at a dock.

Gage climbed out first and helped Hope up. Wrapping an arm around her shoulder, he carried the duffel bag as they walked down the long dock toward a house.

"Why were you in Benediction when you could've been here in paradise?" Hope asked.

"After my team realized that the CIA wanted us dead, we knew we'd be safer apart and scattered. Together we're a bigger target and easier to find. We all had sat phones that the Agency didn't know about. Hunter told us to only call his phone if we were in a jam, something serious, with our backs up against the wall. He'd give us a parachute. But the more of us that pull that rip cord, the more dangerous paradise will become."

A man came out onto the porch and down the steps to greet them. He was around six-two, all solid muscle, and, though a straw hat covered his hair and sunglasses hid his eyes, he was handsome as sin.

Gage dropped the bag on the powdery sand, and the two men hugged like longtime friends. Like family.

"Good to see you, despite the circumstances," Gage said.

"I told you that if you ever needed me, I'd be there for you. For all of you."

Gage stepped back next to her. "Hunter Wright, this is Hope Fischer. It's a long story as to why I brought her."

Hunter extended his hand. "Welcome, Ms. Fischer."

She shook it. He had a strong, firm grip. "Please, call me Hope."

"I look forward to hearing the story. If I had to guess, it's a dramatic tale fraught with danger, probably a little gunfire, but it has a happy ending."

"You would be right," Hope said, smiling. "You must be psychic."

"When you've been doing this long enough, you have to be. Come on inside." Hunter led them up the porch and into the house. The place was light and airy. The furniture modest, but comfortable. "Take a seat." He gestured to the sofa.

A phone rang in another room.

Hunter sighed. "No rest for the weary or the wicked. Please excuse me a minute."

Hope wandered to one of the open windows and stared out at the golden beach and the calm water. "This is gorgeous."

Gage came up beside her and brought her into his arms. He lowered his mouth to hers and kissed her softly, then deeply, tasting her until her stomach fluttered with hunger for more from just one kiss.

Pulling back, he gazed down at her and smiled.

There went those butterflies again.

Hope had lost her sister and, in her pursuit to find a murderer, she'd also found faith in another. Something precious and rare and worth fighting for.

He'd pulled a rip cord, and she'd taken the leap with him. No matter what happened in the days ahead, she'd never regret choosing Gage.

Hope tightened her arms around him and kissed him once more.

Hunter came back into the room. The smile and humor on his face were gone. "That was Zenobia. She's in trouble, too. We'll see her soon if she survives."

* * * * *

*Look for the next book in Juno Rushdan's Fugitive
Heroes: Topaz Unit series,*
Alaskan Christmas Escape

Available from Harlequin Intrigue!

 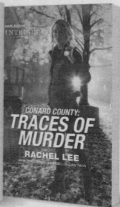

#2037 TARGETING THE DEPUTY
Mercy Ridge Lawmen • by Delores Fossen

After narrowly escaping an attempt on his life, Deputy Leo Logan is shocked to learn the reason for the attack is his custody battle for his son with his ex, Olivia Nash. To catch the real killer, he'll have to keep them both close—and risk falling for Olivia all over again.

#2038 CONARD COUNTY: CHRISTMAS BODYGUARD
Conard County: The Next Generation • by Rachel Lee

Security expert Hale Scribner doesn't get personal with clients. Ever. But having evidence that could put away a notoriously shady CEO doesn't make Allie Burton his standard low-risk charge. With an assassin trailing them 24/7, they'll need a Christmas miracle to survive the danger...and their undeniable attraction.

#2039 TEXAS ABDUCTION
An O'Connor Family Mystery • by Barb Han

When Cheyenne O'Connor's friend goes missing, she partners with her estranged husband, rancher Riggs O'Connor, for answers. During their investigation, evidence emerges suggesting their daughter—who everyone claims died at childbirth—might be alive and somehow connected. Riggs and Cheyenne are determined to find out what really happened...and if their little girl will be coming home after all.

#2040 MOUNTAINSIDE MURDER
A North Star Novel Series • by Nicole Helm

North Star undercover operative Sabrina Killian is on a hit man's trail and doesn't want help from Wyoming search and rescue ranger Connor Lindstrom. But the persistent ex-SEAL is the killer's real target. Will Sabrina and Connor's most dangerous secrets even the odds—or take them out for good?

#2041 ALASKAN CHRISTMAS ESCAPE
Fugitive Heroes: Topaz Unit • by Juno Rushdan

With an elite CIA kill squad locating hacker Zenobia Hanley's Alaska wilderness hideout, it's up to her mysterious SEAL neighbor, John Lowry, to save her from capture. Regardless of the risks and secrets they're both hiding, John's determined to protect Zee because there's more at stake this Christmas than just their lives...

#2042 BAYOU CHRISTMAS DISAPPEARANCE
by Denise N. Wheatley

Mona Avery is determined to investigate a high-profile missing person case in the Louisiana bayou before heading home for Christmas. Stubborn detective Dillon Reed insists she's more of a hindrance than a help. But when a killer wants Mona's story silenced, only Dillon can keep her safe...

SPECIAL EXCERPT FROM

HQN

Meet New York Times *bestselling author B.J. Daniels in*
At the Crossroads,
her next Buckhorn, Montana novel.

Read on for a sneak peek.

At the Crossroads

Bobby Braden wiped the blood off his fingers, noticing that he'd smeared some on the steering wheel. He pulled his shirtsleeve down and cleaned the streak of red away, the van swerving as he did.

"Hey, watch it!" In the passenger seat, Gene Donaldson checked his side mirror. "All we need is for a cop to pull us over," he said in his deep, gravelly voice. It reminded Bobby of the grind of a chain saw. "If one of them sees you driving crazy—"

"I got it," he grumbled. "Go back to sleep," he said under his breath as he checked the rearview mirror. The black line of highway behind them was as empty as the highway in front of them. There was no one out here in the middle of Montana on a Sunday this early in the morning—especially this time of year, with Christmas only weeks away. He really doubted there would be a cop or highway patrol. But he wasn't about to argue. He knew that would be his last mistake.

He stared ahead at the narrow strip of blacktop, wondering why Gene had been so insistent on them coming this way. Shouldn't they try to cross into Canada? If Gene had a plan, he hadn't shared it. Same with the bank job that Gene said would be a piece of cake. Unless an off-duty cop just happened to be in there cashing his check—and armed.

Concentrating on staying between the lines, Bobby took a breath and let it out slowly. He could smell the blood and the sweat and the

"EVERYBODY WHO'S EVER BEEN LOVED BY A DOG WILL ADORE BENJI."
—Liz Smith,
Cosmopolitan

"Benji manages to express shades of love, hurt, joy and sadness so well it borders on the impossible. Throw in anxiety and fear, too."
—Phil Strassburg,
Arizona Republic

"Benji has a face far more expressive than some human actors."
—Susan Goldsmith,
American Girl Magazine

"Benji is probably the most intelligent dog in the world. Introduce him to your children by all means."
—Ann Guarino,
New York Daily News

Mulberry Square Productions
presents

A Family Film by
Joe Camp

FOR THE LOVE OF BENJI

starring
Benji
Patsy Garrett
Cynthia Smith
Allen Fiuzat

special guest star
Ed Nelson

with
Art Vasil
Peter Bowles
Bridget Armstrong
Mihalis Lambrinos

Music by Euel Box

Director of Photography Don Reddy

Original Story by
Joe Camp and Ben Vaughn

Screenplay by Joe Camp

Executive Producer Joe Camp

Produced by Ben Vaughn

Directed by Joe Camp

Filmed in Panavision
Color by CFI
A Mulberry Square Production

FOR THE LOVE OF BENJI

A Novelization by I.F. Love

From the Family Film by
Joe Camp

BANTAM BOOKS
TORONTO · NEW YORK · LONDON · SYDNEY

FOR THE LOVE OF BENJI
A Bantam Book | June 1977
21 printings through December 1979

22nd printing
23rd printing
24th printing
25th printing
26th printing

ISBN 0-553-13692-5

Published simultaneously in the United States and Canada

Bantam Books are published by Bantam Books, Inc. Its trade-mark, consisting of the words "Bantam Books" and the por-trayal of a bantam, is Registered in U.S. Patent and Trademark Office and in other countries. Marca Registrada. Bantam Books, Inc., 666 Fifth Avenue, New York, New York 10019.

PRINTED IN THE UNITED STATES OF AMERICA

I

A voice suddenly broke through the static on the two-way radio rousing the craggy, stone-faced man from a pleasant afternoon nap. He quickly cranked the engine of the Mercedes taxi and followed the ancient stone street to the summit of the Acropolis and down the other side to the Plaka with its maze of colorful shops and taverns.

His name was Stelios and his dark brooding eyes seemed to take note of everything and everybody. He parked the taxi and climbed out into the warm sunshine of Athens. His pace was deliberate and the scowl on his lips caused other pedestrians to move out of his path.

As he turned a corner and walked toward a sidewalk café his eyes narrowed and seemed to search for something across the street. When he found it he gave an almost imperceptible nod and took a table as far away from the other customers as possible.

A heavy man wearing a food-stained apron and carrying several newspapers crossed the street and approached the table. He made no move to sit down but dropped the newspapers in front of Stelios and handed him a large envelope.

1

"The whole world knows now," he said in a coarse voice.

Stelios glanced down at the newspapers. One was Greek, one German, and one English and they all had a picture of the same man on the front page. The headlines announced that a prominent energy scientist had disappeared in Greece.

Stelios said nothing as he opened the envelope. He looked at the first sheet of paper. "Chandler Dietrich," he mumbled and nodded thoughtfully. Then he thumbed through several other papers, finally settling on an eight-by-ten photograph. "What's this?"

It was a picture of a woman, two children —a boy and a girl—and a dog, all staring brightly into the camera.

"The dog is the courier," the man said. "He'll be carrying the code."

"The dog! Why a dog?"

The man in the apron shrugged. "I have no idea. His name is Benji."

Stelios studied the picture again. It was a fairly small dog; a mixed breed of some kind with floppy ears and light-colored hair drooping around the eyes and off the jowls. "Who are the other people?"

"The kids' names are Paul and Cindy Chapman. They're ten and twelve years old. The woman's name is Mary Henderson. She's their governess. They'll all be changing planes in Athens tomorrow and going directly on to Crete."

Stelios sighed, taking a closer look at the brown dog. He wanted to make sure he would recognize him. There was a small tuft of white hair just behind the dog's nose, and his chest was streaked with white.

"Benji, huh?" Stelios mumbled.

The man in the apron nodded.

"Well, Benji, I hope you have a safe trip."

Perched on the ledge behind the back seat of the taxi, Benji couldn't have been happier as he watched the city of Houston disappear behind him. He wagged his tail and turned to look over Mary's shoulder toward the front window. He could already see the big jet planes lined up next to the buildings up ahead.

It had all started about a month earlier when Paul brought home a whole armload of books about Greece for a school assignment. Everybody in the house began reading the books or at least looking at the pictures and Dr. Chapman suddenly suggested they all go there for a vacation.

At first no one took the suggestion very seriously, but when the idea persisted after several weeks, Paul asked the obvious question.

"But what'll we do with Benji and Tiffany?"

"Well, we can't take them along, of course," Dr. Chapman replied. "Maybe we can find someone who will board them for three weeks."

That proved to be an unpopular suggestion indeed. To understand just how unpopular it was, a person would have to know how much Benji meant to Paul and Cindy. They had loved Benji for years, even when he was just a floppy-eared stray who had no family of his own. Now that Dr. Chapman had given his permission for

Benji and Tiffany to live with Paul and Cindy, they couldn't bear the thought of leaving them for nearly a month.

Cindy gave a very convincing argument and the doctor finally cleared his throat and smiled. "Well, let me check with the travel agent. I'll see what kind of regulations they have about taking dogs to Greece."

The taxi suddenly made a sharp turn and Benji took another look through the windshield. They were coming into the terminal now, and there were masses of cars and taxis and buses moving along ahead of them.

"Now let's be careful and all stick together," Mary said. Then she laughed. "I don't want some of us to go to Greece and the others end up in Hong Kong."

The taxi slowed down and Benji glanced out the back window again. Then he stiffened, his eyes fixed on a fluffy cat prancing along the walk in front of the terminal buildings. A woman wearing a fur coat was attached to the leash behind the cat, and both of them had their noses up in the air. Crowds of people were moving along the walk, with men pushing cartloads of luggage between them. Benji smiled to himself. He took one more glance at the cat and then held himself ready as the taxi pulled into a parking place.

"Benji!" Paul yelled as Benji bounded through the window onto the pavement.

Benji didn't respond. He had no intention of getting lost, but cats were arrogant animals, and if you didn't let them know you were around they always seemed to think they owned the place. He let out a threatening bark and scam-

pered across to where the woman was talking to
a skycap. He skidded to a stop and gave two
more loud barks.

The cat gazed indifferently at him, definitely unimpressed. Benji looked puzzled at the
cat's lack of reaction but suddenly felt himself
scooped off the pavement.

"I'm sorry, ma'am," Paul said to the lady,
and then they were bouncing along through the
crowds toward the terminal doors. "Benji, you've
got to cut that out if you want to travel with
us!"

Benji gave Paul's hand a lick.

"Count the bags," Mary said. "Are they all
here?"

"I counted them," Cindy answered. "Have
you got the tickets?"

"The tickets? Oh, dear! They must be in my
purse somewhere."

They all stopped and finally breathed a sigh
of relief when Mary brought them out. She
moved into the line at the counter and Paul and
Cindy stood to the side with Benji and Tiffany.
There seemed to be some confusion over there
being four reservations and only three people.
Mary explained that Dr. Chapman would be coming a week later, and the ticket clerk went off
to check the computers.

"We're going to Greece," Mary said to the
man standing behind her.

He was a tall, handsome man with a little
gray hair at the temples. He smiled politely.
"Yes, I know."

"You do?" Mary said with surprise.

"That's the only place this airline goes."

"Oh," Mary said, "of course." She looked

off behind the counter and then turned back to the man. "I'm sorry this is taking so long. Where in Greece are you going?"

"I'm going to Crete," the man said politely.

"Really? That's where we're going."

The man smiled. "It's a beautiful island. I've been there many times. I'll be happy to tell you the good places to go. My name is Chandler Dietrich, by the way."

Mary smiled and shook his hand. "I'm Mary Henderson, and this is Paul and Cynthia Chapman. And that's Benji and Tiffany."

Just then a pretty girl in an airline uniform came up and asked Cindy for the names of her dogs. Cindy told her, adding that they were going to Crete.

"Well, I'm sure you're going to have a very nice trip, Benji and Tiffany," the girl said. She carefully wrote their names on two tags.

"Are you sure they'll be all right?" Cindy asked.

"They'll be just fine. My cat travels this way all the time."

"Tiffany hasn't been feeling well," Cindy said. "She sort of has a condition."

"Well, we'll take good care of her. I promise you that."

The girl had the tags attached to the cages now and she put Tiffany gently inside hers and locked it up. Benji took a final look at Paul and Cindy and then allowed himself to be lifted from the counter and locked into the cage.

"See you in Crete," Paul called out to both of them and they were placed on a conveyor belt.

As the two dogs passed into a narrow corridor, the noises of the front terminal suddenly disappeared. They moved through a small hole and into a huge room that had baggage stacked everywhere. Now Benji could hear the whine of jet engines and the clatter of machinery and trucks. Benji settled down and rested his chin on the bottom of the cage. Then he looked up quickly.

Dietrich, the man in line behind Mary, was coming toward him, walking fast alongside the conveyor belt. He rested his hand on top of the cage and peered in. "Hi there, Benji boy," he said.

Benji gave him a panting smile of recognition, but the man had already straightened. Benji felt his cage lifted from the conveyor belt and they were moving away. He wondered why the man hadn't taken Tiffany too.

They passed through a door into a room that was crowded with machinery, all of it roaring and banging at a deafening level. Then the cage was placed on a counter and Dietrich was sliding a steel pin into the lock, squinting closely at it. Benji wagged his tail. Perhaps he was going to be let out of the cage. But the door stayed shut.

Benji watched as Dietrich opened the top of a tiny bottle and poured some liquid onto his handkerchief.

"OK, Benji, now just relax. This won't take long and it won't hurt a bit."

Benji hesitated as the man opened the door. Then he tried to turn his head away as the man grabbed his neck and held the handkerchief tightly to his nose.

Benji had never smelled anything like it. The powerful vapor stung his nostrils and sud-

denly made him dizzy as it seeped up into his
nose. He dug his paws into the bottom of the
cage and twisted to the side with all his strength,
trying to wrench his head loose. But his legs
seemed to buckle under him and suddenly his
whole body went limp.

He was flat on the bottom of the cage now
and everything in the room was floating around,
going in and out of focus. Mr. Dietrich had
brought something shiny from his pocket and
Benji blinked woozily, trying to see what it was.
There was a bottle of liquid, then he felt his paw
lifted and the pad of his foot was pressed hard
against the cold metal of the object.

"There you go, Benji. That wasn't so bad,
was it?"

The man was holding a match to the piece of
metal now. It flamed away into nothing. Then
the cage door came shut again, the lock rattling
back into place. Dietrich peered in and smiled.
"Good boy, Benji. I'll see you in Crete in about
twelve hours, huh?"

The problem was Benji couldn't see anything, at least not very clearly. He felt himself
being carried back through the door and bounced
down onto the conveyor belt. Then Mr. Dietrich
was gone and he was moving along the belt, his
head resting between his paws, blinking uncer-
tainly at his surroundings.

"Here's another dog," somebody said. He felt
himself lifted again, this time placed on a big
cart in the midst of more suitcases. A couple of
minutes later the cart was being towed out into the sunshine and Benji closed his eyes. All he
wanted to do now was sleep.

II

The flight from Athens down to the island of Crete took less than half an hour, but the scenery was magnificent. The plane was only half full, so all of them except Mr. Dietrich had window seats and a good view.

The color of the water was amazing: a rich azure that turned to lacy white around the hundreds of islands. It was even prettier than the postcards and travel brochures they had studied back in Silver Creek. Then, as the plane approached the island of Crete, the little whitewashed villages along the coast looked no different from how they must have looked centuries earlier.

Mr. Dietrich turned out to have a wealth of information about Crete, telling them about some of the most interesting archaeological sites in the world. But because they had now been traveling for well over twelve hours, Paul and Cindy had slept through a good part of the history lesson. Now the famous island was directly beneath them and the plane turned and seemed to slow down almost to a stop as they started the descent toward the airport.

The terminal was small compared to those in

9

Houston and Athens, and the passengers were
unloaded several hundred yards away from the
buildings.

"As soon as you're all settled and catch up
on your sleep," Mr. Dietrich said as they
walked across the apron, "I'm treating all three
of you to the best meal you've ever had in your
lives."

Mary gave him a hesitant glance. "You
really don't have to do that, Mr. Dietrich. I'm
sure you have other important business to attend
to."

Mr. Dietrich shook his head. "I won't have
it any other way. I want you to see the best of
Crete."

Mary smiled, not wanting to protest too vig-
orously.

"Will it be Greek food?" Paul asked.

"Very Greek."

"What's Greek food like?" Cindy asked suspiciously.

"I will promise you only one thing," Mr.
Dietrich laughed. "There won't be any fried
chicken on the menu."

Paul laughed, but Cindy thought fried
chicken sounded pretty good right now.

A young man in an Olympic Airways uniform was just inside the door holding a black-
board with Mr. Dietrich's name chalked on it.
Cindy was the only one who noticed.

"Mr. Dietrich, look at that!"

He glanced at the board and stopped abruptly. "Can you believe that? I guess there's no escaping. Why don't you all go on ahead to the
baggage claim area. I'll be right there."

When they moved off Dietrich turned

quickly to the man. "I'm Chandler Dietrich, young man," he said in fluent Greek.

The messenger searched his pockets and brought out a folded piece of paper. "A man left this message for you, sir. He said it was urgent."

Dietrich unfolded the paper and frowned as he studied the message. "Did he leave his name?"

"No, sir."

Dietrich nodded and handed him a tip. Then he moved into the terminal building, angling off toward the baggage area where Mary, Paul, and Cindy were watching the luggage come through on a conveyor belt.

"Is anything wrong?" Mary asked when she saw his dark look.

"Uh . . . no. No, not at all. I just have to make a phone call." He smiled to reassure them. "Look, why don't you and the kids wait for the luggage and the dogs . . ." He searched his pockets for his claim check. "And if you don't mind, watch for my bag too. It's a light tan, about so big."

"Sure," Paul said, "we'll find it."

"I'd appreciate it, Paul. I'll be back in a minute and then we'll all take a cab together so you won't have to fight the language problem."

"That'd be great," Mary smiled. "Thank you."

"Thank *you*," Dietrich said with a smile, and strode off.

He moved along to the last pay phone in the line and stopped, glancing casually at the OUT OF ORDER sign taped across it. He consulted the note again and paced impatiently near the phone for a half minute. Suddenly it rang and he quickly lifted the receiver.

"Dietrich," he said.

The voice was cold and menacing. "Welcome to Crete, Mr. Dietrich. Do you have the coordinate code?"

"I have it. It's in a safe place."

"Good. You will find the map in an envelope taped under the shelf below the phone."

Dietrich bent forward and spotted the bulky envelope. He tore it loose and took the map from inside. "I have it."

"Very good. The project is getting out of hand, Mr. Dietrich, so waste no time. Signal if you need help. We will always be watching you."

"I won't need any help," Dietrich said irritably, "and I don't need to be watched. I'm perfectly capable of handling this alone."

The phone clicked softly and Dietrich rattled the hook. "Hello?"

The man had hung up. Dietrich banged the receiver down and quickly slid the map into his inside coat pocket. Then he looked out at the people crisscrossing the terminal lobby. He recognized none of them, and there seemed to be no one watching him. Then he looked up sharply at the mezzanine.

There standing by another bank of pay phones was a dark, thick-necked Greek. His cold, penetrating eyes seemed to be gazing idly down at the crowds. It was Stelios.

Dietrich wondered if that was the man who had been assigned to watch him. Or was it the man who had called him on the phone? Or was it just another passenger killing time between flights?

Mary and the kids all looked worried when

Dietrich got back to the baggage area. They were the only ones still standing by the conveyor belt and Mary turned quickly when she saw him.

"Chandler! I'm so glad you're back. They're not here! All the luggage came, but there's no sign of Benji or Tiffany!"

"What?" Dietrich snapped, his eyes flashing pointed concern. "Are you sure?"

"We've watched everything that came in," Paul said. "They're just not here."

Dietrich glanced around and found the customer service counter. "They must be here somewhere!" He moved quickly to the counter with Mary and the kids following close behind.

"Excuse me, there's supposed to be two dogs on the flight from Athens. Is it possible they haven't brought them in yet?"

"No," the man said. He glanced at the baggage area. "They would be coming through there, the same as the luggage. Are you sure they were loaded in Athens?"

Dietrich explained that they had come from Houston and then caught the first flight to Crete.

The man smiled. "Well, I'm sure they're all right. They probably missed the plane change in Athens." He glanced at Paul and Cindy. "Now please don't worry. I'll go call and find out for sure. And I promise they'll get the best of care, and be on the next flight."

"When is the next flight?" Mary asked.

"Tomorrow morning."

"Oh, my," Mary groaned. And the customer service man vanished around a corner. "I think I'll go with him," Dietrich said, glancing after the man, "just to be sure."

"Mr. Dietrich!" Mary called as he hurried off, "be sure to tell them they haven't had anything to eat or drink in almost twelve hours!"

"And that Tiffany has a condition!" Cindy added.

Mary sighed as they waited. "I guess we'd better gather up our bags."

"What if they don't find them?" Cindy asked as they moved back to the conveyor belt. "What if they're still in Houston?"

"I'm sure they must be in Athens, sweetheart."

"Yeah," Paul said trying to bolster Cindy's spirits. "They're probably having a big time at the Athens Airport. Benji knows how to take care of himself."

Twenty feet away, Stelios folded his newspaper, studied Mary, Paul, and Cindy for a quick moment, then moved casually from the ticket counter.

For the tenth time in the last hour, Benji's stomach growled and twisted, reminding him that he was hungry. He had been hungry plenty of times before, but he was usually in a position to do something about it. Even a drink of water would help. For some reason the liquid Dietrich had held to his nose in Houston had ended up making his mouth and throat dry, and when he finally woke up three or four hours ago his tongue felt like it was caked with dust.

When they were unloaded from the plane, Benji expected to see Mary, Paul, and Cindy smiling at him, but all he had seen was another cart piled high with suitcases, and then they were towed off to a big room where they were put on a counter.

Although their cages sat side by side and Benji could hear Tiffany's low whimper quite clearly, he had no way of seeing her. Perhaps that was just as well because Tiffany looked terrible. She had barked and whimpered until she was exhausted and now her head rested between her paws as she gazed forlornly out at the stacks of bags and boxes.

Once again Benji rose to his feet and barked and barked until his throat was too dry to bark any more. Somewhere across the room a bell rang ... and continued ringing repeatedly.

Finally, peering between two stacks of suitcases, Benji saw a man in coveralls pick up the telephone.

The man nodded as he listened. Then he frowned and looked off into the room.

He left the receiver dangling and disappeared from sight for a minute. Then Benji saw him moving up the aisle, looking under counters and between suitcases. Benji came quickly to his feet and barked again. Then his heart jumped. The man was looking directly at him, a big smile coming to his face.

The man held up a finger and said something Benji couldn't understand and then went back to the phone. Benji turned a quick circle in his cage, his tail wagging happily, and then he moaned and yelped at Tiffany.

She came to her feet and shook herself awake. Benji peered through the suitcases again and saw the man hang up the phone.

A minute later he was smiling and carry-

ing a bowl of water as he came up the aisle.
Benji barked excitedly. They were saved! The
man grinned and said something to Tiffany as
he peered in at her. Then he set the water on the
counter and said something in Greek to Benji.

Benji cocked his head, listening as carefully
as he could. The man's voice sounded sympathetic, but Benji couldn't make any sense out of the
words. Then the man frowned and pulled at the
lock on Benji's cage. He muttered some more
of the strange sounds and checked Tiffany's lock.

Benji's hopes suddenly plummeted as the
man moved off again, leaving the water just outside Benji's cage.

Benji watched the man go past the telephone
and disappear. Then he stared at the clear, cool
liquid only six inches from his nose. Water had
never looked quite so good to him. He could almost taste it. He moved his nose as close to the
wire cage as he could and thrust his tongue
through one of the holes.

It was hopeless—he was at least an inch
short. He shifted, trying another hole, but he still
couldn't reach. Benji sighed and stretched out,
resting his chin on the bottom of the cage.

He turned his paw and frowned at it, seeing
nothing particularly unusual on the pad where
Mr. Dietrich pressed the metal. There were some
tiny marks; a little square of dots that was hardly visible. Benji licked his paw, tasting nothing.
But the marks didn't come off. He licked at it
again and then gave it up, resting his head on
the bottom of the cage again.

Ten minutes passed and Benji finally closed
his eyes. The man would come back, he told himself—he just had to be patient. He sighed heavi-

ly and waited another ten minutes. Then he heard a door swing open and he came instantly to his feet.

The man was smiling, saying something in the strange language as he came up the aisle again. He was carrying a big pair of clippers. A *huge* pair of clippers. Benji wagged his tail and barked, jumping happily around his cage. Tiffany also rose, panting heavily with anticipation.

The man laughed, talking to both of them as he gripped the lock between the jaws of the clippers. With one movement he squeezed the handles together and the lock snapped and dropped to the counter. The man's face brightened and he laughed again as he reached for the clasp of the cage. Then he hesitated, muttering something as he looked off at the corner of the room.

The telephone was ringing again.

Benji gave the man a hopeful look, but it did no good. The man was moving away, shouting something at the telephone as he strode back down the aisle.

Benji watched the man lift the telephone receiver and start talking and then he pushed his nose gently against the door of the cage. It moved!

Benji pushed again. Slowly he nudged the door open enough to squeeze his nose through, then his whole head. In his earnestness to open the door, he failed to notice the bowl of water now teetering precariously on the edge of the counter.

The crash of shattering pottery sounded like an explosion as the bowl hit the concrete floor.

What happened in the next two minutes happened so fast, Benji wasn't sure what to make of it. As quickly as the water dish shattered he heard a shout from the man at the telephone. And then the man was gone from the phone and striding up the aisle and Benji stood frozen on the counter for an instant. As the man approached, suddenly his foot slipped on the wet pavement and the cage and Benji and the man all tumbled to the floor in a tangled heap.

Benji scrambled to his feet and moved fast. The man was shouting angrily and then groaning as he got to his hands and knees. By then Benji was under a different counter twenty feet away, watching, not certain what to do next. Then a nearby door swung open and another man was peering in.

"I say, is this the baggage storage area?" he asked with a decidedly British accent. "Do you speak English?" the Britisher continued, not seeming to notice that the luggage man was still sprawled on the concrete floor.

"You see, I'm looking for a . . ."

"Κλείνετε τήν πόρτα, παρακαλῶ!" the luggage man shouted and gestured wildly toward Benji. Benji bolted for the door, running right between the Britisher's legs.

"My word—what was that?" he heard the man cry as he raced past a woman who gaped at him and shrieked, "Ronald, it's him! It's the dog!"

Benji didn't go far. After about fifty feet he skidded to a stop on the slippery floor and ducked quickly into an opening under a vacant ticket counter. Then he peered back around the corner.

The Britisher was sitting spread-legged on the floor, having been run down by the baggage man as he rushed after Benji. A woman ran toward him shouting, "It's the dog! Come on!" as she helped the Britisher to his feet.

She was a pretty woman with blond hair and dressed in a neat suit. But Benji decided not to take any chances as all three of them came racing toward him.

"Here, doggie! Don't be frightened, doggie!" the Englishman was calling out behind him.

Benji glanced back and then searched for an escape route. He saw several open doors, but they all looked suspicious. Then he saw one leading into a huge room with tables and a lot of people standing by opened luggage. He made a sharp turn and dashed around the left side of the room.

A man in a uniform turned sharply from the suitcases he was inspecting and shouted something, but Benji kept moving.

The baggage man raced through the door followed by the English couple. They circled around behind Benji. The Englishman smiled and said something to the man in uniform, looking off toward Benji.

"Come on, doggie!" the Englishman shouted.

When he reached the far side of the room Benji stopped and waited, catching his breath for a minute. There appeared to be no good escape route from the room. Then, with the three pursuers almost upon him, he barreled straight across the middle of the room and out the door they had come in.

"Blast!" shouted the Englishman.

Benji glanced around some more as he trotted through the crowded lobby.

"Would you catch my little dog, please?" pleaded the Englishwoman, looking anxiously for help. Her voice sounded sweet and innocent, as if she were some little girl in distress trying to get her pet back.

Benji picked up a little speed and quickly spotted a narrow door standing half open. It was risky, but Benji decided he'd better take the chance.

Behind the door a narrow corridor ran for a hundred feet and then turned. If there was a closed door at the other end, he was going to be in big trouble. He moved faster, trying desperately to outrun the approaching footsteps behind him. Then as he turned the corner his heart jumped. Daylight! And lots of wide-open space.

Eight or ten huge jet airplanes were standing just outside the building, some of them with their engines screeching and whining. There were also a lot of men in coveralls, and three or four trucks crossing the area. Benji took it in with a glance and darted along under the first airplane, heading up the line toward the end of the building. A man shouted, but Benji paid no attention.

A man in a uniform stopped the English couple and was motioning them back toward the corridor. But the baggage man was still coming. Benji watched, catching his breath for a minute, not too worried about the one man catching him in all that open space. The English couple looked upset as the uniformed man shooed them back into the corridor. And the baggage man was puffing hard.

In the other direction, at the far end of the terminal building, a high iron fence ran along the side of the airport runway. But the bars of the fence were wide enough for Benji to easily squeeze through. He threw a final glance at the baggage man and darted across the runway, eased his way through the fence, and disappeared into the traffic beyond.

III

Benji had never seen such a crowded place. The sidewalk was a moving tangle of legs and tramping feet, making it impossible to walk in a straight line. He dodged one pair of limbs after another. He trotted into the gutter now and then before he could find a few inches to slip back into the crowd.

The noise was even worse. Everybody in a car seemed to honk constantly, and in front of every store and shop people were laughing and talking and shouting at each other with their hands and arms waving in all directions. Like the man in the baggage room, their words sounded strange.

He had tried to find some food in a couple of trash cans. The first one had nothing but paper and dirt and splintered pieces of wood, and somebody shooed him out of it the second before he had a chance to get to the bottom of it. Then he had seen a bunch of people sitting at tables next to the sidewalk and his hopes had lifted a little. Most of them only had cups in front of them, or they were sipping some colored liquid out of little glasses. But he had moved among the tables until he sniffed something good, and then he sat down, his tail wagging frantically. The man had reached over and patted his head, and then the woman was smiling and taking something from her plate. But then another man was yelling from inside, rushing out at him and flapping his apron. Benji had ducked around to the other side of the table close to the woman, but the man with the apron followed him, his voice harsh and threatening. Benji knew he wasn't wanted. He hung his head and moved on.

The terrible part was all the water he saw on those tables next to the sidewalk. He had passed five or six such places, and almost every one had glasses and pitchers of water all over the place, and he had seen one of the waiters emptying glasses into the dirt under a potted plant. He stopped briefly, panting up at the man, hoping for just a few drops. But the man looked right past him, staring off at something across the street, and then returning to the café with the empty glasses.

Benji finally stopped walking. He climbed up onto a large windowsill which ran in front of a store window filled with toys. In both directions there were more buildings and more traffic and more people scurrying along the sidewalk. He looked around for a minute and finally dropped his chin in exhaustion. Back home in Silver Creek, he had always known where to find a scrap of food or a cool drink of water. But here, wherever "here" was, he only knew that he was hungry and thirsty and suddenly very lonely.

Suddenly Benji snapped to attention, his eyes riveted on a young girl with blond hair who was getting out of a taxi. An older lady also emerged and took the younger girl by the arm.

Benji barked loudly, leaped onto the sidewalk, and raced frantically down the street, determined not to lose them. He scurried past pedestrians, twisting around legs and jumping over feet. He skidded to a stop, as his last bark died in his throat.

It was not Cindy. The girl was staring down at him, blinking and backing away. The older lady standing next to her yelled at Benji and waved her arm for him to get away. Benji couldn't understand any of her words, but the meaning was clear. He turned and moved dejectedly on down the street.

It came suddenly, and Benji was so surprised he couldn't believe it for a minute. He had turned a corner and walked slowly along with the pedestrians for another block, and then they had all stopped to wait for a traffic light. When he looked up, there it was across the street—a huge fountain with plumes of water shooting high in the air and dropping into a big pond. Benji blinked, then blinked again. His dry tongue quivered. It was the most beautiful thing he had ever seen.

The light changed and he moved along with the crowd, making sure no cars were turning the corner into them. When he finally reached the curb on the other side he broke into a full run, crossing the wide strip of concrete, then the grass, then he leaped up on the ledge at the side of the pond. He took a couple of steps, balancing himself, and then he was drinking, lapping greedily at the cool, delicious liquid.

It was the best water Benji had ever tasted. Even better than the water he and Tiffany used to share from the old birdbath in the Silver

Creek park. Benji reached to lap up some more, but before his tongue could reach the water, he suddenly found himself airborne.

The two strong hands which had interrupted him belonged to a policeman who dropped him back down onto the sidewalk. The policeman spoke sternly to Benji and shook his finger in Benji's confused face. Benji took one long last look at the huge fountain. He'd only wanted a drink.

Benji moped along, dodging feet, circling around in the gutter to pass the more crowded spots. His stomach ached with hunger. He thought of Bill's café back in Silver Creek where he could always manage a handout, and he remembered his favorite trash can in the park. He had no idea where he was, but surely they must have trash cans. At the corner he turned up a narrower street and ducked into the alley that he knew must run behind the many cafés.

A hundred feet into the alley, Benji pulled up short. A huge truck had turned into the other end of the alley and seemed to be coming at full speed, its motor roaring and gears clashing, and it filled the whole width of space between the buildings. Benji edged to the side, but the truck's big tires were scraping along only inches from the brick wall. He backed away a couple steps, uncertain what to do, and then the decision was made for him. A deafening blast that sounded like it came from an onrushing railroad train suddenly vibrated through the narrow chasm, and Benji was running, charging out of the alley as if he had been shot from a cannon.

He didn't stop or even slow down when he reached the street but sped across the bigger boulevard. With the sound of the truck's horn still ringing in his ears, he headed for the hills he had seen behind the city. For the time being, he had seen enough of downtown Athens.

He was dashing across the weeded fields of what appeared to be a collection of very old stones and statues before he finally slowed down a little and took his bearings.

On the hill above him there were a lot of old buildings that looked like they had been shaken to the ground by a big earthquake. A few columns were still standing, but for the most part they looked like piles of rubble, with a lot of statues and carved slabs of marble lying around. Benji finally stopped and caught his breath while he took another look at the city below.

He was no longer so certain now about getting something to eat. This place was a lot bigger than Silver Creek, and maybe the place was so big and had so many people there just weren't any scraps left over for dogs. For a minute Benji wondered if he would ever find Mary, Paul, and Cindy. Maybe he would end up starving to death far from home.

He sighed wearily and glanced around. It was possible, he supposed, that there might be something to eat in these fields.

He finally moved on, sniffing at a few of the statues and fallen slabs of marble. They smelled old. He climbed up some fallen rocks and went over a wall, suddenly finding himself in a graveyard. That too smelled old, and some of the gravestones were so worn that the lettering was almost invisible. Benji gave them a couple of sniffs and trotted along, working his way toward the higher ground at the back. Then he suddenly stopped, sniffing the air.

Did he smell meat? It seemed like it, and the smell came from directly ahead. But it was hard to believe that there could be anything to eat in a place like this. He sniffed again and trotted on, following the scent. Then he came to an abrupt halt, his heart leaping to his throat.

There was food—a big, juicy bone about a foot and a half long, with ragged chunks of delicious-looking meat hanging from all sides of it. There was also a pair of jaws working on it, and attached to the jaws was the biggest dog Benji had ever seen in his life.

Benji was only ten feet away, and surely the animal had noticed him. But he didn't seem to be paying any attention—or at least he wasn't worried about it. He was lying in a kind of nook, with stone walls on both sides of him, and another wall against the hillside behind. One of his huge paws was resting over the bone and his eyes were half closed, not paying any attention to much of anything as he gnawed and chomped away.

Benji would have settled for one tiny corner of the bone, or even one of the good-sized chunks of meat hanging from all sides of it. But he wasn't too sure how to approach the matter. He had very little experience with unfriendly dogs, and if this dog indeed proved to be unfriendly he could probably break half his bones with one bite.

Benji glanced to the sides and to the top of the wall behind the dog. It might be safe up there. He took one more look at the bone and licked his chops. Then, keeping a wary eye on the big dog, he trotted off to the side and scampered up the hill.

He was ten or twelve feet above the animal when he reached the top of the wall behind the nook. He stood looking down at him for a minute and then gave a friendly woof and wagged his tail as if to say "Hello there." Then he wagged his tail, waiting for the dog to glance up.

Could he be deaf? More likely he just didn't care to waste his time with Benji. But what Benji lacked in size, he made up for in persistence. He tried again, making his woof a little louder this time.

There was still no answer, or any indication that the animal had heard him. Benji watched for a couple more minutes and finally moved to the edge of the wall. From there he bounded down to a ledge only three or four feet above the other dog. He barked again.

He might as well have been talking to the wall. There was no question about it—the dog was not friendly. On the other hand, he didn't appear to be mean or vicious either. So what should he do now? The dog certainly wouldn't miss one or two little scraps from his bone. But Benji could hardly jump down there and just grab them. If the big dog knew how hungry he was, and that it was a matter of life and death, would he be more cooperative? Benji glanced restlessly at the top of the wall and back to the dog. He would make one more try, he decided, and moving to the front of the ledge, he jumped down beside the dog, landing as softly as he could. Then he froze, holding his breath for a minute.

The dog was looking at him, his huge head twisted, his jaws dripping saliva, staring at Benji with a faint frown on his face. From the look the dog was giving him, Benji might have been an ant or a water bug, and he was wondering if it was worth the bother to squash him under his paw. Benji opened his mouth and panted, hesitantly wagging his tail.

The big dog didn't appear to be impressed. Without so much as a grunt or a sniff, he returned his attention to the bone.

Benji snorted. If he weren't so hungry, he would have trotted off without a backward glance. But this close the bone smelled twice as good, and his stomach was gurgling and grumbling so loud he couldn't believe the big dog didn't hear it. Benji moved cautiously forward and dropped to his belly, inching alongside the dog's huge shoulder and then to within licking distance of the bone. For a full minute he lay there, watching, listening to the rough scraping of teeth and the hissing and snorting of the big animal's breathing. Finally he stretched out as far as he could reach and gingerly touched a morsel of meat with his tongue.

The bone was gone in the same instant. Without giving Benji a glance the big dog clamped his jaws over it, pulled himself up and turned completely around, plopping his tail right into Benji's face.

It was really very rude and Benji still didn't understand as he trotted back to town. After all, he would have never hesitated a minute to share his food with a stranger. In fact, that's exactly how he and Tiffany had met several years earlier. But that time she had been the one who was starving and Benji had shared his big, juicy bone with her. Dogs must be different over here.

On the way back, Benji kept to the narrower streets, making a quick check of trash cans, pausing only briefly at a couple of doors where there was the smell of food.

There was a strong scent coming from somewhere in the town and he let his nose be his guide, moving deeper into the narrow streets of the city. The scent was growing stronger and suddenly there it was.

He had never seen anything like it back home. In Silver Creek all the markets were inside of buildings, with hissing glass doors and signs and lights. But standing before him now was a whole block full of small open booths, every one of them displaying some kind of food. There were fresh fruits and vegetables and candies and breads and cakes and cookies. In other booths there were things in boxes and cans, while others were stacked high with fish. The smells were incredible, and Benji sat down and licked his chops as he looked the place over. From where he was sitting he could see three meat booths, every one of them packed with all kinds of delicious-looking chunks of meat. Meat was hanging from hooks and resting on counters and packed on shelves and some of the pieces were absolutely huge.

Benji's gaze finally settled on the closest booth. A customer was standing in front of it holding a long string of sausages, waving it around as he talked to the man behind the counter. It looked like they were having an argument of some kind. But the sausages looked delicious, and Benji couldn't keep his eyes off of them. He moved closer, making a broad circle through the crowd, and his eyes suddenly spotted some juicy-looking scraps beneath the counter.

He glanced at the arguing men and then carefully slipped under the counter and proceeded to help himself, completely ignoring the argument, which was growing steadily in both volume and intensity.

The customer seemed to underline each loud complaint with a wild gesture which appeared all the more dramatic because of the long string of sausages held tightly in his fist.

Benji suddenly looked up. The irate customer had accidentally dropped one end of the sausage string and it was now dangling right in front of Benji's face. A veritable feast. His heart was in his throat as he watched the sausages swing back and forth. Should he or shouldn't he? Of course he shouldn't but he was rapidly getting to the point where he couldn't help himself.

As the customer pounded the table top, the long string of sausages once again began to rotate slowly in front of Benji. He couldn't resist a sniff. They must be delicious! Benji glanced up at the customer, still embroiled in the heated conversation. Benji's stomach ached and his mouth watered. The temptation was just too great.

Like a flash, Benji leaped forward, snatched the sausages, and took off at full speed, the wind tearing past his face. Behind him, he heard an angry cry. Then a second and a third man were shouting and suddenly people in front of him were turning and looking as he

sped by. The sausages were bounding along behind him, sometimes flying over his head and
whipping back, but he didn't break his stride. He
was out on a sidewalk making a sharp turn, scooting between the legs of a woman carrying a
basket, then bounding off down a long sidewalk.
The woman screamed and Benji heard the basket
crash to the ground.

If he had looked back, he would have seen a
very curious sight. The customer and the meat
man were standing in the middle of the street
laughing uproariously. It suddenly seemed quite
humorous that a little dog like Benji could throw
an entire market into such an uproar. In fact,
the more they thought about it, the funnier it
seemed. Soon, they were both bent over double
with laughter and curious pedestrians were casting puzzled glances their way.

Suddenly a small sports car screeched to a
halt right behind them. The driver looked off
down the street, trying to spot Benji among the
crowd.

"I'm almost positive it was him," he said.
His companion insisted that they must continue
looking. It was the British couple who had so
recently chased him through the airport.

The big brown dog was in the same spot,
still facing the wall and chewing on the same
bone as when Benji had left him. Benji trotted
up the slope and made himself comfortable. Then
he bit casually into the first sausage as if it was
just one more ordinary meal.

After a minute or so he heard the other dog
quit gnawing on the bone and sniff the air. Then
he saw the big head turn and the eyes glance

from the sausages to himself. Benji paid no attention. He glanced off at the scenery while he chewed, and then he bit into his second sausage.

The big dog finally rose. The huge body came up and the big head and dripping jowls were towering over Benji for a moment as the animal turned and sat down, staring at the sausages now. Benji chewed for a few more seconds and then glanced up indifferently as if noticing the dog for the first time.

There seemed to be a slight frown on the dog's face as he stretched out again and stared. Benji chewed a little longer and finally gave the animal a look of mild surprise as if suddenly realizing his friend might be interested in a bit of sausage to go along with his bone.

Benji didn't hesitate. He was a gracious, friendly, and generous dog, and unlike some others he had met, the last thing he would consider would be to hog all of the food for himself. As if it were the most ordinary thing in the world, he picked up the other end of the sausage string and dropped it on the ground very near the other dog.

The big animal stared at him for a minute as if he couldn't quite believe it and Benji smiled to himself as he went back to his end of the sausage string and resumed eating.

IV

The sun was shining brilliantly when Benji finally awakened the next morning. He stirred uneasily, his paw twitching; he was having vague
dreams about Mr. Dietrich. Then he was whim-
pering, and suddenly he was awake, blinking
across the graveyard and the ruins at the sun-
drenched city of Athens.

He yawned, stretching his mouth wide, and
looked around for his friend. There was no one
in sight. The big brown dog had slept at the
back of the nook, taking up almost the entire
width between the two side walls, and Benji had
curled up near his head. But now he was alone.

Benji moved out to the edge of the nook
where he could see into the graveyard and on the
hill behind. Other than some birds chirping and
a rooster crowing somewhere in the distance,
there was nobody around. He stretched his back
legs and dug at a flea just behind his ear. Then
he scampered up to the top of the hill to look off
toward the city again and his eyes suddenly
brightened.

Quite a distance away and moving up some
steps that led into the city, his big brown dog

friend was loping along with the air of somebody just starting out on his day's business.

Benji moved fast, running down through the
graveyard and over the wall into the ruins. He
scampered through the statues and marble slabs
and then up the steps where he had last seen the
big dog. When he reached the sidewalk he
stopped and looked quickly around.

The big dog was nowhere in sight. Shop-
keepers were opening up for the day, greeting
each other across the street; people were getting
on buses, while others read newspapers as they
walked along. Benji looked in every direction before he finally gave it up.

He was a little disappointed. He had hoped
his new friend would show him around, but the
big dog probably had more pressing affairs to
take care of. Benji took one last look, then
trotted off, glancing at faces and giving a quick
check to side streets as he started his search.

There weren't many people sitting in the
sidewalk cafés that hour, and the loitering waiters all gave him cold looks. So Benji moved on,
heading down to the open marketplace where he
had found the sausages.

Things seemed to be busier than ever.
Truckloads of food were being unloaded and tak-
en to the booths, and customers with net bags
were crowding through the aisles between the
stalls. Benji kept his distance for a few minutes,
studying the situation.

The proprietor of the meat booth with the
sausages was out in front of his stall sweeping a
pile of trash out of the aisle. Benji watched him
and then moved toward one of the other meat

booths, keeping an eye on the man with the broom. Halfway there, the man looked up and Benji trotted quickly to a position behind a stack of crated lettuce. When he peered out the man was sweeping again. Benji gave him a final glance and moved forward, enjoying the mouth-watering aromas.

The shout from behind him came like a bolt of lightning, and Benji's heart almost leaped from his chest. All Benji saw was a quick glimpse of the man from the sausage booth moving quickly toward him. The man had a grin on his face and was waving something in his hand. For a split second Benji thought it looked like a huge meaty bone, but he wasn't about to risk a closer look.

"Ela! Ela!" the man called after him. Benji took off at full speed down the edge of the crowded aisle.

He heard the man scream again, but he didn't look back. He swerved in and out of feet and around packing crates. He slipped and skidded as he tried to turn and avoid a man carrying a huge basket on his shoulder. There was a yell and a crash and Benji was suddenly in a sea of fresh oranges and the man was sprawled on his belly. He shook his fist at Benji and yelled violently.

Benji raced under the booths and up another aisle, going between legs, or around them, or any-place he could see daylight. He had an ominous feeling he was in big trouble this time, and his escape wasn't going to be so easy.

He heard more things crash to the ground behind him and more people joined the shout-ing. He skidded to a halt and reversed his direction again. Two men were coming at him, both crouched low to prevent his getting past. Then he faced another crowd, some of the people yelling at him and some reaching out as he tried to get by.

Benji turned under a booth and scampered out into what seemed like a clear escape route into the open plaza. Suddenly something flashed by in front of his face. He was stopped cold, twisting and tangled in a heavy net. He groped at it, turning and trying to run the other way, but the efforts only made things worse. He looked up.

Towering above him were two very tall policemen. One was wagging his finger at him, and the other was speaking very harshly. Benji hung his head for a minute and then gave the man a panting smile, hoping for a similar response. The man only frowned and didn't lift the net.

The two policemen didn't seem to understand or put much trust in the friendly barks and tail wagging Benji gave them. They kept him tightly closed in the net until a van showed up. Then a uniformed man transferred him to a cage in the back of the van and he was driven away. Ten minutes later a man looked closely at his collar and made some notes, and he was placed in a big cage with a dozen other dogs barking and yelping all around him.

A man came with a bowl of water and put it in the cage. Benji enjoyed the drink, but wished for a little food to go with it. He joined in the barking for a while. Then he gave it up and put his head on the ground, watching the door at the back of the building. Things looked bad, he reflected. Now he was going to find out what they did with homeless dogs in Greece.

Mary held the telephone receiver down for a moment and then picked it up and dialed for the tenth time in the last half hour. She groaned inwardly as the voice answered in Greek.

"Do you happen to speak English?" she asked, speaking slowly and distinctly.

There was a silence at the other end, then the halting voice said, "One minutes, if you pliss."

Less than half of the places she had called were able to find anyone who could speak to her in English, and she'd had to hang up not knowing if they had Benji or not.

"Maybe we just ought to get in a taxicab and ride around looking for him," Paul said now as Mary waited.

"You might be right, Paul. But there are only three more dog pounds listed in the book. We can ..."

She turned quickly back to the phone as she heard someone pick up the receiver at the other end.

"May I help you, madam? I speak English."

Mary breathed a sigh of relief. "Yes . . . that is, I hope you can help us. You see, we're American tourists, and we brought two dogs to Greece, and when we transferred flights to go to Crete one of the dogs ..."

"Is the dog's name Benji, madam?"

Mary almost dropped the phone. *"Yes,"* she cried. "Do you have him there? Do you know where he is? Is he all right?"

"He's fine. He was brought in about twenty minutes ago."

Paul and Cindy were both hovering over her now, their eyes shining. "They've found him," Mary quickly told them.

"We'll be over to get him right away," she told the man. "Are you sure he's all right?"

"Quite sure, madam. Don't worry."

"Oh, thank you so much. I'll . . . oh, dear . . . we'll be right over. Goodbye. And thank you."

Benji watched indifferently as the man came out of the office and walked along between the cages. Then he jumped quickly to his feet and wagged his tail as the man smiled at him and unfastened the clasp on his cage.

"Well, Benji, you're going home." Benji barked, jumped up excitedly, and turned a quick circle as he headed toward the office with the man. When the door was opened he bolted through and then skidded to a stop.

"Well, hello, Benji. How are you, old chap?" It was the English couple!

It was a pleasant-looking place with deep carpets and nice furniture. A stairway at the side seemed to lead up to a second floor and there was a kitchen off to the other side.

"Well, Benji," the man said, smiling down at him, "you seem to be quite a prize. I quite imagine you are the most valuable dog in all of Greece right now."

Benji gave the tall Britisher a puzzled look and began sniffing his way around the room.

"Come over here, Benji," the woman said from the couch. "Let's have a look at you."

Benji moved reluctantly to the couch and let the woman lift him to her lap. She scratched his back for a minute and then unfastened his collar.

"What on earth are you doing?" the man asked. He was across the room at a small bar, mixing drinks.

The woman squinted closely at Benji's collar, then pulled a magnifying glass from a drawer. "I am looking, darling. Of course, it would help if I knew what I was looking for."

The man laughed. "Sometimes you surprise me, Elizabeth. As pretty as you are, I never suspected you might also be intelligent."

"Why, thank you, Ronald."

"Did you really take that as a compliment? In that case, I'll take it back." The man brought a drink to the woman and smiled. "However, I will grant that your suggestion to check the dog pounds was unusually brilliant."

"Hmph. And I hope you realize that I won't be the only one to think of it." She put Benji's collar back on. "And with all the interest in Benji here, I suspect we'll soon be having visitors."

"I'm sure of it. It appears that our hideaway scientist has suddenly become a very important man."

"And very valuable." The woman smiled as she took a sip of her drink. "Let's just hope we get our share of the profits."

Benji felt his ear being lifted. The woman was peering into it with a magnifying glass, pulling the ear from one side to the other.

"Do you see anything?"

"Not a thing." Benji felt the ear drop and the woman frowned at him. "Benji, why can't you talk and give us a hint? You didn't swallow it, did you?"

Benji put his head down on her lap and looked off at the man. He still couldn't figure out if the two of them were friends. By the way they acted, they didn't seem to intend him any harm.

Benji closed his eyes, enjoying the back rub, then he jerked his head up as the doorbell suddenly rang.

The man smiled faintly and glanced at the door. "I say, it appears to be starting already." He put his drink on the table and quickly picked up Benji. "I'll take Mr. Popular upstairs and we'll make a few photographs. All right, Benji?" He glanced at the woman as he headed for the stairs. "Give me a moment to prepare, darling. Then get rid of them."

Benji glanced at the door, but it was quickly out of sight as they went up the stairs and into a bedroom. The man shut the door and put Benji down, hurrying off to a dresser. He brought out a fancy-looking camera and studied it for a minute. Then he crossed to a couch under a window. He pushed the window open wide and leaned out, the camera lifted to his eye.

"I'm sorry, they must be mistaken," the woman's voice echoed clearly up from the porch below. "We haven't been to the dog pound, and we don't have a dog."

"This is your name and address, isn't it?" a man's voice questioned. "Maybe your husband picked up the dog." The voice was deep and a little harsh. Benji didn't recognize it at all.

"No, I'm afraid that is impossible," the woman answered. "You see, my husband hates dogs."

Ronald smiled when he heard that. "Don't you believe it, Benji," he said softly. "Some of my best friends are dogs."

Benji stared at the man and cocked his head, listening to the voices downstairs again.

"I see," the man at the door was saying. "Well, thank you very much."

The door clicked shut and Benji moved across the room and jumped up on the couch next to the Englishman.

"Now," the man said, squinting into his camera, "just turn around, please, so I can have a look at your face."

Out the window, Benji could see the man as he walked down the steps and opened the door of a station wagon. He was wearing an Olympic Airways uniform, and his car had an airline insignia on the door.

The man glanced back at the apartment house and the camera clicked again.

"Ahhh," the Englishman said, "thank you very much." It was a perfect picture. The man was a thick-necked Greek with cold dark eyes. It was Stelios.

"What do you think?" said the Englishman, dropping back on the couch. "Was the gentleman really from Olympic Airways?" He smiled and put a cover over the lens of the camera. "I wouldn't want to bet on it. But we have him nicely recorded."

The man put the camera on the dresser and Benji trotted alongside as he went to the door.

"No, no. I'm afraid you'll have to stay

here, Benji." The man smiled and opened the door only wide enough to squeeze through.

Benji watched it shut and then scratched at the bottom and barked. Why did he have to stay in the room? He scratched again and gave a loud bark.

The door opened, but only a few inches, with the man blocking Benji's escape. "Here, here," he said, "we'll have none of that."

Benji barked again.

"No," the man said. He reached down, turned him around, and gave him a whack on the rear. "Now you might just as well make yourself comfortable, because this is going to be your home for a while."

Benji watched the door close again.

Locked in the room, there was nothing he could do. Until somebody opened the door, or took him out for a walk, he might as well make the best of it. He glanced, sniffed a couple of things and finally jumped back on the couch. He found a soft pillow in the corner and curled up, gazing emptily down at the carpet. He finally sighed and closed his eyes.

As he drifted off to sleep he heard a car door slam, and moments later the doorbell rang.

"Yes?" the Englishwoman's voice said.

"How do you do?" It was a woman's voice. "I'm here about the dog you picked up at the pound today."

Benji's eyes popped open. Was he dreaming, or had he heard a familiar voice? No, he wasn't dreaming. It was Mary. Or at least it sounded like Mary. He jumped onto the windowsill and listened closely.

"I'm sorry," the Englishwoman was saying irritably. "Somebody seems to have made a stupid mistake, and I wish whoever it was would correct it."

Benji stretched out the window, straining to see below, but the porch roof and an awning made it impossible to see the apartment door.

"You're the second person to ask about this," the Englishwoman said, "but we do not have a dog. We have never had a dog, and we did not pick up a dog at the pound today."

Benji looked toward the street where a huge truck was making a loud racket as it climbed slowly up the hill. He could hardly hear the voices anymore.

". . . and my husband hates dogs, so you see . . ."

Benji jumped from the couch and ran to the door, scratching at it again. He barked a few times, but the noise of the truck was growing so loud he was certain no one could hear him. He raced back to the couch and bounded up with his front paws on the windowsill. Then his heart jumped and he almost tumbled out the window as he barked as loud and urgently as he could.

It was Mary! She was walking across the street to a taxi and the driver was holding the door open for her. Benji yelped frantically, his back feet on top of the couch and his front on the windowsill.

He saw the cab door shut and then the big truck was passing, the roar of its big diesel motor drowning out every other sound. But Benji continued barking, leaning far out the window as the taxi pulled out a little and the driver waited for the truck to go by. He barked and barked, putting all the urgency and desperation he could into his voice.

"Benji!" a voice behind him cried.

Benji looked back, almost losing his balance as he turned. Ronald, the Englishman, was just inside the door, moving toward him. He smiled uneasily and came closer. "Now, Benji, just take it easy."

Benji looked out at the street again. The taxi was pulling away from the curb, starting to move slowly up the hill. Benji barked again and again, hoping by some miracle Mary might look out the back window.

"Don't be afraid, Benji," the man behind him said as he came closer, "I'll get you down. Just don't move. That's a good boy."

Benji looked from the cab to the man and back at the cab again. It was halfway to the corner now and behind him the man was getting close. He looked down at the sloped awning eight feet below and hesitated.

"Benji!" the man cried out and lunged for him. Benji jumped.

The canvas awning sagged enough that it was like a net breaking his fall. But the slope was steep and Benji skidded and tumbled, unable to get his footing after he hit. Then he was over the edge, his legs groping at empty air for a minute before he crashed into a heavy shrub.

"Benji!" the Englishman shouted from the window, but Benji didn't bother looking back. He squirmed out of the shrub and was running at full speed when he hit the ground and dashed into the street.

Suddenly, there was a loud screech of tires

and Benji swerved, just missing the front wheel of a small red sports car being driven recklessly by a distinguished-looking man in a dark suit. It was Chandler Dietrich. Benji bolted past the car and kept going, his legs flying and his feet hardly touching the pavement as he raced for the corner at the top of the hill.

Dietrich immediately threw the car into reverse, the gears grinding loudly. Before he could whip the car around he found himself in the middle of three other cars, all trying to go the other direction. He groaned and beat his fist against the dash.

When Benji rounded the corner he could see the taxi picking up speed a block ahead of him. He ran faster, his eyes fixed on the back of the car, his heart pounding wildly.

The taxi was growing smaller and smaller, finally disappearing in the traffic as it sailed along the boulevard. Benji slowed to a trot and finally stopped.

He gazed forlornly at the street for a while and then moved to the sidewalk. He sat down and panted, watching the pedestrians go by.

V

At the end of the alley Benji stopped and surveyed the big cross street. Then he frowned, staring at a taxi waiting for a signal. He could just see the head of someone in the back seat. Could it be Mary? He moved quickly along the sidewalk. He ducked between two parked cars and got up on his hind legs, trying desperately to see into the back seat of the taxi.

The woman in the taxi looked at him through the window and blinked. It was not Mary. The cab moved on, pulling away with the rest of the traffic.

Benji saw a great deal of Athens that he hadn't seen before. There were several large parks in front of huge buildings, and he picked up a few of the tidbits that people were feeding to pigeons. But the people didn't seem to like the idea of his scaring the birds and taking their food, so he trotted on, watching the taxis and the people walking along the streets.

He had just rounded a corner and was enjoying the smells of a huge outdoor flower shop when he almost ran squarely into the two policemen. They were standing by the curb quietly talking and laughing. Benji made a sharp turn and ducked behind a big flowerpot. He stayed there for five minutes before he finally crept out and headed the other way, moving as unobtrusively as possible. He was glancing back to make certain the two men weren't following him when he suddenly banged into another pair of legs. He froze for an instant as he looked up. The legs belonged to a third policeman.

The man smiled and said something to him and then reached down as if to pet him. But since Benji's recent experiences with policemen had been none too pleasant, he didn't take any chances. Before the policeman's hand was anywhere close, Benji ducked and took off at full speed, tearing around the corner and disappearing up the first alley he came to.

As Benji rounded the corner he found himself approaching a huge building with hundreds of windows. But it was not the building which grabbed Benji's attention. It was the constant flow of taxis loading and unloading by the front door. He stopped and took a closer look as three people emerged from the taxi nearest the door.

It was them! Benji was sure of it this time. He had a clear glimpse of Cindy carrying Tiffany, and then Paul and Mary following her through the revolving doors.

Benji moved quickly through the parked cars and watched for a break in traffic. Then he bolted across and raced at full speed toward the hotel door.

He didn't notice the man leaning into the window of the cab giving something to the driver until the man turned toward the hotel entrance. Both Benji and the man came to an abrupt stop.

It was Dietrich.

He glanced at the revolving door through which Mary, Paul, and Cindy had just disappeared. Then an ever-so-slight smile spread across his lips and he began moving toward Benji. Benji looked nervously at the revolving door, then back to Dietrich.

"Come on, Benji," he said. He bent forward a little, holding his hand out. "Come on, boy, I'm not going to hurt you."

Benji remembered his first experience with Chandler Dietrich and moved a few steps back glancing at the door again. He barked at the man, trying to show he was not interested in his friendship. But Dietrich kept coming, moving a little faster now. Benji turned and trotted four or five steps away and looked back. Then Dietrich lunged for him and Benji was at the corner and across the street in seconds.

Dietrich stopped short of the corner and stood staring at Benji, a thoughtful look on his face. He smiled faintly and moved back toward the hotel door.

Benji heard the clank of a garbage can being opened. He stopped and peered up a long dark alley.

A round-faced man wearing an apron was singing and emptying smaller buckets of garbage into the big can. Benji stood still, watching quietly. Then the man saw him. He smiled and said something that sounded friendly, but Benji didn't move.

The man put the lid back on the can. Then he knelt down and smiled again, this time holding his hand out as he spoke. Benji still didn't move, although the man's smile was reassuring.

Benji's stomach was starting to twist and grumble again.

Finally, he began to move slowly, glancing behind him once or twice, ready to run if he had to. As Benji got closer, the man suddenly rose and took a step forward. Benji quickly turned and retreated, watching the man carefully.

The man seemed to understand. He squatted down and held his hand out again, showing Benji an open palm. His voice sounded sympathetic and he spoke quietly.

Benji still wasn't too sure. He tensed as the man rose again. This time the man opened the big garbage can and came out with a tasty looking scrap of meat. He laughed and squatted again, holding it out to Benji.

This was more like it. Benji wagged his tail and moved cautiously forward. He stopped a few inches short of the meat and sniffed it. Then he couldn't resist; he stepped forward and took it, gulping it down.

The man talked quietly as he patted Benji's head. Benji wagged his tail and then hesitated as the man rose and opened the screen door at the back of the building. But the smells coming from inside were so delicious that Benji gave in easily. He wagged his tail and moved inside, glancing cautiously around.

It was a big kitchen, apparently at the back of a restaurant. Benji relaxed a little and gave the man a panting smile as he watched him get a big bowl from a cupboard. The man laughed and talked and put a handful of meat scraps in the bowl. Then he filled another bowl with water and placed them both on the floor.

It seemed like the best meal Benji had ever

had and when he finished the first bowl the man filled it up again. Then he had a good drink of water.

The man wasn't watching him anymore. He was standing at a big stove, pouring something from one huge pot into another and stirring the whole thing. Benji sniffed around the kitchen a little and finally settled down in a corner.

The man smiled at him a couple times, but made no move to turn Benji out. That was fine with Benji. For the present he wanted nothing more than a safe, warm place to catch up on his sleep, and it looked like he had found it. He took a last look around and settled his head comfortably on the floor, closing his eyes with a weary sigh.

When Benji appeared to be comfortably asleep, the restaurant owner smiled pleasantly at him and moved to the wall phone in the corner of the kitchen.

"Ο σκίλος είωαί εδῶ," he said in Greek. He hung up the phone and walked through the door to the restaurant.

Benji looked up sharply as he heard the door swing shut. He glanced around the kitchen assuring himself that he was alone, and closed his eyes again. He thought dreamily about Mary and Paul and Cindy and imagined himself sitting with them on a lazy afternoon in Silver Creek. Then Benji slept soundly.

Benji lifted his head and blinked around. He heard a loud snarl. He stared at the dirty window above his head and instantly jumped to his feet.

A huge, black, vicious-looking dog was looking straight at Benji, his pointed teeth snapping against the window. And behind him, squinting and shading his eyes, was Chandler Dietrich.

The screen door creaked open and clicked softly shut again and there was the rustle of footsteps.

"I know you're in here, Benji boy," Dietrich said softly.

Dietrich paused to let his eyes adjust to the dimly lit room. He looked down to the spot where Benji had been sitting, but there was only an empty bowl. "Come on, Benji. You don't want me to bring that Doberman in here, do you?"

Dietrich walked toward the cupboard. His arm brushed against a broom and it clattered to the floor.

"Come on, Benji. Be a good boy."

He threw open the closet door and quickly slammed it shut. "Why are you afraid of me, Benji? I've never hurt you. Don't you want to see your friends again?"

He paused again. There was no sign of Benji. "Come on Benji. Here, Benji," the voice continued in its soft singsong.

Dietrich cast a puzzled look around the room, then knelt to open the last door of the cupboard.

"Come on, Ben—!"

Like a gunshot, Benji sprang forward, crashing into Dietrich's face and knocking him backward.

Dietrich let out a cry and was on his back as Benji scampered over his legs, going directly for the screen door. Benji lifted his front paws in mid-flight and the door sprang open; he plummeted through it.

If the Doberman had been expecting him Benji probably wouldn't have had a chance to get by. The big black dog was tied to a post just outside the door, and when Benji came flying out his head brushed by just under the Doberman's chin. By the time the big black animal had recovered from the surprise, Benji was halfway down the alley and taking the corner at full speed.

Benji ran for three blocks before he finally slowed down and took a glance behind. He could see no one following him, but he kept moving anyway.

Whenever there was a break in traffic he crossed the street, and then crossed again, hoping to leave the vicious black dog behind him for good.

It was getting dark now, and Benji finally headed back toward the ruins. It had been a long day and he couldn't keep moving forever.

The place looked as dark and lonely as ever. Moving through the ruins he circled a few statues and took a roundabout route getting to the wall and going up through the graveyard.

His friend, the big brown dog, wasn't there. An old, well-chewed bone lay in the corner of the nook. Benji sniffed at it, and then just to make sure about things he climbed up on the hill behind the nook and looked over the graveyard and the ruins below. There seemed to be nobody around, particularly no giant black dogs.

Benji went back down to the nook and made himself comfortable, his eyes fixed absently on the graveyard below. He thought of little Tiffany and wished they had never left Silver Creek. He finally sighed and gazed dully across the graveyard for a few minutes. Then he was fast asleep.

Benji's eyes popped open, and he froze, not daring to move. He was certain he had heard something. He came cautiously to his feet, watching, scanning the ruins beyond the wall. All the dark shapes and shadows now looked ominous, like people and dogs and animals holding themselves still, waiting for him to look the other way.

The graveyard looked even more frightening. Benji hadn't thought much about it when he walked through there in the daylight. But now he was certain he could see thin shadows moving around and hovering over gravestones. He stared, moving his gaze slowly across the dark shapes. Then his heart leaped into his throat and he jumped to the side as a small rock clattered to the ground just beside him.

He froze in his tracks and looked up. High on the wall, the silhouette of a big dog was clearly outlined against the sky and he could see the pale glint of white teeth. Benji looked quickly around, searching for Dietrich, but he could see no other distinct shadows.

Benji backed slowly, almost tiptoeing into a corner of the nook, just under the ledge. More gravel suddenly poured down from above and he tightened himself closer against the wall, pulling his tail close to his side.

There was a heavy *thunk* on the ledge above him. Then he saw the shape land on the ground just beside him. His muscles went limp with relief.

It was his friend. The big brown dog was turning slowly around, looking things over, giving the old bone a sniff. Benji panted and barked softly, saying hello, and stretched out on his stomach.

The dog swung his head over and nudged Benji, giving his face a half lick. He circled a couple of times and made himself comfortable.

Then Benji went back to sleep feeling much more secure with his friend at his side.

VI

Benji watched the hotel most of the morning. He stayed across the street for awhile, moving occasionally, keeping out of sight behind lampposts and telephone poles. He saw no one who looked like Mary, Paul, or Cindy, and nobody brought Tiffany out for a walk.

He considered the idea of marching up to the revolving door and just trotting inside. But there was a uniformed doorman constantly moving back and forth helping people out of cabs and calling other cabs for people coming out of the hotel. He waited, hoping the man would leave for a while. When he finally did, the man who took his place looked meaner than the first one.

Benji finally crossed the street. A narrow stretch of grass with bushes behind it ran along the front of the hotel, and he could lie near the bushes, half hidden from most of the people walking by. He spent another hour there, taking time out only to trot four blocks down the street to a big fountain and have himself a drink. When he got back things looked the same. He finally rose and trotted a little closer to the door, quickly dropping to the ground when the doorman looked in his direction.

He waited as the man opened the cab doors and whistled for empty cabs to stop. Then, staying low to the ground, he scooched up another few feet. The man glanced in his direction, but didn't seem particularly interested.

Benji watched as a taxi with five people and a lot of suitcases stopped. The doorman opened the cab doors and then whistled for some bellhops to help with the luggage. They were all gathered around as the doorman shouted instructions. Benji trotted casually forward.

An empty section of the revolving door was coming slowly around. Benji watched carefully as a woman and two men pushed their way through the door, sending it into a rapid spin. They made it look so simple. Benji cocked his head, made one false start, then headed straight for the door.

"Aaiieee!" someone shouted behind him. Benji skidded to a stop.

The doorman frowned, stomped his foot loudly against the marble pavement, and started toward Benji.

Benji trotted a few steps and looked back. But the man was still watching him. He shouted again, suddenly moving quickly forward. Benji turned and ran.

As Benji sniffed at the screen door and peered inside the kitchen seemed to be empty. He barked and waited, then barked again. No one came.

The door was slightly ajar and Benji studied

it for a minute. He scratched at it, but it didn't budge. He crawled close to it on his stomach, working at it with his nose. It finally opened enough to get a paw inside, and he squeezed through.

The cupboards were all closed again and three or four big pots were simmering on the stove. Benji tried the swinging door, scratching at it, then rising and pushing with all his weight. It opened just enough for Benji to squeeze through.

The inside part of the restaurant was also empty. The tables were all set with napkins and silver, but there were no customers. Benji trotted across the room and stopped at the front door. There were tables everywhere . . . on the sidewalks, across the street, even *in* the street itself. But they were all empty. All except one.

Benji's tail started wagging. It was his friend with the apron who had fed him the day before, sitting at a table directly across the street. He was talking to a second man, a large Greek with black hair and cold dark eyes. Benji didn't seem to remember him, maybe because the last time he had seen him, the man had been in an airlines uniform. It was Stelios.

Benji watched for a break in traffic, then trotted across to the other curb, wagging his tail as he approached the table.

They didn't see him. The man with the apron was leaning across the table, talking in a low voice. The dark Greek was nodding and gazing off in the other direction, his eyes half closed. Benji sat down and barked.

Suddenly he was off the ground, his bark choked off by the tight grip around his chest.

It was Dietrich. Benji squirmed and yelped, trying to push and scratch his paws, but the man was squeezing the breath out of him.

"Don't get up, gentlemen," Dietrich said, "just stay put."

The two men at the table stared at Dietrich, who was pointing a black pistol at them. Stelios looked tense, his hands resting near the edge of the table as if he was ready to jump. "You know your identity is no longer a secret," Stelios said coldly. "Give me the dog and I'll try to see that you come out of this alive."

"That is very considerate of you," Dietrich answered, "but I'll take care of that myself." He was edging toward the street now, glancing back at the traffic.

"You're going to be very sorry, my friend!"

There were no cars coming now and Dietrich laughed. "Good day, gentlemen." And he backed across the street with Benji. When he reached the curb he turned and ran into the café.

Before he reached the kitchen door he turned sharply between the tables and ducked behind a curtained partition that hid a row of coffeepots. Then Benji felt the man's hand suddenly grip his mouth, clamping it shut.

Through the partition Benji could see the other two men come jogging across the street. They separated as they reached the curb. The man with the apron disappeared around the side of the building as Stelios moved cautiously to the door and peered in. Benji felt Dietrich's hand tighten painfully around his throat.

Benji watched, struggling to get some air. Stelios came quickly through the door, glancing around the empty tables. As he crossed to the kitchen door Dietrich squeezed himself and Benji tight around the wall. Stelios didn't look around. He stood at the kitchen door for a minute, listening. Then he pushed it open and disappeared. In the alley, Benji heard a noise that caused him to freeze; it was the vicious barking of Dietrich's huge dog.

Benji heard a chuckle from Dietrich as he headed for the door. His hand was still tight around Benji's nose. When they were out on the sidewalk and striding up the street, Benji struggled again, trying to get air.

"Sorry, Benji," Dietrich said and eased his grip a little. "Just a bit farther."

Dietrich walked a little slower now, trying not to attract attention. He turned a corner and headed toward the end of the alley.

Dietrich's red sports car was parked at a nearby curb. He shifted Benji to the other arm and groped in his pocket for the keys. Suddenly, there was a low snarling sound from behind him and Dietrich spun around. The huge black Doberman was galloping toward him at a terrifying speed, his eyes fixed on Benji.

"No, it's OK!" shouted Dietrich.

The angry red eyes and the glistening teeth kept coming. Benji struggled, trying to spring away from Dietrich.

"Stay!" Dietrich commanded. There was a note of fear in his voice as he backed away, edging along the side of the car. "*Stay!*" he shouted again.

The dog ignored him. His gaze was locked on Benji and he came even faster, then he leaped through the air. Benji struggled free as Dietrich threw up his arms to protect his face and they all crashed down onto the sidewalk.

Dietrich landed on his back and the Doberman skidded past, his legs splayed out in all directions. Benji tumbled over, miraculously landing on his feet and in a flash he was running at full speed back down the alley.

Benji had a head start but he knew he was in great danger. He threw a quick glance behind him as he rounded the first corner. The Doberman was coming, galloping along the parked cars and beginning to pick up speed. Benji crossed another street and headed into an alley.

He could hear the yelps and snarls coming closer, and as he rounded the next corner Benji skidded, almost losing his footing as he made a second sharp turn down three steps which led to a closed door. He quickly fell against the door, hiding himself below the narrow street.

A second later the Doberman flashed by. Benji leaped back to the street level and took off in the opposite direction.

He had picked up another head start but he knew it wouldn't last long. Benji sped on, beginning to feel a little tired. He eased his pace a notch, panting, trying to recover some breath. Then he suddenly slid to a stop as he passed a high board fence.

There was a small hole at the bottom of the fence. He turned and saw the Doberman bearing down on him. He lowered his head and in a flash was through the hole and under the fence.

The Doberman's snout came through the hole. The big animal snarled and bared his teeth and shoved his head through the hole. But that

was as far as he could get. He backed away and
the sharp teeth sank into the wood.

Benji paused at the end of the alley to glance
back over his shoulder. He saw the Doberman's
head and front paws appear at the top of the
fence. He could hear the animal scratching desperately with the claws of his back feet and then
he dropped from sight again. Benji stared as the
Doberman tried again, straining every muscle in
his black, sleek body. This time he made it.

Benji ran as fast as his tired legs would
carry him through the ruins and finally paused
at the top of the hill and looked back. His heart
sank as he saw the big Doberman bounding down
the steps into the ruins.

He took a different route through the ceme-
tery, climbing the hill on the side of his hideout.
When he reached the top of the wall, just above
the nook, he peered down hoping to see his old
friend stretched out on the ground.

The nook was empty. And down in the ceme-
tery the Doberman was coming, following the
same route Benji had taken. Benji was panting,
ready to collapse from exhaustion. He watched
the big animal for a minute; then he jumped
down to the ledge and dropped to the floor of the
nook. He slid under the ledge and looked up,
waiting for the inevitable. He knew he could not
run anymore.

A minute later the Doberman appeared. He
was standing high on the wall above, panting
easily as he looked down. He took his time now,
knowing Benji was trapped. He bounded easily
down to the ledge and then to the floor, flashing
his ugly teeth at Benji.

Then suddenly he stiffened. His head jerked to one side and his look of satisfied anticipation melted into one of fear. For there, under the ledge with Benji, was the big brown dog. The *very big* brown dog. He pulled himself up and began to move toward the Doberman, teeth bared, totally confident. The Doberman blinked and backed away until his rear bumped the wall behind him. Then, in a desperate leap, he went up the ledge and over the wall.

The big brown dog turned to look at his small frightened little friend, but by now Benji was far away, running . . . running through the narrow streets of Athens.

VII

Benji quietly circled around the two rosebushes, looking to see if the doorman was watching. Then he moved along more cautiously, crawling on his belly until he was within twenty feet of the door. He inched up the steps, pausing now and then to lift his head just high enough to look the situation over.

He saw several people going in and out, and then his ears popped up as he saw a door open off to the side. Two bellboys were coming through, pushing a big empty cart. Once they were out, the door swung shut and they rolled the cart off the curb.

The boys took suitcases from the roof of a big airport limousine and stacked them on the cart. A lot of people were getting out of the car and looking the hotel over while they moved toward the door. Benji watched and then looked at the bellboys again.

The cart was almost full now. One of the boys struggled to pull the last suitcase from the roof and finally wedged it into the top of the load. The doorman was bent forward talking to the driver of the limousine, and Benji glanced quickly at the revolving door. It was crowded

with people waiting their turns to go through.
He sighed and looked at the cart again.

It was coming toward the door now, one of
the boys pulling and the other pushing from behind. Benji watched carefully. The bags were
stacked high above the bellboys' heads. Benji
glanced at the door and then off toward the
limousine. The doorman was still bent forward
talking to the driver. Suddenly Benji lifted his
head. He scooched forward a little, never taking
his eyes from the baggage cart.

The cart was about to pass within a few feet
of him. Impulsively, Benji trotted across and fell
easily into step with the cart. He walked as close
to the center of the cart as he could, completely
hidden from the doorman on the other side. The
boy in front opened the door as they creaked
slowly forward. Benji held his breath as they
moved inside.

He passed a large plant, then a row of soft
chairs with two or three people sitting in them.
A man looked at him and smiled and then went
back to reading his newspaper. Then the cart
stopped and Benji stopped with it.

One of the bellboys walked over to the desk
while the other one leaned on the luggage, staring out at nothing. Benji drew his head back and
twisted himself around to face the other way.
He could see several elevators and a glass door
leading to a coffee shop. No sign of Mary, Paul,
or Cindy. He glanced up and blinked.

The bellboy was staring down at him and
frowning as if he couldn't believe his eyes.
Then he cried out and made a lunge for Benji.

The floor was slippery, but Benji got his feet
going just in time. The boy half stumbled and

then lit out after him. Benji kept going, racing across the slick marble floor. There were two bellboys chasing him now, both of them yelling.

Benji's feet hardly touched the ground as he headed for the broad stairway which descended steeply to the coffee shop. Benji took the stairs much quicker than the two bellboys, who stumbled down behind him.

Suddenly Benji heard a familiar voice cry out and his head whipped sharply around.

"Benji!"

It was Cindy, standing just outside the coffee shop, still holding the door open. "Mary! Paul! Benji is here!" she shouted behind her.

Benji couldn't recall ever having moved so fast. He wasn't too sure if he even took any steps. It seemed like he made one giant leap and flew twenty feet across the floor into Cindy's arms.

And then Paul and Mary were coming through the door and Benji was licking Cindy's face and then Paul's and then Mary's as they all crowded around him.

For a few minutes he didn't even notice the bellboys standing in the lobby watching. Mary, Paul, and Cindy were all grinning and talking at once, all of them hugging him and getting their faces licked. Then Mary's face suddenly became very serious and she turned to face the perspiring spectators.

"Thank you very much," she said as if she were dismissing servants. "You may go now."

Tiffany had never looked more beautiful. She was freshly groomed, every hair meticulously in place. Benji couldn't resist a happy bark as he trotted across the hotel room. He gave her nose a gentle nudge and licked her face affectionately.

Cindy laughed and Mary wondered aloud how Benji had ever managed to find *them* when they had looked all over Athens without finding *him*. Mary walked over to close the open door which led to the hall when she stopped abruptly and stepped back from the door.

A man with a heavy jacket was standing in front of her. Benji came instantly to his feet when he got a look at him. It was Stelios.

"Yes?" Mary said, surprised.

The man didn't answer immediately. He moved a couple of feet into the room and his narrowed eyes quickly found Benji. Then he looked at Cindy and Mary and glanced suspiciously at the bathroom door.

"I need to borrow your dog for a few days," he said gruffly. "The brown one on the couch there."

It was neither a question nor a polite request. With his grim face and the cold hard eyes the man looked like he was accustomed to issuing orders and having them obeyed without question.

Paul and Cindy flashed a puzzled look at Mary. "I beg your pardon," she said.

"The dog," the man said. "I need to borrow him for a few days."

Mary blinked incredulously at him. "I don't understand. Who are you, and what are you talking about?"

The man looked slightly uneasy, as if he was suddenly aware that his rough manner had startled everybody. He glanced at Benji again and shook his head. "Believe me, it's at least partly for the dog's own safety, lady. He'll be returned unharmed in a day or two."

"I still don't know what you are talking about," Mary said. She gave the man a hard stare.

"All right, lady . . ." The man reached for his back pocket.

Several things happened at that moment. Chandler Dietrich suddenly appeared behind the man and Benji barked as quickly as he saw him. Mary noticed him too, and with a look of relief she said, "Oh, Chandler, I'm . . ."

At that moment the Greek whirled around, and Dietrich struck him hard with the butt of his pistol.

"Chandler!" Mary cried out as the man crashed to the floor.

Benji was barking; partly at Dietrich and partly from surprise. He sat very close to Cindy, looking from Dietrich to the man on the floor.

Paul moved toward Mary and she reached protectively as she gaped at Dietrich. "Chandler, why on earth did you do a thing like that?! What in heaven's name is going on?"

"It's all right, Mary," Dietrich said. He took a quick look at the fallen man and moved across the room. "Now don't worry. Everything's going to be all right, I promise." He put his pistol in Mary's hand. "Just keep this pointed toward him and call the police. OK?"

Mary gaped at the pistol and back at Dietrich. "It most certainly is not OK! I don't like guns, and I want to know what this is all about, Chandler!"

Dietrich had moved back to the man and was going through his pockets. "I can't say right now." He found a wallet and stood up as he glanced through the contents. "I'm sorry, Mary," he said as he stuck the wallet in his jacket pocket. "I just can't tell you anything about it right now. Please trust me."

"Trust you for what?"

Dietrich hesitated. "It has to do with Benji. I have to take him for a couple of days."

"Why?" Cindy asked. "What's he done?"

"He hasn't done anything, Cindy, and I'll take good care of him. I promise."

"If he hasn't done anything, why do you want to take him?" Paul asked.

"And why did that man want to take him?" Mary added.

Dietrich chewed his lip for a minute and then paced across the room to the window. "Mary," he finally said, "I work for the United States government, and Benji is the key to a very important situation. It's my fault he's involved in all this, and I'm sorry. I had no idea it would become this complicated." He shrugged. "But it has, and I'm afraid that's all I can say."

"Is Benji a spy?" Paul asked.

Dietrich gave a short laugh. "No, he's not a spy, Paul. But he is very important to the United States government right now."

"Hey, that's neat. You mean he'll be famous?"

"It is not neat," Cindy said.

Benji cocked his head, looking from one to the other.

"No, you're right, Cindy," Dietrich said. "It's not neat. But he is important. And necessary. OK?"

"What did he do?" Cindy asked, still not convinced. "Why is he important?"

Dietrich took a deep breath and sighed. "Honey, I just can't tell you right now. I'll explain the whole thing when I bring him back. OK?"

Paul and Mary looked doubtful, but Dietrich smiled at Cindy and waited for an answer. She looked glumly at Benji and finally nodded.

"Good girl," Dietrich said. "And I'm sorry, Mary."

"That's OK—I guess. Just take good care of him."

"I will. Now hurry and call the police. And if the man wakes up be sure to keep the gun on him."

"But I don't know anything about guns," Mary protested.

"All you have to know is to keep it pointed at him. He won't bother you."

Benji didn't like any part of what was going on. He watched as Dietrich came toward him.

Benji tried to turn away, but Dietrich suddenly had him by the chest and lifted him. "I think you'll all be very proud of him," he said as he carried Benji to the door. "And I'll see you in a few days."

"Poor Benji," Cindy said as the door closed.

Paul smiled and shook his head as Mary picked up the phone again. "How about that? Benji's a spy."

"He is not a spy," Cindy protested.

"I'll bet that guy's a spy too," Paul said nodding at the man on the floor. Then he caught his breath. The man's hand was moving to his head and he was trying to pull himself up. "Mary?" cried Cindy and Paul in unison.

Mary looked and quickly clamped the phone between her shoulder and chin, holding the pistol out with both hands.

"Stay exactly where you are," she said striving to keep her voice under control. "Paul and Cindy, go around behind the bed."

The man was up on one knee, rubbing his head. He blinked and looked around the room as if not certain where he was for a minute.

"Hello?" Mary said on the phone. "Yes. Will you please send the police to room seven-oh-one. Yes, that's right, the police. Thank you." She fumbled the receiver back to the cradle.

The man was on his feet now, frowning at Tiffany on the bed. "Where's the other dog? The brown one?"

"He's safely away from here," Mary said. She lifted the gun higher, pointing it directly at the man's chest.

The man's eyes narrowed. "Is he with Chandler Dietrich? Is that who hit me?"

"That doesn't happen to be any of your business," Mary answered. "Just stay there by the door and don't come any closer." The man had not moved, but she wasn't taking any chances.

The man snorted. "I suppose he told you he's an agent of the United States government."

"I told you, it's none of your business."

The man nodded and stepped forward. "Yes, it is my business, lady. You see, Chandler Dietrich's body was found this morning at the bottom of a river in New Jersey. The man who was here is not Chandler Dietrich and he is not an agent for the United States government. Now please put that gun down so I can go after him."

Mary kept the gun up, not sure what to

think. She had seen enough of Chandler Dietrich to know him fairly well, and he certainly seemed trustworthy. She didn't know anything about this man, and his appearance certainly did not inspire confidence. "And I suppose you're going to tell me you *are* an agent?"

The man sighed and shrugged. "What else?"

"I don't believe you," Mary answered promptly.

The man gave her a cold glance and turned away in frustration. "Well, we can wait for the police, and wait another hour for them to check it out. By then your Dietrich impostor can be halfway to Saudi Arabia."

It was clear that the man was getting impatient with her, and Mary wondered what she would do if he just walked out the door. If he did, she knew she couldn't pull the trigger. But she also wondered if he might be telling the truth. If he was, she could never forgive herself if Benji got hurt. She swallowed hard, keeping the gun up, at the same time trying to come to some kind of intelligent decision.

"Of course, it's not terrible important," the man said sarcastically. "I'm just trying to save the life of a top scientist, and preserve a project of worldwide significance. It's no big deal, lady."

Mary blinked, wondering if that was true. She knew about the scientist and how all the Athens police were looking for the man. But that didn't mean this man was on the side of the police.

"Well, say something!" the man suddenly shouted at her.

"I don't know what to say," replied Mary, on the verge of tears.

"Well, you can try saying goodbye to your dog, because that man who took him out of here will probably kill him when he's through."

Paul and Cindy moved closer to Mary, both of them blinking at the man. "I can't believe that," Mary said. "Chandler Dietrich is a very nice man."

"Don't you understand what I've been trying to tell you, lady? The man who has been traveling with you and escorting you around is *not* Chandler Dietrich! He's an international thief, and he's probably a murderer! And what your dog probably has tattooed somewhere on his body is worth nothing to him if anyone else gets their hands on it. Now, if he's killed a person, is he going to stop with a little ... brown ... dog?"

Mary crumbled into tears and Stelios grabbed the gun.

"I'm sorry I had to say those things," Stelios said. "But you won't be." Mary didn't know what to say. She felt a little ill.

The man looked at them for a minute and then disappeared out the door.

VIII

Dietrich kept looking in the rearview mirror as he drove through the city. Benji sat next to him watching the streets and wondering where they might be going. He'd never seen this part of the city before. Dietrich made a lot of quick turns into alleys and narrow streets and then accelerated sharply.

Benji sighed and settled down on the seat, not knowing what to think.

A few minutes later when he sat up and looked out the window again, Benji could see water and hundreds of boats moored in a harbor. It all looked very pretty, and that's where they seemed to be headed.

Dietrich parked the car then, with Benji in arm, he hurried down a long pier which had dozens of huge boats moored on each side. About halfway out he stopped and looked back, then moved up the gangplank of a big cabin cruiser.

"Well, Benji boy, we seem to have made it." He smiled and hurried to a cabin door.

Then a familiar voice stopped him cold. "Do you still plan to dispose of him?"

Dietrich spun around toward the back of the boat.

It was Ronald, the Englishman. He and Elizabeth appeared very comfortable in a pair of deck chairs sipping tall, cool drinks.

"The wife and I sort of like the little chap. We would be quite distressed to hear he was left at the bottom of the harbor."

"What are you doing here?" Dietrich asked angrily.

The Englishman rose and moved slowly across the deck. "Well, to be frightfully honest, old boy, we thought it might have crossed your mind to—as you say—run out on us."

"Run out on you? That's ridiculous. There's nothing to run out on."

Benji looked off at the woman, and then felt himself swung around as Dietrich opened the cabin door and shoved him inside. The door closed quickly behind him.

Benji didn't move for a minute. He glanced around at the fancy leather seats and the big table in the middle of the room. Outside, the two men were still talking.

"There's really no point in discussing it," Dietrich was saying. "You didn't complete your end of the bargain. You let him get away."

Benji moved away from the vent and circled around the table. There were cushioned seats along both sides of the room, with round windows just above them. Benji jumped up and pressed a paw against one of the windows. It was closed tight.

"Yes, of course," the Englishman was saying outside, "I do appreciate that full value was not received. Still in all, a partnership is like a marriage, you know. For better or for worse. And we *did* expose ourselves to an inordinate amount of risk."

From the seat Benji looked around at the rest of the room. Then he jumped up on the table and studied the vent directly overhead.

"I suppose that's true," Dietrich agreed. "However, as I said, you did not deliver the goods."

The Englishman's voice was still casual. "I do hope this is not going to be a problem," he said. "Having become involved in a project like this, of course, could be very costly to us. I should hate to think we might have to recover the costs in other ways."

Benji couldn't reach the vent. He tried two or three times but he could get only his nose that high. He finally gave it up and stared back at the door for a minute.

"Well," Dietrich said after a silence, "I guess you deserve something for your efforts. Shall we say a compromise? Ten percent instead of twenty?"

"Under the circumstances I suppose that's a fair turn. What do you think, dear?"

"I think it's quite honorable of Mr. Thompson."

"Shall we go inside and have a drink on it?" Dietrich said.

"Excellent idea," the Englishman answered.

Benji looked over at the row of windows again and his eyes suddenly locked on one of the curtains. It was moving, flapping gently against a breeze from outside. Benji bounded quickly from the table and jumped to the cushioned seats, pushing the curtain aside with his nose. It was wide open! He peered out, then looked quickly back at the door.

Through the glass he could see a hand reaching for the knob. He pulled himself to the top and struggled through the window just as the door flew open behind him.

"By the way," the Englishman said, "you never did say what you intend to do with the dog."

Benji crept softly along the deck by the side of the cabin. He stopped short of the corner and peered cautiously up through a window.

"After I get the code from his foot," Dietrich said coldly, "the dog goes overboard."

Through the window Benji saw Dietrich step aside to let the couple pass. Then, without warning, Dietrich suddenly lifted a heavy brass telescope into the air. As it flashed forward Benji saw the Englishman disappear and heard a loud thump on the floor, followed quickly by another. Then there was only silence.

"And to keep the dog company," Dietrich chuckled, "the two of you can go overboard with him." Then the door slammed shut.

"Benji?" Dietrich said inside the cabin.

Benji looked behind him and saw Dietrich's head suddenly pop through the open window. "Benji!" he screamed.

Benji was over the railing and onto the pier in one bound. Behind him he could hear the clatter of Dietrich running through the cabin and throwing the door open. But Benji was on his way by then.

"Benji!" Dietrich screamed again.

Benji didn't glance back. He heard the thump of Dietrich jumping from the boat to the pier, and then the running footsteps. By that time Benji was almost to the end of the pier.

As he reached the top of the ramp he slowed

to a stop and glanced around for an instant. Then he jumped to the side and looked back as splinters of wood seemed to explode within inches of his paw.

Dietrich was holding a heavy pistol with both hands, the ugly black barrel pointing directly at Benji. Benji was running at full speed when the next explosion came. He heard the loud bang, and at the same instant there was a click on the pavement just behind him and the bullet went whining into the distance.

Benji quickly altered his course, keeping a row of parked cars between himself and Dietrich. When he reached the top of the hill he looked back again. He saw the door slam on Dietrich's car and then it was backing up, the wheels spinning.

As Benji raced up the street in the general direction of town, he glanced back and saw Dietrich's car. Benji made a sharp turn onto a long street. He heard the screech of tires as Dietrich turned the corner behind him.

Benji had no idea which street he should take to get back to familiar territory but he took a sharp left at the next corner. Behind him he heard the screech of tires from several cars and he glanced back, hoping one of them had blocked Dietrich's path.

Two cars were stopped crookedly in the intersection, but Dietrich had gotten by them and was still coming. He was gaining fast now. Benji rounded the corner.

As quickly as he was on the next street he skidded to a stop, his legs spinning under him. Then he turned and quickly went back to the corner, watching.

Dietrich took a wide angle, crossing all the way to the other side of the street before he came into the turn. His tires were screaming as he sped around the corner past Benji, then screeched to a stop as he saw Benji dash off in the opposite direction.

Benji heard more squealing of tires as he ran on at top speed. He knew the car would be gaining fast. The streets were more crowded now and Benji angled across a corner, tearing by several pedestrians and then between two parked cars. He suddenly felt more hopeful as he raced down the street and saw a broad flight of concrete steps leading off the sidewalk and up to the right. Benji bounded up the steps, taking them three at a time as he heard the car round the corner behind him.

When he reached the top he stopped to catch his breath, and then watched as Dietrich skidded to a halt on the street below. Benji stared at him and Dietrich stared back for a minute. Then Benji took off again, galloping easily along the higher street.

Had he lost him? Benji felt a little more confident now. He went up another set of steps and turned back in the opposite direction at the top. He slowed to a trot to catch his breath.

Then his heart dropped and he skidded to a stop again, staring off at the intersection ahead. Dietrich's red sports car was passing along the cross street. It screeched to a stop and the chase was on again.

Benji darted out, heading in the opposite direction from the car. There were more screeches behind him as Benji rounded the corner.

Up ahead six or seven garbage cans were standing in a cluster near the curb. Benji covered the distance in three seconds, sliding to a quick stop as he ducked in behind them. He stuck his nose out just enough to see the car coming around the corner. Then his eyes widened and his muscles tensed. He couldn't believe it for a minute. But it seemed to be true. Dietrich was coming faster and faster, and he was angling closer and closer to the curb, heading directly at him.

Benji spun and bolted out from between the cans an instant before the car soared over the curb. Then the cans exploded in every direction, sending garbage and trash splattering over the street and sidewalk. One of the lids sailed over Benji's head and went clattering off in front of him as he raced on at full speed.

He wasn't going to last a whole lot longer.

Suddenly, Benji saw a cobblestoned alley sloping up the hill to his right. Behind him he could hear brakes squealing as Dietrich slowed to make the turn. Benji bolted toward the alley and up the steps, finally disappearing around a corner.

Dietrich screeched to a halt at the bottom of the hill, jumped out and started up the steps. But it was no use. Benji was long gone. He gazed angrily toward the top of the hill for a long moment; then a smile began to spread slowly across his face. He hurried back to the car, slid behind the wheel, and disappeared into the afternoon traffic.

Things were beginning to look familiar again. Off in the distance Benji could see the ruins and the hill where he and his big friend had their hideout. He moved faster, wanting desperately to get back to Mary, Paul, and Cindy.

He galloped on through the park, sending dozens of pigeons flapping into the air. Then he rounded a corner and sped past the open flower market.

Only when Benji was within a block of the hotel did he finally slow down a little. He rounded the corner and then came to an abrupt stop.

Traffic was blocked and at least a dozen police cars with flashing lights were parked in front of the hotel. Policemen were all over the place, some of them standing on the grass, others milling around the street or standing across from the hotel. There was a babble of noise from the car radios and the policemen seemed to have an awful lot of guns.

Benji moved along a few feet, trying to get a better view of things. But he still couldn't figure out what was going on. With all that crowd around, it was pretty clear that he would have no chance of sneaking in the door.

He turned and trotted back toward the corner and then stopped again.

Two policemen were standing side by side near the corner, staring directly at him. Benji looked out at the street. More policemen seemed to be coming in his direction, all of them moving slowly and watching him.

What was going on? Benji turned and trotted a few steps the other way and stopped again. Then his ears pricked up as a voice crackled over a loudspeaker echoing something in Greek.

The policemen were slowly closing in on him

from all directions except the direction toward the hotel entrance. He was confused.

He finally turned and moved slowly toward the hotel. Then he stopped again and glanced around. The policemen behind him followed, always stopping within a few feet of him. And the ones in front of him seemed to edge back, clearing a path toward the hotel. Then he tensed, staring off at the entrance.

The revolving door was no longer turning. Two policemen stood on either side, huge guns held tightly in their hands.

"Προσοχη!" the loudspeaker repeated, the voice suddenly very soft. Benji glanced over at a man holding a microphone next to a police car. The man seemed to be looking directly at him as he spoke.

Then Benji saw them—Mary and Paul. They were staring at him from the far side of the hotel door, and they seemed to be holding tightly to each other as if they were frightened. Benji gave his tail an uncertain wag. Then he trotted forward, angling across the walk leading to the hotel door.

"BENJI!"

The voice was Cindy's, and it was a frightened, anguished scream that stopped Benji dead in his tracks.

Then he saw it—Dietrich's red sports car was at the curb about fifty feet away, with all the policemen standing well away from it.

Dietrich was behind the wheel and Cindy was sitting next to him. Benji's heart sank. Dietrich had an arm around Cindy's neck and tears were streaming down Cindy's face.

Then he saw something that gripped his

entire body with an icy fear. In Dietrich's other hand, just inches from Cindy's head, was an ugly black piece of metal.

Benji's thoughts raced back to a dark night in Silver Creek when he'd seen another man hold a gun like that. He remembered the loud explosion, the flash of light, and the smell of gunpowder. And his friend falling to the sidewalk.

"Benji?" Cindy called again weakly. "Here, Benji."

Benji stared for a full minute, scarcely breathing. Dietrich opened the car door and then tightened his grip on Cindy. Benji remembered Dietrich's attempts to shoot him and run him down with his car. Now he had Cindy. And a gun. Benji couldn't bear to see Cindy fall like his friend back in Silver Creek.

Suddenly Benji was in motion, gathering speed as he crossed the walk in front of the hotel. He could see Cindy's anguished look and the smile coming to Dietrich's face, and he was moving faster, digging in with each step, flying at full speed as he raced across the sidewalk. His eyes were fixed on only one thing—the ugly weapon resting in Dietrich's hand. The man was not going to make Cindy cry anymore and he was not going to harm her, and Benji didn't care what happened to him.

He was still ten feet from the car when he leaped, and for an instant he saw the look of doubt and fear cross Dietrich's face. Then Benji was through the opened door and his teeth clamped into the man's bared wrist.

There was a yell as the impact sent Dietrich's arm high into the air and the gun exploded right next to Benji's ear, the bullet tearing harmlessly skyward. Then Dietrich's arm crashed down against the car door and the gun sailed free, clattering down onto the marble steps as Benji's momentum somersaulted him out of the car.

Benji scrambled to his feet, ready to run. But suddenly it was too crowded to run. A dozen policemen were now surrounding the car and rifles were being thrust through the doors on both sides.

It was over. The loudspeaker was blaring out instructions, more policemen were coming at full speed, and Benji edged back, trapped for a minute by the mass of surrounding legs. Then he spotted Mary and Paul and Cindy standing at the curb in front of the hotel. Mary was hugging Cindy, and Paul was looking off at the crowd around the car. Then a big smile suddenly came to his face.

"Benji!" he shouted. "Come on, Benji!"

And Benji did.

IX

Benji had never seen a beach before. When they walked down from the hotel he stood looking at it for a long while, amazed at seeing so much empty sand in one place. He finally trotted to the shore and sniffed the clear, blue water, jumping back when the little waves broke and came chasing after him. Then he raced full speed along the edge, barking out at them, with Tiffany running along behind. The two of them finally jumped in and Benji leaped directly into the first wave that came along, showing off a little for Tiffany. She stayed in the shallow water and barked while he tumbled and thrashed around. Benji finally came back to shore and gave himself a good shake, looking things over again.

It was really a beautiful place. There were palm trees growing in the sand, and there wasn't another person or dog in sight for miles.

Paul and Cindy were in the water now and Benji watched them splash around and jump over the waves for a while. Up on the sand Stelios had strung a hammock between two palm trees and was stretching out in it while Mary sat in a beach chair under one of the trees, slowly swinging the hammock with one hand while fanning herself in the warm sun with the other.

"Benji just happened to be going to the right place at the right time, and for security reasons someone decided to let him carry the coordinate code for a secret meeting with the scientist," explained Stelios.

"Why is the scientist so important?" asked Mary.

"They think he's close to a formula that'll turn one barrel of oil into twelve," Stelios replied. "You can guess how many folks would like to get their hands on that."

"Well," Mary sighed, "the whole thing sounds to me like something out of a James Bond movie."

Stelios laughed. "If it were a James Bond movie, I'd be Robert Redford and you'd be Genevieve Bujold." Mary grinned at the thought and Stelios continued. "Anyway, the whole thing would have worked if Benji hadn't missed the plane change in Athens."

Stelios paused, pushed back his straw hat, and gave Mary a wry smile.

"Hey, you're not living up to your part of the bargain. If I'm gonna talk, you've gotta pull."

Mary laughed and gave the hammock a gentle tug. Behind her, Benji and Tiffany were still enjoying a romp in the cool surf.

"How did the man you thought was Dietrich find out about all this?" Mary continued.

"I don't know," replied Stelios casually. "Security leak, I guess. It happens all the time. We've got spies . . . they've got spies . . . and we're all trying to earn our salaries."

A big wave chased Benji and Tiffany back

toward the beach, and they both took off in the direction of Paul and Cindy, who now sat on a blanket enjoying the ocean breeze.

"By the way, how's Benji?" asked Stelios as Benji and Tiffany trotted under the hammock. "Any signs of wear and tear?"

Mary turned to watch as Benji neared a large picnic basket and nudged the top away with his nose.

"I don't think Benji has ever been better," Mary answered simply.

Paul and Cindy smiled as Benji stood proudly looking into the basket. Inside were four of the handsomest, liveliest puppies they had ever seen. Three were cuddly white, with soft fine fur like their mother's. But the fourth . . . well, he was the obvious heir.

His mixed brown coat was scraggly with a little white streak on his chest and he yapped and growled as he crawled feistily over the other puppies.

Benji reached down into the basket, nudged him away from the others, and gingerly picked him up by the nape of the neck. The tiny puppy gave his proud father a small lick on the nose as Benji placed him carefully onto the blanket.

If ever a son bore the marks of his father, it was this lively, brown puppy who sat looking admiringly up at a very special dog named Benji.

Woof.